The Eleventh Commandment

The Eleventh Commandment

LUTISHIA LOVELY

Dafina
Books

Kensington Publishing Corp.

DAFINA BOOKS are published by

Kensington Publishing Corp.
119 West 40th Street
New York, NY 10018

ISBN-13: 978-1-62490-209-3

Printed in the United States of America

This novel is dedicated to Selena James, the kind of wonderful, true-blue friend you always want in your corner, and in her role as editor . . . an author's dream.

ACKNOWLEDGMENTS

It's the wee hours of the morning and I can't believe it, y'all. I have just completed my . . . drum roll . . . twentieth novel!!! No research assistants. No ghostwriters. Just me, myself, and Zuri Day—in a little over six years—churning out page after page. I sit here amazed, humbled (and after pulling a fifteen-plus-hour day, a little delirious!), but filled with gratitude. I'm so blessed to get to do what I do, to have a career that I love, and a team of wonderfully gifted and talented people who support me.

When I sat down to type the first words to my first book in 2001, I had no idea where that act of obedience to Spirit's gentle prodding would lead me. In 2004, when I felt I'd properly researched the industry and pulled my pennies together to publish *Sex in the Sanctuary* independently, and then channeled E. Lynn by pushing it in barbershops, beauty shops, gas stations, grocery store parking lots, and wherever else from the trunk of my car, I wasn't sure how this whole literary career thing would turn out. I simply did what I could, when I could. And kept believing.

When after a year of ghostwriting and pushing my own product I determined I needed a book deal, and when I took three of my remaining inventory to something I'd heard of called Book Expo and told myself with absolute assurance that I would get a deal there, I had no idea how it would happen. That first entrance into New York City's Jacob Javits Center, where more than ten thousand people were waiting for the doors to open, had a sistah intimidated. But I put faith over fear and began introducing myself to any and everybody as "the best-selling author who'd just sold out my first print run." When I stepped into the Kensington booth, I had no idea that the woman I was talking to, the one who was showing more interest than the other publishers in other aisles, was an acquisitions editor. And when I finally followed up with her two months later, I had no idea that this AE angel, Hillary Sares, had been trying to reach me all that time!

It takes a village to raise an author, and I owe so much gratitude to so many that it's hard to thank them all in one setting. But given the specialness of this occasion, I'd like to thank some now, even if I may have thanked them before. Hillary, thank you. Karen Thomas, who green-lit that first novel, much obliged. To Kensington, the literary family I've grown up in, the Team Lutishia who care so much and do so much and support me all the way: Steven Zacharias, Laurie Parkin, and all the executive staff, Doug Mendini and the sales team, Lesleigh Irish-Underwood, Alex and Alex, and everyone in marketing, Kristine Mills-Noble and the art team for my fabulous covers, Karen Auerbach, Adeola Saul, and the PR staff, Selena and the production team, especially Robin Cook. It would be easier to just reprint the company directory because I'm sure I've left someone out. But thank you, Kensington. Big hug!

To my agent, Natasha Kern, and my promotions guru, Ella Curry. To Debra Owsley, who hooks me up with great giveaway items, and to Jessica Wright Tillis for the wonderful excerpt pamphlets. Appreciate you, ladies! To those authors who are also my friends, who encourage me when I need it and give me a "get 'er done" to cheer me on! You know who you are and I appreciate you, thank you, and love you. See you at the next conference (or on the next cruise, Mrs. Brenda Jackson!). A special shout out to Football Widows author Pat Tucker for the Los Angeles Sea Lions who appear in this book. ☺

I thank my family, who has encouraged me along every step of every journey I've ever taken. And then there is you, each of the readers/fans/supporters who are why I'm able to do what I do. Yes, you, the one who takes a novel that spent about nine months in production (not including the time it took me to write it ☺) and then reads it in one day. Yes, you, who writes me e-mails mad about what some character did and suggests what should happen in the next installment. And you, who tells me that you've seen yourself, or someone you know, in my characters and that what I've written has touched your heart. Or made you laugh. Or cry. Or curse. Or all of the above!

Though there are literally thousands of names that belong

here, these are but a few I've gathered while working on this novel: Shannon Barnett, Doneisha Bridgeforth, Sonja Vann, Nora Hayes-Clark (your long wait is over sistah!—wink—), Kim Knight, and all of the service men and women who read my work while serving our country. Ryan Ivory, Denise Springs, GAYLE Jackson Sloan (yes, I'm shouting!—smile—), Sharon Blount, Denise Williamson-Garrett and her aspiring writer daughter, Sparkle, Norfolk, England's Linda Berry (and all of my international fans!), Shana Smith, Monique Menefee, Angelia Vernon Menchan, Synita Gardner, Allyson Deese, Lacha Michelle, Daphne Foreman, Sandy Barrett Sims, Andrea Corbin Huff, Denise Keese, Marsha Cecil, Eriq Cunningham, Zaundra Lewis-Cooper, Rose Jackson-Beavers, Audra Golson, Carmen Blalock, Angelique Pickett-Henderson, Antoinette Hunter, Denisha Miller, Janette Malcolm, LaKeesha "Missy" Jackson, Aquita Lane, Lynee Jordan, Nia Stanley, Angela Varnado, Nikisha Wallace-Smith, Valerie Butler, Tennille Madden, India Watson, Sharmon Lynette, Dionne Payton, Kandi Graham, Charliene Crowder, Christy Pantel, Valerie Martin, Charles Henry Hall, Monique Matthews Waddell, and Kenneth and Nicole Royal. To Yolanda Gore and Orsayor Simmons, who without my asking have gone above and beyond in promoting my work.

Book clubs! I can't forget you: Readers of Paradise (Chi-town, yeah, baby!), Claritta Stinson and Sistahs of Color Book Club, Nikisha Wallace Smith & In the Company of my Sisters, Readers by Choice, Chi-Town Reading Circle, Readers in Motion, Deirdre Newsome and Beyond the Reading, Tanesha Mapson and AOOA, Bonita Thornton and Sistahs Thoughts from Coast to Coast, Black Faithful Sisters and Brothers Book Club, Lashaunda McKinley and Ebony Pages, OOSA, Sharon Blount and Building Relationships Around Books, Turning Pages Book Club, Yasmin Coleman, Priscilla Johnson, and all the reviewers and members of APOOO, Ebony Pages Book Club, Sisters United and Lisa Renee Johnson and Sistahs on the Reading Edge. A thousand thanks to all of you and a thousand more to those book clubs who've read me and I don't know about and/or didn't mention. Let me know so that I can give you a shout out! To Lissa Woodson and the Cavalcade of Authors. Chicago was a blast!

Spirit, the All That Is, You are indeed everything to me. Thank You. To my angels . . . I soar to success on your wings!

Whew, all that and I'm sure I still forgot somebody. I told y'all it takes a village. But don't trip. If you're not in here it just means I've got to write another book. So let me get to it! Book number twenty-one, here I come!!!

The Eleventh Commandment

It's Lutishia Lovely coming to you with a little ditty that I
Wrote while I was hanging out in the city.
It's the hook for my latest lit release,
Another hallelujah love about to hit the streets.

It's got drama, twists and turns, humor, inspiration,
Both characters and readers gonna get some revelations.
We know there's ten commandments, not five, six or seven,
Well . . . Now there's about to be eleven.

You should know yourself,
And uphold yourself,
And let unconditional love be the only kind
That you show yourself. (repeat)

You've heard you should not steal and that you shouldn't kill,
And that you shouldn't bow down to an image outside Spirit's will,
That you should not take the name of the Lord in vain,
And to keep the Sabbath day holy and free from strain.

Don't lie on your neighbors or envy what they've got,
Honor your mama and your daddy, whether they're good or not.
You should not creep and sleep with another's boo,
and I'll add: do to others what you want done to you.

** Eleventh Commandment**

This is the eighth installment of Hallelujah Love,
And I'm still getting story lines from up above.
So don't worry that this is the last—not quite;
I don't see an end to this series up in sight.

If you've heard or read or tried to follow, understand,
This is my own interpretation of the ten commands.

And you don't have to agree with me for you to get to heaven,
But I sincerely suggest you try number eleven...

You should know yourself,
And uphold yourself,
And let unconditional love be the only kind
That you show yourself. (repeat)

The Eleventh Commandment

1

Friendships and Fatherhood

"Ooh, yeah, just like that, just like that!" Frieda Moore-Livingston cooed as expert hands moved up and down her bare back, across her shoulders and back down... kneading, rubbing, before coming to that sensitive dimpled spot just above her juicy assets. "That... feels... so... good." "Oohs" and "aahs" surrounded each word that oozed from her lips. Strong, lean fingers continued down her thighs, paying special attention to the calves and feet before heading back the way they'd come, lingering at the small of her back, switching to feather-light strokes as they splayed across her shoulders and along the nape of her neck. Frieda felt as though she'd have an orgasm right on the spot. It had taken her a while to understand the hype. But now she was a true believer: there was nothing better than an afternoon massage.

"We're done, pretty lady." Tyson, the masseur to the stars and to those with star quality (translated, plenty of cash), tapped Frieda lightly on the shoulder to signal the end of their session. "See you next week?"

"Of course, baby," Frieda said, turning over and getting off the table, shamelessly letting the towel fall on the floor. More than once Tyson had suggested she wait until he leave to begin dressing, but Frieda had other plans. Often, she'd wondered how it would be to have other body parts massaged during these sessions, but so far her not-too-subtle hints had only been met with a patient smile. The first assumption had been that he was gay. After all, who would turn down what Frieda called "pussy on a platter"? But her friend Stacy's baby daddy, Darius, had told her that Tyson didn't get down in that club and since the platinum-selling R & B singing sensation was patently homosexual and very much a part of that world, Frieda thought that he would know. If not for the fact that she was now headed to a thick link of sausage not far from her old stomping grounds, she might have been insulted. As it were, she simply laughed as Tyson quickly averted his eyes and left the room.

Moments later, Frieda clicked the locks on her shiny new Lexus LX and slid inside. Ever since she'd purchased the pearl wonder with light tan seats, she'd given to wearing outfits and/or accessories in the same color, often finished off with Louboutin pumps and pearl-colored Gucci shades. Frieda's picture could have appeared next to the word *materialistic,* but she didn't mind. She'd learned how in LA image was everything. She had faked it until she made it and snagged a doctor in the process. Thinking of Gabriel, the hardworking husband and sponsor of the designer duds she wore, caused a tiny tinge of guilt as she turned down Martin Luther King Boulevard and headed toward where she used to live. Passing row after row of modest apartments much like the one she'd rented upon arrival from Kansas City, she reflected on her journey from then till now, and how far she'd come in less than five years. When she'd left the Midwest and a drug-slinging boyfriend to join her cousin and best friend, Hope Taylor, in the City of Angels, all she'd hoped for was a good time. And now here she was a wife and mother, living in a tony Westside neighborhood amid five-thousand square feet of luxury, a bank account courtesy of her husband that never boasted less than five figures, credit cards with no limits, a chef, a maid, and a nanny/house manager. Sometimes she had to pinch herself to make sure she wasn't dreaming. And sometimes she had to do what she was doing now. . . . go slumming for something that money couldn't buy—a thick piece of sausage.

"Get in here, girl," a tall brothah said as he opened his apartment door. His island accent was as sexy as his long thick locks, his ebony skin, his straight white teeth, and his washboard abs. "You know me don't like to wait for ya."

Frieda was nonplussed as she threw her purse on the couch. She kept silent as she unzipped the front zipper on her pearl-colored mini and let it fall to the floor. Her cell phone vibrated, but she ignored it as she reached behind her and unclasped her bra. The youngblood's eyes narrowed, and he licked his lips. *That's right,* she thought. *This caramel goodness is worth the wait, isn't it?* Her nanny/house manager's son, Clark, could say whatever he wanted just as long as he did what she told him to. And he did. Long and hard. Every single time. "Stop sulking and get over here," she said, looking fierce while wearing nothing but a wispy thong, five-inch pumps, and a smile. "And show Mami how much you've missed me since I've been gone."

Two hours later a totally satiated and satisfied Frieda left the hood and headed back toward the Westside, and her appointment at the spa. The man was a beast, and she needed professional help to wipe the just-been-sexed-to-within-an-inch-of-my-life look off her face and body. It would be the last appointment of the day before heading home to a quiet evening, probably alone. Even though it was likely that Gabriel would work well into the night, Frieda always scheduled a spa visit after her romps with Clark. She never wanted to make her husband suspicious and had learned early on that the astute doctor didn't miss much. No, tonight she was not in the mood for a lecture on what he sometimes called "behavior inappropriate for a doctor's wife." There was already enough on her mind. Like Clark, and how she was going to continue to have her cake and eat it too.

Her phone rang and as she looked at the dash, she again felt a twinge of guilt. The last thing in the world she ever thought would happen was that she'd go soft. The old Frieda wouldn't have given two hoots about what anybody else thought or felt. Undoubtedly her cousin would attribute it to the Holy Spirit that Hope swore never left Frieda's side. *I hope that Brothah took a break just now. Otherwise, He got an eyeful!* Frieda thought it was less likely divine intervention and more probably motherhood that had unearthed the heart she'd buried during her teenage years, fending for herself on Prospect Avenue, perhaps dug up by the three-year-old who had both his parents wrapped around his finger. *Or maybe it's you,* she thought, reaching to connect the call. She could honestly say she loved the somewhat stodgy, somewhat geeky doctor whose work was his passion. Even though he bored her to tears.

"Hello." Frieda turned down the sounds blasting from her speakers as she spoke.

"Where are you?" Gabriel Livingston's voice was just short of curt. "I've called you three times."

Just then Frieda remembered that her phone had vibrated earlier, when she'd been so focused on...well...various types of massages, and she'd forgotten to turn it back on. "I've been out running errands," she said, the beginning of an attitude creeping into her voice. Having basically been on her own since she was fifteen years old, she wasn't too used to having to report her whereabouts.

"Cordella said you've been gone for hours."

That nosy nanny needs to mind her own business! Frieda made a mental note to speak to her at the next opportunity. Sistah-girl wouldn't get fired as long as her tenderoni son was handling that pipe like he did, but his mama was definitely going to have to put her mouth on lock. "After my workout I went to get my weekly massage, then went shopping"—*screwing but hey, they both have eight letters and start with an S*—"so yeah, I guess I've been gone for a while."

"You can't keep doing this, Frieda. Spending your afternoons gallivanting while Cordella watches our child. In the two years that she's worked for us, I'm beginning to think Gabe considers the nanny his mom."

"Did you call to make me feel bad about taking care of myself?"

Gabriel's exasperated huff came through the phone. "I called to tell you about a dinner engagement tonight with a prominent couple from DC. An unexpected change of plans has them here for the evening, time enough to make an impression that will hopefully result in a large donation for the new oncology ward." He told her the name of the restaurant. "Reservations are at eight."

"Looks like it's a good thing I'm on my way to the spa," Frieda purred. "So I can look good and help impress your guests."

By the time the call ended, Frieda knew that she'd flipped the frown that had undoubtedly marked Gabriel's face when the call began. She turned up the music again as she thought about how opposite she was from Gabriel in so many ways, and how her vibrant personality was what had drawn him to her like a hummingbird to sugar water. He was often exasperated with her, but a witty quip, flirty phrase, or naughty innuendo could usually brighten his mood. *He's so easy to manipulate.* And when it came to fathers, there were none better. That heart that Frieda liked to ignore constricted a bit. She really did love Gabriel. He'd do anything for her, and even more for his namesake, the namesake that every day was looking less and less like the good doctor and more and more like one of the men Frieda used to know.

2

The Ex Factor

It was a picture-perfect evening in La Jolla, California, an upscale suburb of San Diego. Cy and Hope Taylor sat on their ocean-front patio, sipping wine and enjoying a sunset that was painted by God. The chilled wine they'd uncorked was a rare vintage that Cy had procured on a recent trip to Italy, vino that Hope had unashamedly poured into sensibly priced crystal wineglasses purchased at a discount chain. God had blessed her with the good life, a life beyond her wildest dreams. But she wasn't bougie. A no-nonsense mother, matter-of-fact father, and an upbringing in a tight-knit Baptist church community in Tulsa, Oklahoma, had planted her designer-clad feet firmly on the ground. "Don't get so high that you can't see low," her mother had told her on more than one occasion, like after church when mothers fawned over a song she'd sung or a dance she'd choreographed. Or when the teachers commented on the well-mannered pretty girl with big brown eyes, thick braids, and good grades, Pat would remind Hope that God had given her the ability to have those things, that they'd not been achieved simply through actions of her own. Even now, this down-to-earth mother was in La Jolla, passing down that same wisdom to Cy and Hope's four-year-old twins, Camon and Acacia. Hope and Cy relished the quiet time, and each other.

"It's been a while since we've done this, huh?" Cy reached

over and took his wife's hand in his, held it up to kiss the back of it.

"The world is so quiet when they are gone; I almost can't remember what life was like without them. For years, I thought I'd never have children. I'm thankful for them every day." She leaned over and kissed her husband on the cheek, still reveling in his star good looks after six years of marriage. His tall stature, dark caramel skin, soft curly hair, and cocoa eyes framed by ridiculously long lashes never ceased to make her heart skip a beat and her panties grow wet. Cy Taylor had been one heck of a catch, another blessing that was above and beyond what she ever dared dream.

Cy turned and took the chaste kiss Hope had intended to another level, brushing his lips across hers before running his tongue across the opening of her mouth, and when she complied, slipping it inside. The headiness of their love matched the potency of the wine and within seconds, the lovebirds were caught up in a dance they'd perfected over time: lips touching, tongues twirling, hearts beating as one. He looked up through desire-darkened eyes and gazed upon the woman he loved—her chocolate skin, big doe eyes, and thick lips parted with wanting.

"Let's go inside." The insistency in Cy's voice hinted of a desire to take her here, now, on the smooth slate stones of the patio.

"Mama will be back with the kids anytime," Hope replied. At Cy's sigh, she smiled. Their lovemaking schedule was forever changed when the kids came, and getting it in where fitting it in had taken on a whole new meaning. "I know, me too," she finished, with a final peck on his lips before sitting up, reaching for her wineglass, and taking a cooling swallow. "Don't worry. I'll take care of all of that"—Hope gestured at his obvious erection—"later tonight."

"All right." Cy stretched his long legs in front of him to offer a bit of relief to the long leg in the middle. "Best to change the subject then. Otherwise, Mom Pat will walk into a situation best not seen by mothers-in-law."

"Not to mention our children."

"Remember that time—"

"The twins coming in the room..."

"Standing at the end of the bed—"

"Eyes wide, wondering..."

"And then little Camon pipes up, 'What y'all doin'?' "

Cy was really laughing, doubling over in his seat. "I look down and all I see are two sets of eyes barely able to peer over the mattress."

"And my response to their question—'We're just playing.' "

"Good thing I was riding it low and slow, instead of punching you like a time clock with your legs thrown over my shoulders."

"Not exactly our idea of a teachable moment, huh?"

"No, baby. Not especially." They were silent a moment, both reflecting on what had been one of the funniest incidents of their parenthood. "You know what, baby? I had no idea how much having children would change our household, or being a father would change my life."

Headlights coming up their quarter-mile-long drive signaled the end of the couple's alone time and Pat's return with the twins from their outing. As they left the patio, Hope looked at Cy, noting the look of contentment on his face. It mirrored her own. For years, more than a decade, she'd prayed (cried, begged, bargained) for a husband and children. It had been her singular goal for most of her adulthood. And here she was, living out the answer to that prayer. *Thank you, God. Thank you for everything that I have, and all that I am. Thank you for my family, my parents, my friends. Bless those whose prayers you have yet to answer, Lord. Bless them with the desires of their heart, the same way you've done for me. Amen.*

On the other side of the country, in a beautifully restored brownstone in the Edgecombe area of Harlem, New York, another woman had just finished a prayer. She was still reeling from news received a month before, news that had caused her to take stock of her life. Highlight accomplishments, acknowledge regrets. The latter was why she'd just typed an e-mail to a man she'd not recently seen but had never forgotten, the first and only man she'd ever truly loved. Reading the letter one more time, hoping that it contained the right mix of casualness and desire, her finger hovered uncertainly over the button before she finally pushed SEND.

Okay, God. I've done what I can do. What happens at this point is up to You . . . and Cy Taylor.

3

Sistah-Girls, Sistah-Chats

The next morning, Hope bounded out of bed at seven a.m., wanting to be ready when her personal trainer, Yvette, arrived. The popular LA trainer, who came at a hefty one-fifty an hour, had proved herself well worth the payment; Hope was smaller than she'd been before getting pregnant, actually in the best shape of her life. Yvette combined several popular training modules—Pilates, aerobics, Zumba—along with her own brand of stretch and cardio. She achieved in forty minutes the same results that usually required sixty to ninety minutes of working out. The routine was grueling, fast paced, relentless, and aside from time spent with her husband and/or children, the absolute best time of Hope's day. She donned workout gear and then walked over to the other side of the second floor to check on the twins. Satisfied that they slept soundly, she walked downstairs and into the kitchen for a bottle of water, smiling as she spotted a note on the fridge.

Baby, I hope your workout this morning is half as good as the one we gave each other last night. Have I told you lately that you're amazing? Hope these meetings go quickly. I already miss you. Cy.

"I miss you too, baby," Hope murmured, as she ran her hand over the note. It was a habit they'd started in the early days of their marriage, leaving each other notes in various parts of the house, but most often on the kitchen fridge. Even with the popularity of texting, e-mails, and the old school phone call, there was nothing quite like seeing pen having been put to paper, hearts hastily drawn, or an "I love you" scrawled in Cy's bold handwriting. *Bold. Strong. Yes, that's my baby.* She remembered how well he'd sexed her last night and then again this morning before leaving on his New York business trip. During the downturn in the nation's economy and the subsequent falling real estate prices, Cy had greatly expanded his company's portfolio, picking up several prime pieces of land and property from the eastern seaboard all the way down to the Florida Keys. He and one of his newest business partners, Jack Kirtz, had also secured property outside the United States, including ocean-front property in South Africa on which they'd built a sanctuary for children orphaned as a result of war and disease. The simple yet sturdy housing complex was comprised of one-thousand units and included a school, gym, playground, general store, and medical facility. It was one of Cy's proudest achievements and since she and Jack's wife had been a part of the planning process, it was Hope's pride and joy as well.

"Perfect timing!" Hope opened the side door that led directly to the area of the mansion that housed the gym, game room, laundry room, and maid's quarters.

"The traffic cooperated this morning," Yvette replied. "A good thing since your neighbor hates it when I'm late." The ladies continued chatting as they walked the short distance to the gym, and Yvette replaced sandals with athletic shoes. "I still don't get why you and Millicent don't work out together."

"It's a long story," Hope replied, placing her water on a nearby bench before stretching her hands high above her head. "Besides, I like our one-on-one routine."

"That's just it. The routines I've designed for both of you are very similar; it would be less work for me and more fun for you. I'd even give you a discount. So what's the story?" Yvette asked when Hope continued stretching in silence.

"You don't want to know and probably wouldn't believe it if I told you. Millicent and I have known each other for a long time and while we've learned to coexist quite nicely, we'll never be BFFs, okay?"

"Okay." Yvette knew when she was coming close to a line she dared not cross. She walked over and placed her iPod on the dock. Soon, Adam Levine and Maroon 5 were talking about moving like Jagger. "Let's get to work."

An hour later Hope had finished her workout, showered, helped the housekeeper and part-time nanny dress the kids, and had made sure they were settled in for their Spanish lesson followed by lunch and their daily "wear them out so they'll take a nap" romp in a nearby park. Ironically enough, her housekeeper Rosie was a member of Open Arms, the church pastored by Cy's business partner, Jack. Jack was also her former nemesis Millicent's husband, and she had been the one who, after Hope had mentioned her desire to have someone help her with her growing and increasingly rambunctious children, suggested Rosie as a perfect fit for the job. She'd been right. The forty-five-year-old mother of four grown children had melded into the Taylor household right away and quickly become invaluable to Hope's running of it. In addition to housekeeping and babysitting, she taught the children her native language. These days in California, and increasingly in other parts of the country as well, knowing Spanish was not an option, but a necessity.

Hope was in the kitchen and had just downed a bagel with her daily superfood smoothie when her cell phone rang. "Hey, cuz! How's the doctor's wife?"

"Bored as hell," Frieda grumbled. "Gabriel has me at this vanilla-ass breakfast with some snooty-ass women flaunting their husbands' millions. I had to come out for some air before my face fell into the eggs Benedict."

"It's probably a very nice breakfast." Even as Hope said this, she could barely keep from laughing. Her ride-or-die former hood rat cousin wasn't much for high-class hobnobbing.

"Please," Frieda responded, proving Hope's point. "There's enough silicone and bleach in this room to open up a business on the black market. Wish I'd known what kind of paper would be in here. I could have had one of my former neighbors jack this joint and walk away with diamonds worth at least five mil!"

"Frieda, you don't mean that."

"Hell, if I hadn't stopped carrying my piece like you told me, I could have robbed these bitches myself!"

"Ha!" Hope knew her cousin was playing, mostly.

"The best part of the whole morning was the mimosas. I know my man Dom when I taste him."

Hope could hear that Frieda had brought "her man" out with her and was now taking a healthy gulp. "We're not drinking and driving are we?"

"We're not. I am. But don't worry. I'm not driving far. Heading back to the house as soon as this is over so I can get my groo— Never mind."

"Since when have you been coy about lovemaking? You'se married now," Hope continued in her best Shug Avery voice. "Sex is allowed."

"What are you doing?"

Hope didn't miss that Frieda was changing the subject, a red flag since it was one of her cousin's favorites. "Wait. Why do I feel there is something you're not telling me?"

"Nothing, girl."

"Frieda . . ." She heard her cousin taking another drink.

"Aw, hell. I might as well tell you since I might need you to cover for me one of these days." A pause and then, "I've got a new boo."

"What?"

"A tenderoni, girl, with a big, thick, black dick that he knows how to use!"

"Frieda!" Hope jumped off the bar chair where she'd been lounging. "Tell me you're not serious."

"As serious as a blod clot on its way to the brain."

"Frieda, Gabriel is a good guy, a wonderful man. He's the man supporting your lavish lifestyle, the father of your child!"

"Maybe..."

"Whoa!" Hope's voice went from a low G to a high C in no time flat. "Okay, I know you're joking but, girl, that's not funny.... You are joking, right?" Before Frieda answered, Hope's phone beeped, indicating an incoming call. "Don't hang up," she warned Frieda before switching over. "Hello?"

"Hey, girl."

"Stacy!" Hope was glad to hear her bestie's voice. "Hold on a minute—Frieda's on the other line talking crazy. Let me do a three-way."

"Okay."

Hope clicked back to the other call. "Frieda, you there? It's Stacy. I'm going to click her into the mix. Frieda? Cuz, you there?"

Cuz wasn't there. Cuz had dropped two bombs and then left the building.

4

Sistah-Girls, Sistah-Chats, Part 2

Hope clicked back over to Stacy. "She hung up."

"Oh, dang. I was looking forward to talking to her. You know it's been way too long since the three of us have gotten together."

It was true. Six years ago, when they all lived in Los Angeles, Frieda Moore-Livingston, Hope (Jones) Taylor, and Stacy Gray-Johnson were as thick as thieves and as close as triplets, chatting by phone almost every day and getting together at least once if not several times a month. Stacy had been busy chasing her baby daddy and dreaming of living life with this R & B star. Frieda had been footloose and fancy-free with no desire to have husband or baby, and Hope had wanted the latter so badly that she'd nearly lost her mind. Actually, some (specifically her neighbor, Millicent, her husband, Cy, her mother, Pat, and her therapist) would argue that she had lost it for a moment. Thankfully, therapy, prayer, and the twins had calmed her down and brought her mind back from crazy to normal. A true testament to the fact that life happened while people were busy making plans.

"So what is she tripping about today?" Stacy was all too familiar with Frieda's wild antics.

"You don't even want to know," Hope said, repeating what she'd earlier told her PT when it came to her history with Millicent Kirtz. "I think she was joking anyway." *At least I hope to God that Frieda wasn't being serious about having an affair. And Gabriel Jr.*

being someone else's baby. The three women shared everything, but if and when Stacy heard this madness, it would be from Frieda and not her. "So what's going on in Phoenix, besides the heat?"

"You said that right; not even July yet and today we're already at a hundred-five degrees. It's ridiculous. Makes me think about moving back to Cali."

Hope's ears perked up. She'd love nothing better than to have her best friend move back to LA, or even San Diego, which would be better still. "You guys thinking of moving?"

"I don't know what we're going to do. Tony is still pretty upset at being cut, doesn't want to face the fact that his days in the NFL may be over. That's one reason why I'm calling you. We'll be in LA at the end of next month."

"Really? Why?"

"He's hoping to do a walk-on at the Sea Lions' training camp."

"That's great, Stacy! Cy loves sports; his company has a suite at all of the major venues. Tony playing in that beautiful new stadium might even make me come out and watch a game!"

"I know, right? So far I've gotten along with the wives well enough, but it would be hella fun to hang out with you and Frieda, especially if the Sea Lions follow everyone's prediction and make it to the Super Bowl. Tony even joked about Darius singing the "Star-Spangled Banner," if LA ended up in the top two spots."

"Can you believe it, Stacy? How much all of our lives have changed, and how blessed we are? There was a time when I couldn't have imagined you and your son's father being able to hold a civil conversation, let alone becoming friends."

"Tell me about it. Not to mention that I'm also friends with his *husband*. He's even teaching me how to cook, passing down his Aunt Gladean's guarded recipes."

"Gurlll . . . how is Bo?"

Bo Jenkins was the legal partner (translated, husband) of America's R & B darling and Stacy's ex, Darius Crenshaw. "As crazy as always. Running behind Darius and swatting away fans, groupies, and wannabe lovers the way that a cow's tail swats away flies."

"You've got to give it to them. They've been together what, six, seven years now?"

"Together for eight, married for four," Stacy corrected. "Longer than some heterosexual marriages last."

"Shoot, I might need to hang out with Bo myself, ask him what his secret is to their long-wedded bliss."

"Why? Is the bliss starting to wear off at your house?"

"Not hardly, darling. Cy and I are happier than ever; I fall more and more in love with him every day."

In the perfectly appointed premiere Central-Park-view suite of New York's Mandarin Oriental, Cy sat at a small table, next to floor-to-ceiling windows offering views of the Manhattan skyline, whose bright lights had just begun to twinkle against dusk's tranquil blue sky. It was a stunning sight, but even as Cy gazed upon it, he didn't really take it in. No, his mind was filled with a variety of thoughts and emotions, all dredged up because of the e-mail that he'd just read. Standing, he walked over to the counter and placed the iPad on it. After pouring himself a glass of cabernet, he read the note again:

> Dear Cy: Hello, stranger. It's Trisha Underwood, or Tricky as you called me back in the day. If this note reaches you, I can only imagine what you'll think, especially since at one time I had planned to never speak to you again. Life is funny, huh? Which is probably why the adage "never say never" was coined. As I sit here looking at the invitation for our class's fifteenth-year reunion, I'm reminded of what once was, and wondering how you are. I hope this e-mail reaches you, and that you answer. If so, I hope that we can communicate. I trust that life has treated you well, and I would love to catch up.
> Until then, Cyclone . . .
> Tricky

To say that Cy was surprised would be an understatement. He was floored. For years, he'd thought about Tricky, had looked for her and inquired of her whereabouts. Her sorors had been tight lipped, understandably so considering what had happened to break them up: the one and only time in their relationship that he'd been unfaithful. At that time, Cy had been sure that Trisha Underwood would become his wife and the mother of his children. They'd spoken of spending a lifetime together, had shared dreams and goals, met each other's families, and before that crazy night when a woman who'd long envied Trisha's seemingly effortlessly successful life duped Cy into her bed, he'd been very close to buying a ring. He'd hated that other woman for a long time, had temporarily entertained the idea of swift retribution. But at the end of the day, no one had put a gun to his head to make him have sex; he'd been over twenty-one and in full charge of his faculties. He'd pulled out all of the stops to win Trisha back, mounted a campaign that would have rivaled President Obama's in its tenacity. But Trisha had grown up in a household where infidelity was tolerated and had sworn to never become that woman. At least where Cy was concerned, she'd kept that promise.

Cy took his glass of wine and walked over to the oversized windows. He placed a palm against the glass and took in the high-rises across the way and the antlike people scurrying on the streets more than fifty floors below. Sipping, he pondered this unexpected event that had unfolded at the end of a long yet productive day, a day full of meetings where he'd not checked his e-mails until moments before. Included among the business associates, club memberships, professional organizations, real estate info, and spam mail was a correspondence that caught him totally off guard. Trisha Underwood. *Her maiden name.* Cy wondered whether she was one of those independent women who refused to take on her husband's name. Remembering how feisty and headstrong she'd been in their college days, Cy had no problem believing this was true. He also thought of the possibility that she'd divorced and reclaimed her maiden name or, although highly unlikely, that she'd never married. Remembering their lovemaking, and what a sexual creature his first true love had been, Cy found this last possibility improbable. *Cyclone, her pet name for me. What's that about?* Cy read the ending more than once. And why refer to herself as the name he used to often call her in the throes of lovemaking? What had happened to make her seek him out after all these years? And then there was the most important question of all. What if after talking she wanted to meet? Would he? Should he?

As Cy walked back over to the counter and picked up his iPad to type a reply, he already knew the answer.

5

Expensive Toys and Pretty Boys

Darius Crenshaw sat watching the gargantuan screen in his theater room, praying that Bo would stay in the kitchen. He watched the movie intensely, not at all caring about the suspenseful story line about a spy who'd infiltrated the White House. The story line didn't capture his interest, but the man who played the spy very much had his attention. Pascual Demopoulos, the half-Italian, half-Greek heartthrob known simply as Paz, who in less than two years had taken America and the big screen by storm. A seasoned actor who'd been a European celebrity for many years, he had broken into America's homes and most females' hearts with last year's breakout role that starred him as a single father with a precocious, nine-year-old daughter. The movie, *Nine Times Over,* was a critical and popular smash, leading to an Oscar nomination and his being given the coveted crown of Sexiest Man Alive by *People* magazine. *They got that right,* Darius mused as he watched the actor, looking dashingly bad-ass in a tailored black suit as he accompanied the "president" as part of the Secret Service detail. His stunningly blue eyes were hidden behind dark glasses, but Darius knew exactly how they looked. He'd committed those orbs to memory when they'd met face to face six months ago.

"First class is the only thing that makes traveling overseas bearable," the handsome man said as he sat next to Darius in seat 3B.

"I hear you, man." Darius barely looked up in answer, so busy was he texting his legal partner, Bo. This trip had come up unexpectedly, but when royalty called, you answered, and Darius's presence had been requested at the wedding of a princess. It was a rare trip where Bo hadn't accompanied him, staying behind to attend meetings for a Fourth of July concert happening in Central Park and a New Year's Eve Celebration he was headlining at Kingdom Citizens Christian Center. Even though the latter gala was still several months away, it was the first major event Darius had held for them since resigning his minister of music position the year before, a move that had been necessitated by both his demanding schedule and the time he spent in Phoenix to be near his son. He wanted everything to be perfect, and the only person he trusted absolutely to make that happen was Bo. "It's only seventy-two hours," Darius had pointed out when Bo complained of not going with him, as he always did. "I'll be back before my side of the bed gets cold."

Because he'd barely acknowledged the stranger, who'd spoken as he placed his carry-on in the bin above him, the first thing Darius had truly noticed about Paz was his scent: a combination of something earthy and sexy and mysterious and wild. The second thing was his eyes.

"Paz Demopoulos," he'd said with hand outstretched, once seated and firmly secured by the requisite seat belt.

"Darius Crenshaw."

"I thought you looked familiar. I love your music, man!" Paz immediately pulled out his smartphone and showed Darius how the music catalog was loaded with songs by D & C, Darius and Company. "That new album is flawless. I know that 'Power' is the song climbing up the charts, but 'Subtle Sexy' is my personal fave. 'Subtle sexy, you vex me, arrest me with your charm while on my arm...'" Paz sang the lines with a surprisingly smooth voice, showing that he was not only a great actor and model, but could possibly hold his own behind a mike.

"I'm sorry, but I haven't seen your work," Darius said, once Paz finished the lyric. "Heard about it though. Congrats on the award nomination."

Paz's smile reflected straight white teeth and the hint of a dimple. "Thanks."

After learning that they'd both been summoned to the same party, the two men had conversed comfortably on their trip to Dubai. Darius had only been mildly surprised to learn that Paz swung both ways. More unexpected had been the A-list actor's not-so-subtle interest in a fling with him, something that Darius had found flattering, but had flatly turned down. "I'm married," he'd explained, when Paz had pushed the issue. "I'm determined," Paz had softly replied. Nothing had happened in Dubai. But Darius was all too aware that if Paz had his way . . . something would happen stateside. And soon.

"You're watching that piece of crap movie again?" Bo entered the theater carrying a tray from which a decadent aroma wafted. "If I didn't know better, I'd say you were trying to have a crush on someone other than your wife." He reached the coffee table and sat down what would be a light yet fulfilling lunchtime treat: Portobello mushroom burgers with roasted red peppers on focaccia bread, and a warm, wilted green salad. He reached for a cloth napkin that had been thrown over his shoulder, placed it on Darius's lap, and placed his own plate on the table beside his mate.

Darius reached for the remote and wisely changed the channel along with the subject. At the time he'd thought it best to tell Bo about meeting Paz on the trip to Dubai. Now, given how jealous Bo acted whenever the man's face or name came up, he wasn't so sure. "This smells good, baby. But where's the meat?"

"The mushroom replaces it. Remember I told you about watching Dr. Oz and deciding for us to try and cut our beef and pork intake a little bit."

"Yeah," Darius replied around a bite of food. "This tastes good, even without it."

"I aim to please," Bo replied.

"You aim too, please!" they said simultaneously, laughing at the reference to a poster that used to hang in the gay spot where they met. "Um, babe," Darius said, after another healthy bite of the sandwich. "What kind of cheese is this?"

"Gruyère," Bo replied. "Saw it on the Food Network."

"Oh, you've been watching *your* on-screen crush again?" Darius took full advantage of further defusing Bo's fixation with Paz by bringing up his own professed heartthrob.

"Honey, I love me some Toussaint Livingston. But his ass is as straight as the highway to heaven." The Food Network's latest darling, Toussaint Livingston, was one of the heirs to a large barbecue dynasty in Atlanta, Georgia, whose riches had been garnered largely through their grandfather's secret sauce recipe, a restaurant chain called Taste of Soul, and the tremendous entrepreneurial success of the third generation.

"Word is their food will be featured at this year's Music Muse Awards. So watch it with the compliments or I'll take someone else with me." Darius leaned over and kissed Bo's pouting lips. "Stop it. You know nobody looks as good next to me as you do."

Even after all this time, when a man as fine as Darius made a big deal over him, Bo couldn't help but preen. Not that Bo had any lack of confidence. Though his frame was slight, a mere five foot nine to Darius's bulkier six feet, Bo had a pretty boy face, flawless butterscotch skin, baby fine hair, and bow-shaped lips most women would envy.

The Crenshaw landline rang and Bo reached over for the handset. "Hey, Spacey."

"Hey, Little Bo Peep," Stacy answered, in her and Bo's ongoing mutually exchanged digs. "Darius there?"

"He's eating. You ready for us to pick up Junior?"

"I told you not to call him that! I hate that name!"

"Are you ready for us to pick up Darius's son?" Bo's tone was way too syrupy to be sincere.

"I'd prefer Darius to come and get him, but I doubt you'll want him out of your eyesight long enough to let him come alone."

"Hmph, Darius isn't the one I'd worry about, witch."

"Please, Bo. Nobody wants Darius but you."

"Except everybody who doesn't have him, including your husband." There was silence as Bo imagined Stacy remembering how to breathe. "Ha! I thought that would get you. You never know about those professional athletes."

"Ease up, Bo." Darius interrupted the verbal war that was sure to happen whenever his child's mother and his male wife crossed paths. "Tell Stacy I'll be over there in a half hour."

The two men finished their meal and, contrary to Stacy's assumption, Darius then left the house alone to pick up his son. A good thing, since his text indicator vibrated shortly after he got into his SUV for the short drive from the home he'd purchased for the sole purpose of being near his son to the abode that Stacy shared with her ex-NFL football player husband, Tony Johnson. When Darius reached a stop light, he pulled out his phone.

I'll be in Phoenix tomorrow for a photo shoot. Can you get away?

Darius sighed as he punched the voice-activated responder on his cell. "Not a good idea," he said, enunciating slowly so that the device would type in the correct words. Lord knew he was interested in Paz, who hadn't been far from his thoughts since returning from Dubai. But when it came to Darius and anyone wanting to get next to him, Bo seemed to have a bloodhound's nose, a sixth sense if you will, a gift that could be part of the reason for Darius's faithfulness. Bo's love for Darius was almost legendary, his devotion unparalleled. Bo was already suspicious. If he knew how actively Paz had been pursuing him, there would be hell to pay.

The text indicator beeped. You know I won't stop until I have you.

Darius couldn't help but smile as he spoke his answer: "I know."

6

A Welcomed Distraction

Paz was still on Darius's mind as he knocked on the Johnsons' door. Stacy answered wearing a tube top and a pair of cutoff jeans. As always, she was a distraction. This time it was a welcome one.

"Hello, Stacy," he said as he entered, stopping to wrap his ex in a light hug. "How are you doing?"

"I'm okay."

Her answer caused Darius to stop in his tracks and turn around. He looked at her closely, noted the slightly dark circles under her eyes and the fact that she seemed to have lost some weight. "Are you?"

"Of course. Why wouldn't I be?"

"Daddy!" An ever-growing five-year-old burst of energy entered the room, wrapping himself around his father's legs. "Are we going to the park, Daddy? Remember, you promised. Are we going to go to the park and race cars?"

Darius looked down at his spitting image, his heart overflowing with love as he gazed into wide brown eyes staring from a body that seemed all arms, legs, and a smooth round head. "We'll see, little man. Did you pack the cars in your bag? Are you ready to go?"

In answer, Darius Jr. darted around the corner, into his room, Darius presumed. "He's growing up so fast," he said, shaking his head as he looked from the corner his son had turned and back into Stacy's eyes. "I can't believe he'll be starting kindergarten in the fall."

"According to his preschool teachers he's more than ready." Stacy walked over to some video games that had been left on the floor, idly picking them up and stacking them on a nearby table. "He has scored high in all of the tests given so far." She turned and faced Darius. "Your son is a very bright young man."

"Just like his mother."

Stacy's chuckle was light, and a bit hollow. "Just like his dad."

For a moment, time seemed to reverse, and both Darius and Stacy remembered warm and genuine feelings that had once existed between them. Stacy saw the man who for years she'd chased in hopes of being his wife. Darius looked at the only woman who'd been able to arouse him to orgasm, the only woman he'd ever loved in a romantic fashion. "You sure you're all right?"

Stacy nodded, again busying her hands by picking up the few toys that were strewn around the room. But before Darius could focus on Stacy's seemingly distracted state of mind two things happened: his son reentered the living room and Stacy's husband, Tony, came through the front door.

"Hey, baby!" Stacy walked over and hugged a scowling husband.

To Darius, Stacy's greeting seemed forced, a bit too cheery. But then again, while he and Tony had developed a cordial enough relationship, it wasn't like they were best buds. Darius felt it best that he take his son and leave the premises, give Tony the space he needed in his own home. "All right then, Stacy. I'll bring Darius back on Monday morning, if that's okay."

"Sure." Stacy knelt down to hug her son. "You be a good boy, okay?"

"Yes, Mommy."

Had Tony not been there they would have hugged, but considering the tension that was in the room, Darius simply nodded his good-bye. Stacy walked them to the door and stayed there waving as Darius and his son backed out of the driveway. Once they'd driven down the street, she turned to see that Tony had left the living room and walked into their bedroom at the end of the hall. Stacy took a deep, calming breath, placed a hand on her stomach to still the fluttering, and followed behind him.

"How was your day, baby?" She leaned against the closet door jamb, watching as Tony took off his shoes and socks.

"What was he doing here?"

Not quite the response she'd hoped for, but Stacy tried to keep things light. "Just doing what he does every other weekend, picking up his child."

"You know I prefer that to happen before I get home, right?"

"I'm sorry, Tone. I didn't know that you'd be home early. If I had, I would have suggested dropping off DJ instead." She watched as Tony rolled one sock inside the other before hurling the pair into a basket in the corner of the large, walk-in closet. *Oh no, another bad day. The interview must not have gone well. God, give me strength.* "I thought about grilling some steaks. You hungry?"

"Why in the hell would you want to fire up the grill when it's a hundred degrees?"

Stacy shrugged. "I won't be out there long. The steaks only take around five minutes on each side. I've already prepared a salad and have some ears of corn that can also go on the grill." Tony remained silent as he stood, unbuckled his belt, unzipped his tailored black trousers, and let them drop around his ankles. She knew there was nothing she could say that would elicit a positive response. "I'll go and fix us a drink." She turned and left their master suite without waiting for an answer.

A half hour and two tumblers of Courvoisier later, Stacy felt it safer to broach the subject in which she was really interested: Tony's employment. Hopefully soon. She walked from the patio into the dining room, holding a tray of medium-well steaks and perfectly grilled corn. "So how did it go today, baby?"

"How do you think it went?"

Okay, perhaps I should have waited for that third glass to go down.

Her calm demeanor totally belied her inner angst. In the months since Tony had been unceremoniously released from the Cardinals and passed over by every other major team in the NFL, Stacy had learned the hard way how to read his moods and mask her own emotions. The laid-back, even-keeled man she'd married looked nothing like the one she'd lived with for the past few months. And she didn't even want to think about the Ponzi-type scheme that had drained most of Tony's finances—the one she'd warned him against, which was another reason for his ongoing chagrin. "I think they should have hired you if they have any sense. Nobody knows defense the way you do, Tony." She placed a tong's portion of salad on white porcelain salad plates, and then placed a steak, corn on the cob, and a piece of toasted bread on matching dinner plates. "And definitely there is no one more handsome." She walked over and placed Tony's plate in front of him, leaning down to kiss his temple in the process.

Tony's scowl remained, but Stacy could tell he was somewhat pacified. "I'm too young to become a talking head for that jive-ass network." He poured a generous amount of Italian dressing on his simple salad, and then angrily jabbed his fork into the mix. "I don't need them to tell me that when it comes to sportscasting I'd be on top of my game."

"Sounds like the interview went okay."

"All right, except they want to offer me pennies on the dollar for what I'm worth."

"I'm sure it's nowhere near what you made on the field, or what you're worth."

"How in the hell would you know what I'm worth?" Tony asked, in an explosion of emotion.

"Baby, I'm just saying that whatever they offered you, I'm sure it wasn't enough."

Without another word, Tony scraped his chair back from the table, grabbed his plate of uneaten-food and half gone drink and left the dining room.

Stacy kept her head down, pushing lettuce, tomatoes, avocado, and black olives from one side of the plate to the other. No one wanted Tony to get picked up by a professional team more than her; no one prayed harder. And their financial situation was only part of why she wanted him to be gainfully employed. His happiness was the main reason. She knew from previous conversations that her husband had eaten, drank and slept football since he was eight years old. Being an athlete wasn't just what he did, it was who he was. If what she was seeing was who he would become once his career ended...she didn't even want to go down that road of thought.

After he'd left the room, Stacy emptied her uneaten salad into the compost device and placed her uneaten steak and corn into plastic containers before putting them in the refrigerator. Her mind went back to three years ago and how happy she'd been when Tony asked her to be his wife. Now she knew that the honeymoon was definitely over, and only hoped that her dream of a marriage wouldn't turn into a complete nightmare.

In the game room and out of earshot, Tony put down his plate and retrieved his cell phone from his belt clip. He scrolled down to a name he'd only entered about a year ago, the name of the one person who might be able to help him save his career. "Yo," he said when the call was answered. "That supply come in yet?"

"Was going to call you later," was the gruff reply. "It arrived this afternoon. I can overnight it tomorrow."

"Do that."

Tony picked up his plate and attacked the perfectly done steak and juicy ear of corn. His appetite had returned, along with his hopes that he would end this limbo nightmare and once again live his NFL dreams.

7

Doctor's Orders?

"Where's my son?" It had been a long day with back to back surgeries, but Dr. Gabriel Livingston had barely stepped into his Beverly Hills home before summoning the love of his life.

"Cordella!" Frieda knew how much Gabriel hated her hollering instead of using the intercom or, even more civilized, walking into the room where the nanny played with their son, but right now, with everything that was on her mind, she didn't care.

Moments later, a petite, dark-skinned woman wearing a baby blue uniform, polka-dotted head scarf, and sensible shoes walked into the room, holding the hand of a handsome little boy. "Good afternoon, Doctor." Her lyrical accent floated through the tension in the room, bringing a smile to Gabriel's face in spite of his mood.

"Good evening, Cordella. Good evening, son."

The little boy looked up at Cordella, whose subtle nod was the impetus he obviously needed to speak. "Good afternoon, Dad." The voice was soft, tentative, an adorable addition to the caramel-skinned cutie with thick curly hair, big doe eyes, and rosy cheeks.

"Come here, Gabe." Gabriel's voice was raspy with emotion as the boy walked into his arms. A sworn bachelor until his literal run-in with Frieda at a Beverly Hills mall four years ago, he'd had no idea how much having a family would change his life. He loved his little boy with all his heart and, God help him, but he loved his son's crazy mother as well. "How's my little man doing, huh?"

"Good, Dad." Gabriel Jr., whom they all called Gabe, was a study in way too much seriousness for a three-year old. His was a quiet, contemplative countenance, one that totally reminded Gabriel Sr. of how he was at that age. After a moment of studying his son, his eyes slid up to the woman who vexed him. She was looking decadently gorgeous in pants too tight, hair too flipped, and a halter top that showed way too much. He adored her. "What about you, Frieda? What did you do today?"

Got sexed to within an inch of my life, is what she thought. "Went to another boring meeting about the charity ball," is what she said. "With those women who look at me and see yet another charity case."

"If you dressed like that, you didn't help the situation. I've purchased you an entire closet of clothing befitting a doctor's wife. I don't understand why you insist on dressing like a stripper."

"There was a time when you liked how I looked," Frieda quipped..

"There is a time and place for every outfit, Frieda. What you have on is not appropriate for a meeting with the other doctors' wives"

"Oh, slow your roll, dude. I looked totally appropriate for those blue-haired heifahs." When Gabriel continued to look doubtful, she continued. "I didn't wear this. I wore the black Armani suit paired with a floral knit top that covered everything. And those loafer-looking heels that only belong on someone going to a funeral, or to church. I couldn't wait to get out of that stuffy getup. But you'll be happy to know that Mrs. Goldstein actually complimented me on my outfit. That should insure at least another half a million for your cause."

"*Our* cause, darling," Gabriel said, motioning Frieda over to his side. She complied and once in his arms, he kissed her gingerly, nothing like the Neanderthal manner in which Clark often grabbed her hair and pinched her nipples and butt cheeks. In a moment of conscience, she felt bad for missing the mistreatment.

"Dr. Klaus will be retiring at the end of the year and I am a true contender to head up the oncology unit. Your relationship with the wives matters in the decision-making process. I want you to think of us as a team, Frieda. It's not just you against the world anymore, remember?"

Frieda nodded at her geeky husband's one nod toward the hip-hop world she loved, his knowledge of rapper Tupac's music, and her surprising discovery of a couple of his songs on the doctor's iPod. She rubbed her hand across the crotch of his pants. "Someone won't let me forget."

Later that night, Frieda methodically stimulated her husband's penis to a respectable erection, something that given his long hours and distracted mind-set was not always so easy to do. She heard his breathing shift, becoming more intense and labored. She only hoped that she could climb on and ride a second or two before he climaxed and passed out, something that was totally understandable given the fact that he'd been in surgery for ten hours today. She rolled her body toward him, placing her leg over his thigh. He responded by turning his head toward her and engaging her in a sloppy wet kiss. *Better hurry this up,* Frieda thought, as she listened to her husband's breathing get even more erratic. *Another couple tugs and this gun will fire.* She removed her hand and placed her body over him, expertly lowering her wet heat over his hard shaft. Throwing her head back she set up a sensuous rhythm, licking her own palms and rubbing them over her hardened nipples as she rocked back and forth over Gabriel's body. He grabbed her hips and guided her up and down his slightly above-average member, his breath now coming in short bursts.

"Ah!" He flipped them over, spreading Frieda's legs and plunging into her paradise.

"Ooh, yeah, baby," Frieda said, with all of the excitement of an average starlet in a B-list movie. "Um, feels so good, baby. Ah. Yes. Yes!"

The performance was good enough for its audience, a fact evidenced by Gabriel's increasingly rapid hip movement accompanied by a prolonged "aw" and a sustained hiss before he collapsed on top of his pride and joy. In what had become typical fashion, he gave grateful pecks to Frieda's cheeks, lips, and forehead before turning on his side away from her and quickly falling asleep. Frieda waited for just a moment before rising from the bed and heading to the shower. She set the temperature as hot as she could stand it, then soaped her loofah sponge and ran the uniquely refreshing scent, a strawberry/coconut/vanilla combination she'd had created just for her, over her skin. Closing her eyes, she remembered another lovemaking session earlier in the day, one that had probed deeper and gone longer than her husband could have ever dreamed. What surprised her was the fact that she wanted him now, again, even as she washed the scent of her just sexed husband off her skin. *Damn, Clark. You got me whipped.* Frieda had been around the block enough to know that this wasn't good. She was supposed to have him wrapped around her finger. Instead, it was exactly the reverse.

8

No Place Like Home

"Camon! Stop splashing your sister!" Hope tried unsuccessfully to prevent water from touching the hair that in anticipation of her husband's return had been pressed bone straight by her San Diego hairdresser just hours before.

"Why, Mommy? I like it!" Obviously four-year-old boys had no concern for hundred-dollar dos.

"I like splashing!" Acacia cried, mimicking her brother in word and deed.

"Stop it, you two!" Hope scolded, but the laughter that followed belied the severity of her words. Cy always warned her that when it came to their twins, she was a complete pushover. He was right. Hope's mother, Pat, said it was because of how long Hope had wished for children, and how hard it had been to get pregnant. Hope chose to believe it was because her children were perfect. But she also readily admitted her bias to anyone who asked.

"Look, Mommy!" Acacia held up a colorful floating block.

"No!"

Too late. The block that Acacia held quickly became a splashing weapon, coming down hard in the water and effectively soaking Hope's hair, face, and top.

"Hahaha!" Camon loved his sister's antics, so much so that he copied them exactly.

Their giggles filled the bathroom, and Hope simply couldn't be mad. *If you can't beat them, join them.* "All right, you little boogers," she exclaimed, reaching for one of the foam toys and squishing the water over Camon's head. "You think bath time is fun time, huh? Huh?" Water splashed over the side of the tub, soaking the towel and rug beneath her knees. "Sorry, Rosie," Hope murmured, thinking of her housekeeper, who would clean up the mess she and her children had made. After a minute more of splashing, Hope decided they'd had enough. "Come on, you dolphins! Out of the water."

Just as she reached over to unplug the tub, a voice boomed into the room. "What's going on here?"

Three pairs of large, brown orbs looked at each other before Hope and the twins simultaneously exclaimed, "Daddy!"

Cy entered the room, chuckling as he took in the motley crew.

"Ooh, baby, you're home early," Hope said, unplugging the tub with one hand while reaching for a towel with the other. "I planned to have the twins in bed and be dressed all sexy for you when you got home."

Cy took in his disheveled wife, hair half straight and half curly from being splashed, T-shirt wet and sticking to perky nipples, his twins behind her, wet from head to toe. "Baby, right now I can't imagine a sexier scene." He walked over and, taking no regard for his eight-thousand-dollar suit, wrapped her in his arms. They shared a quick kiss before each parent wrapped a towel around a kid and scooped them up in their arms.

"Where you been, Daddy?" Acacia wrapped her arms around the man who was totally and completely in love with her, and the first man she'd ever loved.

"Daddy went to New York, baby."

"What's New Work?" Camon asked.

"New York," Cy corrected, enunciating the word. "It's a city that is far, far away." Cy looked over his shoulder at Hope. "Haven't they been working with the lighted globe?"

"Please. They've been working with some of everything."

Thirty minutes later, Hope and Cy walked the children to their bedroom, dressed them for bed, and read them a bedtime story that promptly put them to sleep. The couple had retired to their bedroom where Hope now rid herself of the clothing that was almost soaked to the bone as her husband lustfully eyed her.

"What?" Hope asked, fully knowing the answer to why her husband wore the expression he did. It was for the same reason her va-jay-jay was vibrating like a ten-dollar dildo. Amazing that after being married all this time her man could still almost make her come with a simple look, a warm smile. Yet here she was, draped in a towel as she prepared to step into the shower, about ready to explode before her husband had so much as touched her.

"This here," he said, reaching out to tweak her hardened nipple. "And this." He ran a strong index finger from her weighty breasts down to her navel, even as he leaned in for a soft kiss on the top of her head. His arm went around her, pulling her closer to his still-clothed body. "I missed you," he whispered, before covering her mouth with his.

She felt his heat rise and harden. "Me too." Words dissolved under the intensity of their reconnected desire, as hands sought and found various body parts: shoulders, hips, backs, buttocks.

Cy took her juicy booty in both hands and pressed her against him. "Mind if I join you in the shower?" he asked against her opened mouth.

"I'd love for you to join me," she purred. "You can tell me all about your trip."

He took off his black cotton boxers and nine inches of stiff goodness bobbed and weaved its greeting. "Oh, you want to hear about New York. Is that the only reason?"

Hope looked down at one of God's gifts, before glancing up shyly. "Not the only one." This time she didn't resist when Cy reached for her hand and led them into the shower, one of her favorite places in the house. With six shower heads strategically placed on the ceiling and walls, the bather could literally be massaged from everywhere.

But with the way Cy's hands were molding themselves to her frame, there was no need for any other type of massage. He ran his hands through her wet hair, slid his tongue over her lips, and ran a finger down the crease of her buttocks. She gasped, and he used this opportunity to thrust his tongue into her mouth, grinding against her pelvis as he backed them to a wall. With one swift movement he'd lifted her off the floor. "I need you so badly, Hope. Are you ready for me?"

She nodded, and it was all the encouragement he needed. He made them one with one fell swoop, buried himself deep inside her wet, pulsating warmth, guided her legs around his waist, and plundered her mouth while he plundered her sex. Hope gave as good as she got, rotating her hips to make sure that no area of her pleasure went untouched. "Ooh, baby, you feel. So. Good."

"It's you," Cy countered, pulling out so that his throbbing head pulsed against her sensitive spot, just the way he knew she liked it.

"Oh, baby! I'm coming!" Hope screamed her pleasure, surprised at how quickly she'd reached her peak, and how ready she was for yet another round. "I love you." Her legs shook as he gently placed her feet on the floor, showering kisses on her face. Her breath came in short, deep spurts as she tried to regain her equilibrium. No one could get her discombobulated as quickly as her husband, a fact that he proved again in short order. Her breath returning to normal, she lay her head against her husband's wet shoulder. "You're too good to me," she whispered.

Cy's chuckle was that of a secure brother who knew he'd just given his woman the ultimate pleasure "You ain't seen nothing yet."

After making quick work of their shower, with Cy using his tongue as effectively as he used the sponge, and then applying lotion to his wife's body before she returned the favor, they retired to the custom made king-sized bed that anchored the master space. Hope climbed into the middle of the bed, knowing that that was exactly where her husband wanted her. After another, more leisurely round of love-making, Hope snuggled into Cy's embrace as they lay spoon style.

"Thank you, baby," she said.

Cy yawned as he asked, "For what?"

"For loving me so completely and unconditionally. I don't want to ever take what we have for granted."

"Me either, love."

"I did once, you know. When I was so obsessed with getting pregnant, making your life miserable with my crazy paranoia."

"If I remember correctly, someone was already pregnant and dealing with some serious hormonal fluctuations."

"I know but—"

"Uh-uh. No buts. Those days are behind us. Let's just enjoy what we have right now."

"You're right." She turned to face him, lightly kissed his lips. "I love you, Cy."

"I love you, too."

It was true. Cy adored her, not only as his wife, best friend and confidante, but also as the mother of his children. Which is why no one was more surprised than he when during those last seconds of wakefulness his mind was not on Hope, but rather on Trisha Underwood . . . his long lost love.

9

No Friend Like an Old Friend

The next morning Hope figured that her husband was as ravenous as she was. They'd made love almost all night long, recreating their favorite positions like it was the first time they'd been together instead of a couple that had been married for many years spending just three days apart. Cooking for him was almost as satisfying as making love, and she hummed as she placed the fruit salad she'd just prepared in the refrigerator and pulled out farmfresh eggs and extra-sharp cheddar cheese for the vegetable omelet on the menu. In a nod to both of their vows for healthier eating, several slices of organic turkey bacon lay on a grill pan, ready for the broiler. When she heard footsteps on the stairs, she poured a glass of grapefruit juice and placed it next to a setting where two superfood capsules lay waiting to be consumed.

"Good morning!" She took in her handsome husband, dressed in a casual tan suit, mandarin-styled shirt with no tie, and loafers, and once again thanked God for the life in which she'd been blessed. "Do you want toast or English muffins?"

"Toast, please." Cy walked over to kiss his wife, checking his smartphone for messages as he did so. "Somebody's responsible for my late start today. I need to leave here in about half an hour."

"Well, whoever that somebody is needs a spanking." She turned as if to prove her point, dressed in white boy shorts, a cropped white tee, and barefoot.

"Woman, don't tempt me. I've got a full day ahead."

"Ha!" Hope added fresh vegetables to the frothy egg and cheese mixture and within minutes placed two piping hot plates on the table. After pouring her juice and topping off Cy's glass, she joined an obviously hungry man who was devouring his food.

"This is good, baby."

Hope laughed. "I can tell."

"Used a lot of calories last night."

Hope cocked an eyebrow. "God be praised."

"Ha!"

"We never did get around to talking about New York.," she began after taking a few bites. "How was your trip to one of my favorite cities?"

"Very good," Cy said, with a nod. "And somewhat interesting."

"Really? How so?"

Cy told her about the interesting proposition he'd gotten regarding partnering on some property in Harlem and also near where the World Trade Center used to stand, a space now occupied by the newly finished Freedom Tower. "And then there was the e-mail I received from an old classmate."

"From high school or college?"

"College."

Hope finished her bite of omelet and reached for her mug of tea before sitting back against the breakfast booth. "What did he want?"

Cy hesitated only a second before correcting her. "It was a she, e-mailing about our fifteen-year reunion coming up."

"That isn't really so unusual, babe. I remember months ago seeing a Facebook post about our high school reunion. I naturally started thinking about people I'd gone to school with and what they were doing now. Maybe that's what happened with her."

"Maybe so, but there's a little more to it than that, love." Cy finished off a piece of bacon, reached for the napkin and wiped his mouth. "We dated."

"Oh." The way Hope held out the two-letter word showed

that she fully understand what this meant. She'd just spent a night with one of the most talented dicks in the world and knew that any woman who'd encountered it had never forgotten its skills. "So you think this old flame is trying to stoke the fire that kept me warm all last night?"

"I wouldn't say that. The e-mail was pretty straightforward, saying she'd gotten my e-mail address from a mutual friend who's on Facebook, and wanted to know how I was." He flipped through his e-mails and showed her what had been written.

Hope read it quickly. "Trisha, huh? So just how special was she all those years ago?"

Cy shrugged. Later, he'd ponder on why he'd hedged the question. But in this moment he was only interested in moving on to the next topic before leaving for his office near San Diego. "She and I dated for most of our college years, before one of her supposed friends set me up."

"Set you up? With someone other than Trisha?"

"She set me up to sleep with her knowing that Trisha would find out."

"So Trisha found out and dumped you?"

"It sounds pretty harsh being described like that but, yes, in a nutshell that's what happened."

"You've got to respect someone who values herself."

"True."

"So how do you feel about hearing from her after all these years?" Hope asked.

"I don't know. A bit curious, I guess, wondering how life has treated her after all this time."

"So you responded?"

"Yes," Cy replied with a nod. "And she replied. Turns out she lives in New York and I told her that I happened to be in her city. But I didn't hear from her again before I left so . . . who knows if anything will even come of this."

"Her correspondence doesn't make you want to attend the reunion?"

"It's put the event on my mind, no doubt. But I haven't been to one in ten years." Cy leaned over and kissed his wife. "Who knows, it may be time to check another one out, show off my trophy wife."

They finished breakfast and by the time Cy left for his city office, the twins were off for a romp in the nearby park before having their Spanish lessons with Rosie. Hope knew she'd have at least two uninterrupted hours of quiet time. She didn't intend to waste them. She'd just gone into her office, fired up her computer, and put a name into the search engine when her home phone rang. "Hello?"

"Hello, Hope."

"Hey, Vivian!" Hope always loved hearing from Vivian Montgomery, first lady of Kingdom Citizens Christian Center, Hope's church home. She oftentimes thought this pastor's wife whose husband oversaw a megaministry had a sixth sense when it came to knowing one's need for having a sistah-girl conversation.

"You sound chipper this morning. Any particular reason for the good mood?"

"Cy was in New York for a couple days. He came home last night."

"Ah." Vivian's one-word response held a lifetime of marital understanding. "Well, I won't keep you. Are you busy right now?"

"Not really. Just doing a little investigative work."

"Oh? Do I want to know why?"

"Probably not, but I want to tell you anyway. Her name is Trisha Underwood. She's a former college mate of Cy's from New York, who contacted him while he visited there. She reached out on the pretense of discussing their fifteen-year reunion, but you know how skeptical I can be when it comes to Cy and women."

"Our minds may take it there a time or two too often, but our intuition never lies. What have you found on her?"

"I just started, but so far, nothing really. An article or two about some social organization with which she's involved, and her participation in the alumni association at Howard University."

"Any pictures?"

Hope smiled, thankful for the woman who'd counseled her through a variety of ups and downs. Vivian was a Christian who kept it real, whom you could talk to without censoring your thoughts or words, a woman who not only believed in enjoying every aspect of marriage, but made sure that she was taking care of all of her husband's needs. "You know me too well," she said at last.

"No, I know what I'd be looking for." The smile on Vivian's face was evident in her voice.

"Several images came up under the name, but none of them were connected to the stories I think are tied to Cy's classmate."

"Do you feel that there is anything to worry about?"

Hope's answer was quick and unequivocal. "No. They exchanged a couple e-mails but that was it. For all I know, she's one of the coordinators reaching out to everybody, not just Cy, especially since Cy hasn't seen her for fifteen years, since he graduated."

"You're probably right."

Hope switched from the screen containing Outlook to her Facebook account. "What about life in Beverly Hills? How is Derrick doing?"

"He's fine, thanks for asking. We continue to take it one day at a time, and his last doctor appointment showed no return of the tumor. In fact, the doctor feels that Derrick is healthier than he's ever been."

Everyone even remotely connected with Vivian and Derrick's church knew that the past year had been quite challenging. Derrick had faced a major illness that attempted to derail his ministerial career, and even though Hope and Cy were an hour away and not nearly as active in the church as they'd once been, they were still very involved with the ministry. It's where they continued to tithe and where they tried to worship at least once or twice a month. Other Sundays were spent at Open Arms, a church in San Diego led by their neighbor, Jack Kirtz, with help from his capable first lady wife, Millicent. And then other mornings Hope and Cy worshipped God in unusual ways, such as by taking their children

to the beach or the park, and thanking God for nature's workman-
ship that they enjoyed.

"I'm so glad to hear that, Vivian." Hope looked at the clock,
noted that time was passing faster than she'd like, and that she still
had several things she wanted to accomplish before preparing the
children's lunch. "What can I do for you, sis?"

"I'm calling about the e-mail I sent you last month. About the
specifics of the Sanctity of Sisterhood's The Woman I Am Summit
happening this fall."

"Yes, I received the material. Just by the title I'm liking it already."

"Thanks, Hope. Even though this is a minisummit, since it's
regional and lasting only one and a half days, I want it to pack as
much punch as our full-blown ones. It's going to be a mini-KCCC
reunion of sorts: you, Millicent, and a few other ex-members
who've relocated and I haven't seen in awhile. Since I know you
keep in constant contact with your cousin, I'm hoping that she and
Stacy will also be able to participate. If possible, a highlight of the
final service would be an appearance by our former minister of
music and Stacy's baby daddy, but I know his schedule stays booked."

"I'll be talking to Stacy later today and will definitely mention
it. No promises on whether or not Darius can show up, but hey . . .
nothing beats a failure but a try."

"I'm so proud of you, Hope. It seems like just yesterday that
you showed up at our church as Cy's fiancée. And now here you
are a wife, mother, and mover and shaker in your part of the world.
Yours is a prime example that dreams can come true, and that God
does answer prayer. That is why I'd like for you to be one of the
speakers on Saturday. Have you share your story to the extent you
feel comfortable. When it comes to the theme, The Woman I Am,
you are an embodiment of an answered prayer." Vivian continued,
sharing in more depth how she'd like Hope to contribute to the
conference. "Do you and Cy have plans for the fourth?" she'd
asked, when finished.

"We've talked about going to LA," Hope answered. "With the

holiday falling on a Tuesday, I'd like to get into town that Saturday, hopefully spend time with Frieda and Stacy, attend church on Sunday, and then play both Monday and Tuesday by ear."

"Perfect! Then I can go ahead and pencil in you two to attend the barbecue we're planning. Very casual, and the only thing you need to bring is yourselves."

"That sounds great, Viv. I'll run it by Cy and confirm later this week."

"And if Frieda and Stacy want to join us, either with their husbands or alone, they too are welcome."

"I'll be speaking with both of them this week if not later today, and will let them know."

"It'll be good to see everyone again."

"I agree, Vivian. See you soon."

10

The Woman I Am

Hope finished checking her e-mails and, instead of balancing the household checkbook as she'd planned, then looked up the foundation scripture to the upcoming conference. It was an interesting one, taken from the third chapter of Exodus when God commanded Moses to go before Pharaoh and demand that the children of Israel be let go. When Moses had asked God what his name was, and who should he say had sent him, God answered, "I Am that I Am." He told Moses to say that I Am had sent him. Vivian had told Hope to study the Hebrew word for this passage. She'd been the one to suggest that Hope purchase a Hebrew-Greek Bible. It had been the best study guide Hope could have imagined, had helped her deepen her understanding of the scriptures and in doing so, to strengthen her relationship with God.

"*Hayah.*" Hope practiced the Hebrew word on her tongue as she read its literal meaning: to breathe. Immediately she began to get excited. *God was her very breath?* She continued reading aloud, literally feeling the Spirit as she did so. "This verb means to exist, to become, to come to pass, to happen, to be finished." She stopped, pondering that definition. It came to her that what God had spoken was already done, that the end was known from the beginning. She also felt that God was saying that whatever Moses needed God was, and by default, since humans were made in the image and likeness of God, that whatever people desired was inherently already inside them. The revelation sat Hope back in her chair. Could that be true? Could the power to realize all of her desires have existed inside her all along? If so, why had it taken so long for it to happen, for her to meet Cy and have children? And what about all of the single women out there, good women who wanted marriage and motherhood, yet found it so difficult to find the right man? As more questions than answers came to her, she kept reading. "The key meaning to Jehovah/Yahweh is found in this word. I Am that I Am means I Am He who exists: timeless, ever-present." Fingers drummed against the mahogany table as she thought on these words, asking God what she should say at the conference, how she could use these words and her life to encourage someone who was in the shoes she'd occupied for a long period of her life. "Help me, Jesus," she murmured, rising from the table and stretching long and hard. She looked at her clock, knowing that the kids would be coming back soon. It was also workout day, one of three times a week that Yvette came through to torture her into retaining the lean, tight body that Cy loved.

Just enough time left to try and catch my girls. Reaching for her phone, she walked from the kitchen area toward the great room, to the covered patio beyond it. It was a favorite hangout place for Hope, a smartly appointed area anchored by an outdoor kitchen on one side and an infinity pool on the other. Beyond it was the expertly maintained garden from which Hope filled the house with flowers: hydrangeas, orchids, lilies. Also growing were large bird-of-paradise plants that she admired but refused to cut. Beyond the garden was what drove up the property's value—an unobstructed view of the Pacific Ocean. She and Cy had spent many amorous evenings on this patio. Her cootchie tingled just thinking about them, so she forced away these thoughts as Stacy picked up on the other end of the phone.

"Hey, Hope."

"Hey, girl. What's wrong?"

"Nothing. What's up?"

"Uh-uh. That's not how we do things. I'm your girl, Stace. Talk to me."

It was true. Hope and Stacy had become fast friends after Hope relocated to Los Angeles from Kansas City. Stacy admired her lifestyle, especially the fact that she'd snagged KCCC's most eligible bachelor, right out of Millicent Kirtz's—then Millicent Sims—crosshairs. Hope later found out it hadn't been quite that way, that while Cy had dated Millicent a couple times they'd never been intimate. At any rate, Hope truly appreciated Stacy's friendship, the only woman she conversed with other than her cousin, Frieda. Hope had been Stacy's confidante regarding her obsession, Darius Crenshaw. She was the first to know that Stacy was pregnant with his child, the first to whom Stacy finally admitted the truth that he was gay, and the one who helped her pick up the pieces when Darius, who'd finally married Stacy following the birth of their son, then had their marriage annulled to be with his true love, Bo Jenkins. On the other hand, Stacy had been a much-needed sympathetic ear during Hope's attempts to have children, had been her cheerleader when Hope began to lose the essence of her name. She'd helped pull Hope back from the brink when she'd become obsessed with the fact that Millicent had had a child before she did, and then was convinced that Millicent was after Cy. Her paranoia had resulted in her racing to a hotel where Cy was meeting with Jack Kirtz and a contractor about the surprise dream home where she now sat. Unfortunately for Millicent, when her husband knew he'd be delayed for the meeting, she offered to bring the plans and get things started. Hope found Cy and Millicent alone in the room and had held a San Diego tea party, tossing a pitcher of the cool drink in Millicent's face. Stacy and Hope had been through their share of drama and if there was some more brewing, they'd face it together.

"What's going on, Stacy?" Hope prompted her friend to open up about what was bothering her. "You know you can tell me anything."

"I'm worried about Tony."

"Still no takers?"

"No, and that's the problem. No team has shown interest in picking him up for the upcoming season. Tony is not dealing well with the fact that his career may be over."

"That's got to be rough."

"It is. I've talked to some of the other wives whose husbands have retired. Things can get tough. Some men get depressed and withdrawn, others have divorced their wives, left their families."

Hope swallowed her nervousness, forced herself to sound calm. "Are you worried that Tony will do that? Leave you and DJ?" She'd liked Tony Johnson from the moment she met him, and in hopes of helping Stacy move on from Darius, had encouraged her to date the strapping football star. Tony was a big, solid guy, over two hundred pounds of muscle and bone.

"If you'd asked me that six months ago, I would have said no way. But he's changing, Hope, becoming more distant and moody, just like what some of the wives said would happen. It's like nothing I say is the right thing. If I share my optimism that he'll get picked up, he tells me I don't know anything about the business of football. Which is right, I don't. If I tell him that he has a great future postplaying, remind him how various stations have shown interest in him doing game analysis or even hosting his own show, he gets angry and quiet. Tony likes to live large, so I know he's also concerned about our finances. I don't mind it, but I don't think my husband will want to change our lifestyle, a necessity once the big checks stop coming in. I want him to talk to Pastor Derrick, but I'm afraid it will make Tony too angry if it's suggested he get counseling, that *we* get counseling. But I hate to see him in pain, Hope. I hate to see the man I married becoming someone else."

"I'm so sorry, Stacy. Tony is a good guy. I can't help but think that y'all will get through this challenging time." Hope was quiet, her mind racing with possible ways to help her dear friend. "Do you think it would be too obvious if Cy called him? If I talk to him, I think he'd be open to helping Tony break into real estate. He's always looking for partners he can trust."

"Thank you, Hope. I don't think Tony is open right now, but that's a possibility to keep in mind."

"Well, maybe Cy can put it on his mind." Hope told Stacy about her convo with Vivian, the upcoming Sanctity of Sisterhood minisummit and her open invitation to their Fourth of July bash.

"Oh my God, girl, that would be perfect! It's just what Tony needs to get his mind off the game, and what is or isn't happening. Please thank Vivian for me and let her know that if at all possible, Tony and I will be there."

"I can send you guys plane tickets if it'll help; tell Tony that it's an early anniversary present."

"Let me talk to him. That man is so proud. If he smells anything close to charity, he'll not only clam up, but he'll know we've talked. So don't say or do anything unless I say so."

"Okay. I'm praying for you, sistah."

"Thanks, Hope. I need it."

"I've got you. If you and Tony come up the weekend before the fourth, we can hang out at Frieda's and do some serious shopping." Belatedly, Hope realized that suggesting they spend money might not be the best idea. "My treat."

"Tony's home, I'll talk to you later."

"Okay, Stacy, keep me posted. You know I'll worry about you. Take good care."

11

We'll See What's Up

Stacy sat in the living room, listening to the sound of Tony's footsteps as he entered the kitchen from the garage. She heard them stop, and knew that he'd opened the refrigerator and pulled out a beer. It was a daily ritual, popping a cold one as soon as he got home. He'd only have one beer a day, max. He was too aware of staying in shape to drink more than that. Cognac, however, was another story. After she heard the beer can top pop, she heard Tony's steps continue. Hiding the paper she'd been reading within an *Essence* magazine, she called out. "Hey, Tone."

"Hey." Instead of turning right, toward the living room from where she'd greeted him, he went left, and up the stairs to the bedrooms above. Not a good sign, but not a total surprise. He was home earlier than usual, which typically meant one of two things: he'd run out of potential opportunities to track down. Or he was in pain. Or both.

Stacy didn't know what to do, didn't like this state of flux that she'd felt for months, ever since the Cardinals had released Tony from their roster. This life was so different from the one she'd imagined when they met. The living room and bright Phoenix sunshine faded behind her memories of that better time—when their friendship went to another level and both decided to give the relationship a try.

Things had gotten off to a rocky start. After showing genuine interest in her at one of the Montgomerys' legendary Sunday dinners, Stacy had thrown a hitch in the giddyup when after Darius and Bo had shown up at the same dinner she began overtly flirting with the defensive back. Tony immediately peeped her try-and-make-Darius-jealous game and made it known that he didn't want to play. He'd cooled things until the day he'd seen her leaving a hospital as he entered, the day she'd found out that a lump in her breast was malignant. Tony had recently had his own indirect battle with the C word, had almost lost his mom to cancer. His understanding and compassion thawed the ice between them, and as he cared for her during and after her lumpectomy, their friendship began to grow. And then there was his proposal that brought the heat and changed the game! Stacy smiled, remembering. It had started with a date at the Getty Museum, after learning that both she and Tony had a love for art. Even so, she'd never visited the museum and hadn't been able to ignore her man's class in choosing such a location. They walked the grounds, opening up even more about their feelings for each other. Then they'd heard a jazz trio playing, and had moved closer to listen to them.

"Shall we?" Tony asked.

Stacy looked around. "We can sit here?"

"Why not?"

"It looks like it's reserved."

"Baby," Tony said, leaning over a bit, "my knee is acting up. If it is reserved we can sit down until whoever's got the table gets here."

They sat down at the center table, and soon the couple were taken to paradise on the wings of smooth jazz. A card on the table informed them that the group, the Musical Messengers, were on a twenty-five-city tour and would be at the Getty only this weekend. When they broke into a jazzy rendition of Marvin Sapp's "Never Would Have Made It," Stacy unexpectedly teared up.

"They're playing gospel," she whispered, wiping her eyes. "I love that song."

"Me too," Tony said. He kept his arms around her as the trio played. After the bridge, the saxophone player stepped to the mike and began reciting an original poem:

> *"Never would have made it, without God in my life,*
> *And now I don't want to go on without you by side.*
> *You are the air I breathe, the sun that shines,*
> *And I'd be so grateful if you'd be mine because . . ."*

Tony, getting down on his knees, began speaking along with the saxophonist and then finished the poem he'd written and then given to the musician when he set up this whole surprise. The saxophonist dropped out and Tony continued.

> *"I never would have made it, and I don't want to*
> *   take it,*
> *Take life without you. Stacy, baby, you turn my gray*
> *   skies blue.*
> *You have my heart. I love you. Will you marry me?"*

He reached into his pocket and pulled out a ring. Stacy could barely see it for crying.

"Tony!"

"I know it may feel like I'm moving too quickly. But I've waited my whole life for you. I know we can work. Because even now, before we're lovers, you're my best friend. Marry me, baby. And make me the happiest man on the planet."

"Yes," Stacy whispered, and then again, louder, "Yes! I'll marry you!"

"You'll be my wifey, baby?" he asked as he slipped the ring on her finger.

"Yes, baby, I'll be your wifey."

★ ★ ★

Stacy wiped her eyes as she came back to the present moment, her heart beating faster with the blessed memories of that event. In that moment, she recommitted to Tony, and to God. *I'm right here, baby. You and me together, we can do this. We'll get through this. . . .*

"Why are you crying?" Tony leaned against the living room's entryway, an unreadable expression on his face.

Stacy hadn't heard him descending the stairs. "Babe!" She hurriedly wiped the tears from her eyes. "I didn't hear you come down."

Tony walked into the room, sat in a chair opposite the couch where Stacy reclined. "What's the matter?"

Stacy looked over at the only man she'd ever loved, besides her baby's father, Darius Crenshaw. She hoped that the love she felt in her heart showed in her eyes. "Would you believe I've just taken a nostalgic walk down memory lane? I was remembering the night you proposed. It is singularly the most romantic thing anyone has ever done for me." Her voice dropped to a whisper. "What can I say? Now, as then, it brought me to tears."

Tony rose from the chair and joined her on the couch. He took the woman he'd loved enough to give her his last name in his arms. "That was a good day."

"The best."

"You know I love you, right?"

She shifted her body to face him, and wrapped her much smaller hands around his large ones. "I love you too, Tony. And I'm so proud of you."

Tony's demeanor immediately changed.

Oops. Wrong words. *Who knew?*

Tony removed his hands and jumped up from the couch. "What do you have to be proud of me about? Huh? I'm an out of work ball player trying to come back from what is looking more and more like a career-ending injury. I'm being courted by half-ass networks for half-ass sportscaster jobs. We're getting ready to see our net worth decrease exponentially, which means my child support payments will have to go down, which means their mothers will start tripping even more than they do now!" He came and stood over Stacy, causing her heart to leap into her throat. "What part of that equation do you find worth being proud about, huh? Huh?"

Stacy took a deep breath before she looked into her husband's somewhat scary face. She didn't like how he was standing over her, didn't like the fear that bubbled from her core to her stomach and from her stomach to her head, bringing on the hints of a migraine. She'd shared with Hope how some retired athletes couldn't handle the transition, becoming different men than the ones the women had married. *Are you worried that Tony will change like that?* That's what Hope had asked, and right now...? Stacy simply did not know what Tony was capable of doing.

"I remember a sermon where Pastor Montgomery quoted that it wasn't what happened to us, but how we handle it," she finally answered, forcing her voice to remain calm and steady. "In the face of some pretty challenging circumstances, you are still a strong, good man. That is why I'm proud of you."

Tony continued to hover over her with a silent intensity. Stacy eyed him steadily before looking beyond him, noticing a pair of sparrows frolicking in her wilting rosebushes. She abstractly remembered that the gardeners would come tomorrow and water the bushes drying prematurely under Arizona's relentless sun. It was only June, but she already knew the summer would be a scorcher. She only hoped that her husband's anger wouldn't outdo the record-breaking temperatures that Phoenix expected.

"That's bullshit," he finally said, turning and walking toward the window in time to see the birds that Stacy had observed leave the rosebushes and fly off in pursuit of each other. "But I know you're trying to make me feel better. I appreciate it."

"I married the man you are, not what you do."

"I know that. I believe that."

After a roller coaster of emotions within minutes, they'd reached a tender moment, one that had been rare in the last few months. Stacy didn't want the moment to end, so she mentioned something safe, something that almost always put a smile on Tony's face. "I've been thinking about the Fourth of July holiday, maybe spending it in LA and being able to spend at least part of it with Shea, Justin, and DJ, all of us together doing something fun."

Tony looked out the window for another moment before turning to face her. "It's funny that you should mention LA. I finally got the call and will definitely be doing a walk-on at their training camp."

"That's great, baby! I know you'd love to be back in LA. Me too."

It was true. Tony had loved playing in California. And now that this new team had been formed, and the Coliseum rebuilt, he'd like nothing better than to end his career in the City of Angels. "I'm not getting my hopes up but . . . it's a shot."

"I talked to Hope today and she'd just gotten off the phone with Lady Viv. She's putting together the next Sanctity of Sisterhood conference and wants my help. She told Hope that if we were in town for the fourth, we were welcome to their barbecue."

A slight frown scampered across Tony's face before he settled his features into an unreadable mask. "We'll see what's up." Without another word, he walked away.

Okay, what just happened? These mood swings were throwing Stacy off balance; one second the two of them could be in a great place and the next second he'd be filled with attitude. Walking on eggshells was an understatement. Anything could set him off. Stacy opened the *Essence* magazine and continued reading the paper that she'd hidden inside it when Tony came home. She was an optimist, but she was also a realist. If anything shaky jumped off between her and Tony Johnson, she planned to be prepared.

12

Happy Family, Happy Meal

Darius sat with a smile on his face, watching his son consume a Happy Meal. For the life of him he couldn't figure how a little toy inside a colorful box could make chicken nuggets and fries such a hit, but his son had turned down Bo's slap-your-mama spaghetti in favor of the popular children's fast food meal. D.J. walked the action figure across the granite island top as he munched on a fry, his legs swinging freely beneath the bar stool. Darius continued to watch him, amazed that doing what mothers around the world did every day all day—taking care of their children—could bring one such joy.

DJ took a break from the imaginary war happening on the table and turned to find his dad watching him intently. "What is it, Daddy?"

"Nothing. Just watching you eat."

DJ scrunched up his face. "Why?"

Darius laughed. "No reason."

DJ pondered that comment a moment, then reached for another fry and aimed it toward his father. "Do you want one?"

"No, he does not," Bo answered, turning from the stove with two plates of sausage spaghetti. "Nobody in this house eats that fake food but you."

"It not fake!" DJ protested.

"It isn't as good as my spaghetti," Bo countered.

"It's *better* than your spaghetti!" DJ said, as his voice rose an octave.

Bo leaned against the island, coming face to face with the little boy he loved like his own, which, in a way, DJ was. "Do you like how tall your father is?" DJ nodded. "What about his face; do you think he's handsome?"

DJ looked at Darius. Another nod. "Yes."

"Well, you know how he got so tall and so fine?" Bo's voice became an almost-whisper. "By eating *real* food like my spaghetti!" Without waiting for a reply, he flounced over to pull the parmesan-garlic toast from the oven.

DJ laughed. "Uh-uh. That's not true, Daddy . . . is it?"

"No, son, that's not true. You are going to be way more handsome than me." This, Darius believed was true. When it came to his son, he felt that he and Stacy had given him the best of themselves. DJ's facial features were almost carbon copies of Darius, but his lean body, keen mind, and sparkling personality were courtesy of Stacy Gray-Johnson. Yes, he'd been given awards, charted platinum albums, and toured the world, but the five-year-old wunderkind sitting across from him was by far the best product he'd ever created.

Bo placed the toast on the island and then joined them. Once he sat down, Darius reached for his fork. "No," Bo said, eyeing DJ as he took a piece of toast and tore it in half. "You're going to grow up looking like either a chicken nugget, hamburger, or French fry because that's all you eat." After finishing a forkful of spaghetti, he added, "But don't worry. You'll be the finest chicken nugget the world has ever seen. In fact, that's my new name for you: Nugget. You okay with that?"

DJ was crazy about Bo, but in this instance adopted an appropriate look of chagrin before forcing out a begrudging, "Not really. I like DJ."

"What if I tell you that the next time you come over we're going to create a special cookie and call it a Nugget, named after you. Would you be okay with that?"

"Yes!" A pause and then, "To go with my Happy Meal, right?"

They laughed and the conversation meandered from DJ's lengthy dissection of the movie they'd seen the day before to Darius's upcoming tour that kicked off with the musical benefit in New York's Central Park. They made quick work of devouring the vittles and while Bo tidied the kitchen, Darius and DJ went to pack for DJ's return to Stacy. As father and son chatted, Darius offered up a prayer of thanks that he and Stacy had been able to finally come to terms about custody. Because of Darius's hectic schedule, DJ stayed mostly with his mother, but when he was available, Stacy never turned down a request from Darius to spend time with his son. Last year, DJ had even traveled to New York with Darius and Bo when they went to visit the extensive family Bo had there. *Yeah, buddy,* he thought as he watched his son zip up his Transformer-decorated carry-on, *your life can't get much better than this.*

"You ready, little man?"

"Do I have to go home, Daddy?"

Darius's brows creased. This was an unexpected comment. He sat on the bed. "Don't you want to go home and see Mommy?"

"I want to see Mommy, but Tony's acting funny."

Darius tensed. "What do you mean by funny?"

DJ shrugged. "He just acts mad all the time and hardly plays with me anymore."

Darius relaxed. A little. "Aw, little man, don't worry about that. Tony likes to play football, remember?"

"Uh-huh."

"He's not playing right now and is probably a little upset about that. So just hang out with Mommy and give him his space, okay?"

"Okay."

They walked from DJ's bedroom back into the living room. Darius grabbed his keys from the fireplace mantel. "All right, Bo. I'll be right back."

Bo looked up from the TV show he was watching. "Okay. You

got a hug for me, Nugget?" DJ walked over and hugged him. "Okay, baby, hurry back."

As they walked out the front door to the Infiniti SUV waiting in the driveway, Bo went into the kitchen for a soda. Seeing a cell phone on the counter, he snatched it up, ran toward the front door, and opened it in time to see the brand new sporty BMW turn onto the road. "Darius!"

But it was too late. Darius hadn't heard him and, knowing how loud his husband played the car stereo, Bo knew why. He also knew that Darius hated going anywhere without his phone. He often even took it with him when he used the john. *Oh, well. He's just dropping off DJ. I guess he'll live without it till then.* Bo watched the car until it turned the corner and then walked back into the house. He was just about to set the phone down on the one-of-a-kind, stainless steel coffee table in front of him when it chirped in his hand. Someone had sent Darius a message.

"Bo," he said to the empty room, in a voice laced with warning, "you go looking for shit, you're going to find shit."

But it was a temptation he couldn't resist. He tapped the message indicator envelope. His jaws tightened when he saw the sender's name. "Muthafucka, you are just like herpes. You won't go away!" With anger mounting, he tapped the screen to open the message, and read it:

Hey, Handsome: Heard the commercial where you're going to be in NY on the 4th. Me too. Leave Bo at home and let's do the town . . . and then each other. Let me know.

"Oh, you've got this shit real twisted, nucka." Bo scrolled to the beginning of the message thread and saw that there had been several. While most had come from Paz, there were some that had been answered. "What? An independent project with my baby providing the sound track? Oh, H-E-double-L to the muthafuckin' no! You think it's that easy? You think you're going to dangle some money and take my man?" Bo's ire now had him walking the floor, boxing with an imaginary adversary. "You mess with him, Paz, and that will be your ass. You don't want none of this Brooklyn-born playa. You don't want none. Of. This."

As soon as Bo sat down to plot out his husband-saving strategy, an angel landed on one shoulder and a devil made himself at home on the other.

Angel: He didn't respond to the flirtatious e-mails, only the business ones.

Devil: But that don't mean he hasn't called him, or met him somewhere.

Angel: Except for Stacy, in all these years, he's never given you a reason to doubt him.

Devil: He's never given you a reason *that you know of.*

Angel: Don't make a mountain from a molehill, Bo.

Devil: Today's Mr. Cool, tomorrow's fool.

Bo jumped from the couch. "Both of y'all shut the hell up!" Walking to the back of the house to the great room where the bar was located, Bo made quick work of pouring a shot of Courvoisier and slamming it down. It felt so nice, he did it twice. "Think, Bo." And he did, back to the days and months following DJ's birth, and Darius's dilemma about who the person was with whom he should spend the rest of his life. His heart had said Bo while his head had screamed Stacy and their newborn son. It had been one heck of a tug-of-war, but eventually soul mate love and Stacy's histrionics had pushed Darius right into Bo's waiting arms. Now they coexisted amicably—Darius, Bo, Stacy, and DJ. Tony, not so much. The gay couple was tolerated because Darius was DJ's father, but Tony had let there be no mistake made when, during a visit shortly after he and Stacy married, he informed Darius and Bo that "he didn't get down with anybody who got down like that."

Bo had retorted, "Then I guess since your wife's baby daddy is gay, you're not getting down with her?"

Stacy's intervention had prevented an episode of *Fisticuffs, Beat-*

downs, and Curse-Your-Ass-Outs, but since that confrontation, Tony had refused interaction except when absolutely necessary for the sake of the child. Meaning that if he were home when Darius dropped off DJ, he'd eke out a "how you doing" and then promptly leave the room.

No, Bo. Don't be a bitch about this. Don't make waves until you know for sure there's another boat in your harbor. Plan of action decided, he picked up his phone, stored Paz's number, and cleared the screen just as he heard Darius's keys jingling in the door. Bo poured another Courvoisier, this time on the rocks, fixed Darius's favorite drink, and walked toward the living room to meet him. Halfway there he changed course and took the drinks into the bedroom. He was too happy and life was too good for anybody to think for a minute that he'd give any part of it up. Couldn't nobody love Darius the way that he did and when it came to this fact, Bo believed that he could show him better than he could tell him.

13

Nosy Nannies

Frieda heard the doorbell ring. She wasn't expecting anyone and assumed that Cordella would send whoever had the nerve to solicit at her doorstep on their merry way. Having decided to end the suspense in at least one area of her life, she was busy researching DNA-testing companies. Earlier, she'd retrieved a few hairs from the comb that Gabriel had recently used and had placed them in a plastic bag. Gabe looked a lot like her, true, but the "good hair" on his dome was not the product of a texturizer, conditioner, or either person listed on the child's birth certificate. There were a couple of past partners whose genes could have been the source of that trait. She hoped it was Shabach, a multi-platinum gospel hip-hop artist—because in the event of a divorce, he'd keep the paper rolling—but it could be Gorgio, her former running buddy and casual sex partner for many years. Either way, a sistah had to know. Raised voices from the foyer area brought her out of her musings.

The female voice was clearly that of her house manager, Cordella. "I don't care what she told you. This is my place of employment and you cannot come strutting through the front door as though it's your due. Why didn't you call and tell me you were coming?"

The mumbled male voice sent a squiggle through Frieda's

nana. *Clark!* She closed the browser of her latest search and made quick work of the distance between her shared office with Gabriel and the front part of the house. "It's all right, Cordella. I asked Clark to come here." Actually, she'd had no idea that her lover would show up on the front door of the home she shared with her husband but...okay. Gabe was sleeping, his father wouldn't be home for several hours, and it had been two days.

"What?" Cordella looked at her with both scorn and skepticism.

This witch has been tripping with me ever since I checked her about helping Gabriel get all up in my business. She made up a story on the spot. "The last time he was here he, uh, told me about a new computer program. I asked him to come over and teach me how to operate it." The lie came so quickly and so easily that had she been more limber, Frieda would have patted her own back.

"Forgive me, Mrs. Livingston, but I don't believe it is proper that my son visit you in this way."

"And I don't think it's *proper* for you to question my behavior! Three months ago, when you needed to quickly get money to your grandchild, you didn't believe it improper that I gave you an advance on your salary, and that your son came over then, did you?"

"No, missus, I didn't."

"Then don't try and check me on what I do. Your son helping me is working to your advantage. Do you understand me?" Silence. Frieda took a step forward. "I said, Do. You. Understand. Me?"

"Yes, Mrs. Livingston," Cordella replied, hands clasped, eyes shifted downward. "I understand. My apologies."

"And just so we're clear, I don't need you reporting back to my husband about this visit, just like I didn't need you running down my schedule to him before. If there is anything happening in my life that Gabriel needs to know, I will tell him."

"Mrs. Livingston, I simply told him what he asked me."

"If he asks you another question with my name in the sentence, you refer him to me. Okay?" Cordella nodded. Frieda was tempted to curse out the help, but considering the tongue-lashing in store for her lover, she chose not to die on this particular hill. Instead she fixed Clark with a pointed look and said, "Come on back to the office." She turned and began walking, not waiting to see whether or not she was being followed. Her actions had clearly told him that he'd messed up. His obeying was a given.

As dramatic a move as it was, it may have been worth her while to look back. Had she done so, she would have seen the daggers that Cordella was shooting at her back. Unfortunately, out of sight was not out of mind. She'd feel more than the tip of these knives before long.

Frieda remained quiet until she and Clark had reached the office and she'd closed the door. Then she rounded on him like a boxer. "What the fuck are you doing?"

"What? Me wanna see you."

Trying to not let that sexy-ass accent, those juicy lips, or the outline pressing against his shorts get her off track, she continued her line of questioning. "Coming to my house without calling first, and ringing the front doorbell? Have you lost your damn mind?"

"Have you lost your nerve, woman?" Clark crossed his arms and anyone looking would have sworn that his chest grew another inch as he puffed it out. "You told me that you got it handled over here, that you were running things. Don't look like it, the way you're acting right now."

His audacity was as sexy as his accent. Standing in her house, in her office, reminding her of words she'd boasted and making her feel like she was on the defensive in the process. *How did this script get flipped?* Frieda didn't know, but she was definitely getting ready to get the train back on track.

"Look, you got some good dick, but it's not the biggest one, the longest one, or the only one in LA. Don't think I'm sprung on your ass, 'cause I can blink my eyes and move you to the left faster than you can roll a blunt. . . . Feel me?" Clark lost that extra inch of chest that it looked like he'd gained moments before. "Your boy

Spencer was looking pretty good when we were at the club last week. Don't think I won't hollah at him. As you know, since I met you because your mother is my nanny, I don't have a problem keeping it in the family."

Mentioning Spencer was like striking a match. Born only months apart, Clark had had a love/hate relationship with his cousin—feeling he'd readily take a bullet for him, yet kill him at the same time. He closed the distance between himself and Frieda in one long stride. "What the hell you telling me, girl?" he asked as he placed a viselike grip on her arm and pulled her into his hard chest. "He say something to you?"

Umph. Ain't nothing like a take-charge man. This type of delicious friction would never happen between her and Gabriel. He was too logical, too civilized. But this, this animalistic palpitation in the room, the sexual tension, the inevitable argument that precedes incredible makeup sex . . . only came with someone like Frieda dueling with someone like Clark. She knew this and, for whatever it was worth, Clark knew it too.

"No, he didn't say nothing. I'm saying that *I* might say something."

"Don't push me, girl. . . ." Clark loosened his grip on her arm.

Frieda took a step away from him. "You better check yourself."

"So what . . . you kicking me out? You want this to be over? Or do you want me to"—he gave her the once-over while stroking his rod—"show you how to work that new computer program?"

Frieda got to within inches of Clark's face and dropped her voice to a low growl. "Don't you ever come to my place again unless I personally invite you. Not to see your mother, not because you're in the neighborhood, not for any reason. Do you understand me?" She pointed a finger in his face for emphasis.

"I understand this," Clark drawled as he tweaked the hardened nipple beneath Frieda's strappy top.

She cursed the spontaneous wetness that occurred in her panties at Clark's touch, then swatted his hand away. "I'm not playing, Clark. This is my life we're talking about."

"Your life . . . or your lifestyle?"

"Whatever it is, it's mine, nucka. You want to play with Frieda, you play by my rules. My way or the highway. Now which one do you want?"

Clark's response? Not a word. Just closed the gap between them with one step, and without breaking eye contact, wrapped his muscular arm around her waist and pulled her to him. It was a surprise move, and Clark swallowed Frieda's gasp in a bruising kiss, forcing his swordlike tongue into her mouth in a merciless assault. She wore a twelve-hundred-dollar Mondo original, but Clark scrunched the skirt up around her waist like it had been purchased on the clearance rack at a garage sale. His hand found her booty and squeezed each cheek before pushing her closer, slamming her pelvic area against his massive hardness. Swirling his tongue inside her moistness, he walked them over to the large cherrywood desk that anchored the left side of the room. Pushing books, files, and medical periodicals to the floor, Clark lifted Frieda by her booty and placed her on the desk. He stepped between her legs, slid a finger up her thigh and began circling motions precariously close to her heat. The oral assault continued.

Frieda shivered, totally caught up in the wave of feelings overtaking her senses. It was a heady combination of shock, anger, lust, satisfaction, and overwhelming need. For this. Sex. Hot, hard, and with Clark. A strand of her thoughts toyed with the question of what it was about this particular brothah that had her so twisted. A finger sliding between her drenched folds combined with a wet tongue creating a trail from her neck to her tank top provided a partial answer.

"Why didn't you call me back?" The voice was low, almost growling, breath hot and pungent—Newport Menthols—against her stomach.

The words, or at least their sound, wafted between the haze of her desire. *Huh? What? Did he just ask me a question? Does he actually believe I can think right*—"Ooh." He'd parted her paradise to slide a long thick middle finger inside.

He slid his face closer to where his finger lounged. "Huh? Why didn't you call me?"

"Couldn't," Frieda panted as she grinded against his finger. *Wait a minute. I'm in control, mutha*—"Ahh." His tongue had found out where his finger was hanging out.

"When I call, you need to answer." His breath teased the inside of her thighs. "You know who this belongs to." As she spread her legs to allow better access, Frieda was vaguely aware of a knocking sound. It crept into her lust-filled conscience, a nagging distraction that gained in intensity even as Clark's tongue strokes gained in speed. *What is that? His legs against the desk? My head next to the . . . no . . . wait . . . it's the door!* She placed her hands on the sides of Clark's head, forcing him to stop. "Shh!"

The knock again, followed by a rattling of the doorknob. "Mrs. Livingston, your husband is on the phone."

Damn! Thank God I locked that door! "Okay, Cordella. Thanks." With both sets of lips quivering, Frieda slid off one side of the desk and wobbled over to where the phone sat on the other side. "Hey, baby." Her voice was far more breathy than she'd hoped, but it was what happened when one was literally at the peak of orgasm, and then unexpectedly interrupted.

"Frieda? What are you doing?"

"I just ran into the house from outside—trying to catch my breath." Five seconds passed. Ten. Twenty. "Gabriel?"

"You were outside?"

Frieda knew the deal; Cordella had disobeyed her orders and again talked out of school. But just how much did Gabriel know? "Yes, I'm working in the office, but heard a weird sound out by the pool and went out to investigate. I didn't see anything so . . . maybe it was a bird or something." No back pat this time; the answer was lame at best.

"What's going on, Frieda?"

"Why do you think something is going on? I told you what I was doing so what do you want?"

"Never mind."

"Gabriel, wait!"

But he didn't. Dead air was Frieda's confirmation that he'd ended the call. Frieda charged to the door.

"Where are you going?" Clark asked.

"To fire your mother."

He closed the distance between them in three strides. "Wait! What did she do?"

"She needs to mind her own business, but keeps getting into mine!"

"Come here, baby," Clark said, once again enveloping Frieda in his long, strong arms. "Let me talk to her." When she squirmed a bit he continued. "She needs this job, baby. My brother's back home and you know my sister's baby has been sick. . . . She's their only support."

Frieda's eyes narrowed as she gave Clark's body—tall, lean, taut—the once-over. "Cordella has one more time to cross me, Clark," she huffed, one lone finger in the air for emphasis. "One more time to get out of line and she is out the door."

Needless to say, the thrill was gone, so Clark left within minutes. But the moment would prove pivotal for everyone involved.

Frieda decided that along with a DNA specialist she needed to shop for a new nanny/house manager.

Cordella decided to begin collecting proof of what she believed were her employer's infidelities.

Clark decided it was time for Frieda to know who was really in control.

And Gabriel decided it was time to spend less time with his patients, and more time with his wife.

14

Friends and Facebook

Cy sat in his office, sipping a cup of green tea and staring at the computer screen. He'd had a restless night, due in no small part to the conversation he'd had yesterday. With Trisha. The fact that she hadn't immediately answered his e-mail to her, the second one he'd sent the day after she'd decided to reconnect with him out of the blue, had left him thinking that he wouldn't hear from her at all. But he had. Yesterday. She'd told him she'd been busy, had expressed her excitement that they'd reconnected, and ended the e-mail with her phone number. He'd had an appointment in Los Angeles and when he arrived at his LA office . . . he'd called her.

"Trisha Underwood."

A long pause and then a question. "Who's calling, please?"

Cy smiled, realizing that the feisty skepticism that Trisha possessed had not diminished. "Trisha, it's Cy."

"Cy! Oh my goodness!"

I don't remember your voice being so hoarse, but then again, it has been almost twenty years. "How are you, Trisha?"

Again, a pause before answering. "I'm okay. Wow, after all these years of thinking about how you've been and where you are, I can't believe I'm actually talking to you."

"I've thought about you too . . . over the years."

There was a palpable intensity to the moment, even though both struggled to sound casual and nonchalant. Later, both would learn that it was for very different reasons.

"So, Cy Taylor, what have you been up to the last decade?"

"Ha!"

"I should add besides becoming a very successful businessman. That's how Jeannetta tracked you down, you know."

"You can't possibly mean Jeannetta Harris."

"The one and only."

Now it was Cy's turn to pause as memories rushed in. Jeannetta Harris, the woman who'd lured him into her bed while he was dating Trisha. What he hadn't known at the time was that Jeannetta was insanely jealous of Trisha and would do anything to dim the sunshine that seemed to follow Trisha around. Simply put, she set him up, and made sure that Trisha found out about it. To say she was hurt was an understatement. Trisha not only broke up with him, but during the remainder of their college years acted as though he was not alive. For years Cy had detested Jeannetta as the cause of the breakup with his first true love. Even after graduation he'd tried to obtain Trisha's whereabouts, but her friend's lips were tighter than Spanx on a fat chick. Finally he gave up and moved on.

"Jeannetta?" he finally said. "You've got to be kidding."

"I ran into her a couple years ago. She'd found God and I guess as a result of that, was full of remorse about what she'd done. She asked for my forgiveness, and whether you and I had kept in touch with each other. When I told her no, she told me that she'd seen your name from time to time on various social media sites, namely LinkedIn, which I'd never joined. Lately, she saw you on Facebook and gave me your e-mail address."

Cy knew there was a reason he'd held out on joining the popular website. There were some people from his past with whom he'd rather not reconnect. Trisha was not one of them. Jeannetta was. "Wow, I don't even know how to respond to that story. After the one and only time we were together, and after I found out her true motives, she and I were never even in the same room, much less talked to each other."

"Well, you may be surprised to know that she is living on five acres of rural land in North Carolina, married to a cattle rancher, and the mother of three rambunctious boys."

"I'm very surprised."

"I saw her at the ten-year reunion, but we didn't talk. Then a couple years ago she looked me up on the classmate Web site, reached out, and I responded."

"Why?"

"Beyond anything else, Jeannetta and I are not only sorors, but we're human. She asked for my forgiveness, I gave it, and she felt that reconnecting us was a sort of restitution."

"I must say I was more than surprised to get your e-mail, but after all these years, it is truly a pleasure to talk with you again." A comfortable silence ensued before Cy continued. "I notice you're still using your maiden name, Trisha. Are you one of these new age women who maintain their independence even after marriage?" This time, there was no mistaking the pause. It lasted so long that Cy checked his connection. "Trisha?"

"Nope, never married. No children."

Thinking of his wonderful wife and beautiful twins, Cy was immediately uncomfortable, and somewhat saddened. "Well, you always were a go-getter. I imagine you opted for the successful career."

"Not exactly."

Hmm. Cy wondered what he was supposed to do with that response.

Turns out, he didn't have to do anything with it. Trisha wasn't finished. "I never stopped loving you, Cy."

The raw energy surrounding her honest answer caused Cy's stomach to clench. "You can't possibly be saying that your single status, all these years later, is because of me."

Trisha chuckled to try and lighten the moment. "I guess I was always trying to find someone to replace you. And no one ever did." Cy had absolutely no answer for that, so he remained quiet. "I'd like to see you, Cy."

"I'd like to see you too," Cy responded, with no hesitation. "I'm married with children and happily so, but I never forgot you, always wondered how you were doing and prayed that life had given you what you wanted. Has it?"

"In a way. Seeing you would be a great booster."

"Then it's settled. I've got business that will have me in and out of New York for the next few months. The next time I'm headed that way, I'll let you know."

Cy hadn't told Hope about this conversation. It wasn't that he was trying to hide anything, but having had his share of experiences with women, he just felt that whatever was said to Hope regarding Trisha would be delivered on a need-to-know basis. Cy looked down at the one-sentence message he'd discovered upon opening his e-mails this morning.

I need to see you, Cy. As soon as possible.

The words were simple, but for whatever reason, Cy felt an urgency beneath them. He wanted to see Trisha, felt that he *needed* to see her. And when it came to his wife, his heartbeat, Hope Jones Taylor, this situation was now a definite need-to-know.

15

Assuming the Best

"You were an early bird this morning." Hope placed a glass of orange juice and two superfood pills in front of her husband, who was seated at the breakfast nook. It was seven-thirty in the morning, more than an hour since Cy had read Trisha's latest e-mail, and mere minutes since Hope had washed her face, brushed her teeth, and come downstairs to prepare breakfast for her husband.

"Yes. I didn't want to wake you so instead of tossing and turning, I decided to just get up."

Hope's hand hovered for just a moment above the French toast that she was about to flip. She took a breath, flipped the thick French bread awash in whipped eggs seasoned with sea salt, raw sugar, and cinnamon, and lowered the heat before she turned around to get a look at the reason for her breathing. "What's on your mind, babe?"

Cy finished drinking the orange juice Hope had given him. "I talked to Trisha yesterday."

"Oh?" The marital counseling sessions she'd had with First Lady Vivian Montgomery before her marriage, and the conversations they'd recently shared, caused her to absorb this news without so much as a flinch. *Always assume the best about your husband.* That's what Vivian had told her. And that's what she'd do. "How'd that come about?"

"I responded to the e-mail she sent me and she responded with her phone number."

Hope lifted the French toast from the cast iron skillet that had been a wedding gift from her mother, added several links of organic veggie sausages, and walked the plate over to where Cy sat. "I remember you saying that you two were pretty serious in college," she said, her voice light and airy as she placed a single piece of toast on her plate, along with a couple links of sausage. After getting the maple syrup from the microwave she joined her husband at the table and said, "I'm sure that that was an interesting conversation."

"It was." Cy spread butter on his toast, added a liberal amount of syrup, and after slicing it into uniform cubes, took a bite. "This is delicious, baby."

Hope dressed her plate as well, but instead of reaching for her fork, picked up her orange juice and leaned back in the booth. "What did she say? Why is she contacting you after all these years?"

Cy gave Hope the condensed version of his conversation with Trisha.

"So she's never married, has no children, and admits that she still loves you. I'm finding it hard to see the positive angle of her desire to reconnect." She picked up her fork, cut off a generous piece of French toast, and enjoyed the bite. "Um, this *is* good."

"I'm baffled too, not only because it was Jeannetta who told her how to contact me, but because I thought this was all about the reunion. But now, I just don't know."

"So what are you going to do, baby?"

Cy devoured a sausage link. "She wants me to call her the next time I'm in New York."

"Where she lives, right?" Cy nodded. "And if I remember correctly, your next trip there is scheduled for shortly after the Fourth of July."

"The following week."

Hope took a couple more bites. "Are you going to meet with her?"

"It depends on whether or not you have a problem with that."

Hope finished the food that was on her plate and downed the juice in her glass. "I guess a brief meeting in a public place, with no physical contact, for old time's sake, would be okay."

"Dang, baby. I can't hug a person I haven't seen for years?"

Hope thought for a moment. "I guess a very brief church hug would be okay."

Cy smiled. He knew what kind of hug Hope was talking about—where the upper bodies touched but the lower half was at least a foot apart.

"I wouldn't want to come off as a possessive, jealous female who doesn't trust her man."

"I appreciate that, baby. Like I said, I'm curious about what she could want after all these years."

"Well," Hope said dryly as she reached for his plate, then got up from the table and walked over to the sink, "with all the effort she's put into finding you, I'm sure that she'll tell you."

The rest of their conversation was aborted as Rosie brought down the twins, who enjoyed the French toast and sausage as much as their parents. Afterward, Cy left for LA and Hope spent a couple hours with the children before Rosie's Spanish lessons and time at the park. After Yvette arrived and put Hope through a rigorous workout, Hope watched an episode of *Conversations with Carla,* a popular television talk show hosted by Sanctity of Sisterhood member and former first lady Carla Chapman. Then she placed phone calls to both her parents. Pat, who was still glowing following her return to Oklahoma after a long weekend in La Jolla, and Earl, who much to his daughter's surprise and delight was touting the benefits of less meat and more leafy greens, a diet encouraged by his current wife. Just after she'd conferred with Rosie about the dinner preparations, she got a call from Vivian.

"Hello, Hope. I don't have much time, but I wanted to call and see if you'd had a chance to study the theme of the upcoming summit, and the scriptures I'd mentioned."

"Sure have. I Am. Who knew those two small words could mean so much? I researched some of the foundation scriptures and will look at the rest of them when we return from LA. I also have an idea for a praise dance, using a song by Rickie Byars called "In the Land of I Am."

Vivian instantly loved the idea, surprised that she herself hadn't thought of it. Hope had been involved in praise dancing from her youth and when she relocated to Los Angeles, had added this component to KCCC's worship arts. "Hmm, haven't heard it," she replied.

"One of Cy's associates turned him on to her work some time ago. She's Reverend Michael Beckwith's wife."

"Why does that name sound familiar?"

"He's the founder and pastor at Agape."

"Of course—the one who was in *The Secret*."

"Yes. His wife is a force to be reckoned with in her own right: minister, author, and amazing recording artist. They wrote this song together."

"I love the idea of a praise dance, Hope, and I'd like to hear it."

"It's on my iPod. I'll make sure and bring it when we come over."

"So you and Cy are coming for sure? That's excellent."

"Yes, we'll be there."

"Telling me about Rickie's song reminds me of another song that came out years ago. It was on a CD produced by a ministry here in LA, Bam Crawford. The song is called "I Am the I Am." Do you know it?"

"No, I don't think I've ever heard that."

"We'll also give that one a listen when you come to town. I can't wait to see you."

"I need, I mean, want to see you too."

"Okay, Hope. What aren't you telling me?"

"Something that I'd rather discuss in person. I could use your counsel."

"In that case, let's carve out some time when you and I can chat."

"Sounds good. I miss being at KCCC every Sunday, Lady Viv. I'm looking forward to seeing you guys."

"And I look forward to seeing you as well."

After ending the call, Hope poured herself a glass of sparkling water and went out to the patio . . . her favorite place. She looked out over the Pacific Ocean, the beauty that surrounded a life that had exceeded her expectations. As she thought on the I Am, she counted many things that she was: happy, fulfilled, and madly in love being among them. And whatever it was that Trisha had on her mind, Hope didn't plan on giving up any of the things for which she was thankful.

16

Bump the B. S.

"Frieda!" Stacy walked into the private dining room of a Beverly Hills hotel, feeling more joy than she'd imagined she would at seeing an old friend. They met and hugged. "It's been too long, girl. How are you?"

"Girl, we need to order drinks before I answer that question," Frieda quipped, sitting down and taking in Stacy's picture-perfect outfit but telltale face. A tale that wasn't picture perfect. "When did you guys get here?"

"Flew in last night." Stacy sat down. "So what's going on, girl?"

"We might as well wait for Hope so we don't have to repeat the same stories twice."

"I'm surprised that I beat her, especially since I know they drove up from La Jolla last night, too. She's usually the timely one."

"That was before she had two crumb snatchers to lug around. Speaking of, how is your Junior?"

"Growing up too fast." Stacy picked up the menu. "How is your Junior?"

"Three going on thirteen. He loves preschool and is already reading."

"The kids these days come in on another level. DJ was reading by that time, too."

"It's crazy how fast they learn... computers, video games. But life moves way faster than when we grew up. Kids these days have to be on top of their game." Frieda took a sip of her cocktail. "What are you drinking?"

"I'll have what you're having."

Stacy had just received her banana split martini when Hope came through the double doors. "It's my girls!" Both Frieda and Stacy stood so that they could all get in good hugs. Hope sat down on one of the remaining empty seats. "Sorry I'm late. Had to get Rosie and the kids settled in the condo."

"Where's Cy?"

"Went over to Kingdom Citizens Christian Center to meet with Pastor Derrick." Hope squeezed both of her friend's forearms. "It's been way too long since we've done this, all three of us together."

"You're right about that," Stacy readily agreed. "Oh, and thanks, Hope, for the offer to purchase our plane tickets. You know Tony, though. Not only did he not go for it, but he had to use some of our dwindling bank account to book us in first class." She shook her head. "I must say that the timing for the trip is perfect, though. Tony is using the extra time to work with a friend of his who is also a personal trainer, doing some last-minute tweaking before his tryouts coming up. He's so excited to try out for the Sea Lions; I just hope he isn't setting himself up for disappointment."

"His knee is totally healed, right?" Hope asked.

Stacy nodded. "Yes, he's been back to his full workout for a while now."

"Tony's one helluva defensive end," Frieda offered. "I think any team would be lucky to have him."

"I agree," Hope said, signaling the waiter to bring over another martini. "It would be wonderful having you back in our neck of the woods."

The small talk continued until the waiter delivered Hope's drink, and they placed their orders. Then in typical bump-the-bullshit fashion, Frieda shifted the conversation from possible vacation locations to more dramatic situations. "Stacy, what are y'all going to do if Tony doesn't get picked up?"

Stacy's voice dropped and her eyes became sad. "I don't know. His agent lined up sportscaster interviews, but Tony isn't ready to think about life beyond football. It's making things tough at home."

Frieda's brows creased. "How tough? He isn't violent, is he?"

"No, Frieda! Why would you say that?" Even as she responded with indignation, the image of his menacing frame recently standing over her flashed into her mind.

"I hung out with a player for a hot minute and became friends with his best friend's girlfriend. She used to get beat on the regular. Finally left him. The paper he threw her way wasn't worth the punches he also threw."

When Stacy continued to remain silent, Hope continued probing. It wasn't simple nosiness. She was the one who'd encouraged Stacy to date Tony, hoping that by doing so she'd get over Darius. Now Hope prayed that she hadn't sent her friend from the frying pan into the fire. "So things are still tense on the home front?"

"Yes. I'm trying to be the understanding wife, but every time I attempt to offer a positive perspective, it backfires." Stacy shrugged. "I don't know how to help him."

"Maybe he can talk to Pastor while he's here."

"That's a good idea, Hope. But I'll have to find a roundabout way to make it happen. Tony isn't too keen on anybody thinking something is wrong with him right about now. To hear him tell it, his present situation is everyone's fault but his."

"If you'd like, I can talk to Lady Viv, or have Cy mention it to Pastor."

"Yes, please do that. Having Pastor Derrick talk to him will probably help some, but the only thing that will bring my old Tony back is him being back on the playing field."

After a thoughtful silence while the ladies processed this news, Stacy said, "Speaking of playing the field, Frieda, what's going on with you that had you dodging a three-way?"

"What?"

"Don't 'what' me. Hope pulled me into a three-way and when she clicked back over to reach you, there was only dead air." When Frieda acted as though she didn't get the meaning, Stacy spoke straight out. "You'd hung up."

"Yes, Frieda," Hope added. "I'd like to know more about that too."

The waiter delivered their salads and Frieda waited until he'd left to address Stacy's and Hope's comments. "I already told you, Hope," she said, taking the double helping of balsamic vinaigrette dressing that she'd asked be served on the side and pouring it over her organic micro greens. She looked at Stacy. "I have a new boo."

Stacy stopped in midreach of the container filled with honey-mustard dressing on the side of her plate. "You're having an affair?"

"Girl, you might call it an affair; I call it an alternative. I've been faithful to Gabriel since we got married and believe me, it hasn't been easy. He works almost around the clock and when he comes home, nonstop effing isn't what he has in mind. I love my child's father, but the doctor is boring with a capital B."

"Cousin, that's no excuse to commit adultery."

"Hmph. Christians commit adultery. Heathens like me just fuck."

"Frieda!"

"Ha! I'm messing with you, Hope. I knew that would get you going. I didn't go looking for Clark. It just happened. But the way I look at it, my man on the side may be the very thing that helps me stay married."

Hope wanted to shake sense into her cousin's foolhardy head. But she forced herself not to lecture. She'd done that too many times and knew that, for the most part, any advice she gave her cousin went in one ear and out the other.

Stacy finished her bite of salad. "Where'd you meet him?"

"He's my nanny's son."

"What?" The one-word question was in stereo.

"Cordella called him one day to bring something over to her. And, baby, I took one look at that six-foot-three-inch collection of muscle and bone and became interested in one bone in particular. Something about his swagger said that brothah was packing." She pointedly looked at Hope and then Stacy. "Why are you y'all looking at me crazy? He is!"

"You've got a good thing going, Frieda," Stacy said. "A good man. Do you want to throw it all away for good sex?"

Frieda finished her salad and pushed away the plate. She didn't answer.

Stacy's voice was filled with concern. "Just be careful, okay?"

"Don't worry. Gabriel is too busy working to know what I do." After the waiter had delivered their entrées, Frieda turned to Hope. "What about you, cousin? What's going on in your picture-perfect, Cinderella world?"

Hope shook her head as she finished the bite of grilled tenderloin on toasted foccacia bread. "I'm not perfect, Frieda; and neither is my world."

"So what's up?"

"Cy got a blast from his college days past."

"Let me guess," Stacy said. "A female."

"Not just any female; his first love."

Frieda was immediately indignant. "What in the hell does she want?"

"We don't know, but we'll soon find out. She lives in New York and Cy will more than likely meet her when he goes there next week."

Frieda crossed her arms. "Are you crazy?"

"Hope, I've got to go with Frieda on this one. Stirring the coals of an old flame is never a good idea."

"Believe me, I'm not too thrilled about it, but at the same time I have to trust my husband."

"Yes, but do you trust her?" Frieda finally picked up her fork and began eating her baked salmon. "You know how scandalous we can be. Cy had better be on guard at *all* times."

After that cryptic warning, the conversation moved on to less stressful topics including plans for a play date after church the following day so that their children could better get to know each other. Because of dinner plans with her brothers and mom, Stacy declined Frieda's invite to meet later on at her house. Hope gave a tentative acceptance, as long as Cy hadn't already committed them to something else.

With tentative activities outlined, the ladies soon wrapped up lunch and went their separate ways. Before long, they would learn that they were not the only ones making plans.

17

Flashback to the Future

"I know you love La Jolla, but, man, do I miss you being in the ministry full time." After a grueling three-hour meeting about the church's expansion, Derrick and Cy sat in Kingdom Citizens Christian Center's private dining room, enjoying a lunch that had been prepared by one of the kitchen staff. "Your consulting on this project is invaluable, but I miss you having my back on Sundays."

Last year, Cy had resigned as an associate minister at KCCC, a position that Derrick had talked him into in the first place. "Honestly, Dee, I've been too busy to miss much of anything, but I know Hope wants us to try and start attending service on a more regular basis. If she had her way, we'd be here every Sunday. Jack wants us to move our membership to his church, but while Hope and Millicent have reached a level of civility, she could never be my baby's first lady."

Derrick chuckled. When it came to some of Millicent's and Hope's past drama, he'd had a front row seat. "I'll never forget the first time you brought Hope to church."

"Oh, Lord. Don't remind me."

"I haven't thought of that incident in a long time. When Millicent appeared at the back of the church in that dress? It was all I could do to keep my jaw from dropping to the floor."

"Imagine how I felt. First time I'd invited Hope to California, still in the early stages of our relationship. I wanted the Lord to come right then, to save me from Hope's anger and to save Millicent from herself!" Cy shook his head at the memory of Millicent walking down the aisle during a packed Sunday morning service, in full wedding regalia, demanding a stunned Cy Taylor join her at the altar.

"Husband, come to me!" Derrick mimicked the words that Millicent had somberly intoned on that fateful day.

"Aw, man. The cool way Hope handled that situation and her total belief in what I'd told her was further confirmation that she was the one." After a pause, he continued. "You know, it's funny that you should mention that fiasco. It's making me think twice about another woman."

Derrick leaned back in his chair. "Talk to me."

Cy recounted the surprise e-mail he received from Trisha and his plans to meet her next week. "After all of these years, I'm curious to see her," he finished. "Hope doesn't object to my meeting her as long as I limit any physical contact to a church hug."

"Smart woman. But even with your wife's approval, for lack of a better word, do you think this is a good idea? She could turn out to be another stalker."

"No, not Trisha. She's got too much pride for that." The room became silent for a few moments, as the men ate their food and marinated in their thoughts.

Derrick finally reached for his napkin, leaning against the chair as he wiped remnants of perfectly fried chicken from his mouth. "If you don't have other plans, you and Hope are welcome to join us for Sunday brunch tomorrow."

"I'll talk to her and let you know. I'm just glad to see that you're still looking good and doing well. It's almost like the tumor never happened."

"God gets all the glory," Derrick responded. "And I'll forever be indebted to Keith Black."

"Absolutely. That man is definitely operating in his gift; his skill as a surgeon is something you can't get from education alone.

I went online to find his book and—Oh, wait a minute." Cy reached for his vibrating cell phone. He looked at the number, then shifted his eyes to Derrick as he answered the call and put it on speakerphone. "Trisha!"

"Hello, Cy."

"I'm having lunch with my pastor. What's going on?"

"Your pastor? Wow, you have changed. I never would have pictured you as a churchgoing man."

"I know, huh. Considering all of those times you used to try and drag me to church. A lot can change in fifteen years."

"Who is your pastor?"

"Derrick Montgomery, senior pastor of—"

"Kingdom Citizens Christian Center."

"Oh, you've heard of him?"

"I'm a PK, Cy, remember? Derrick Montgomery is a big name in the Christian world. Of course I've heard of him."

At her mention of being a preacher's kid, Cy asked, "How is your father?"

"He's had some health issues but overall, he's fine. Look, right now I only have a few minutes to talk. I just called to see if you were still coming to New York next week."

"Yes. I'll be there on Wednesday."

"Will we get a chance to meet?"

"Yes. I talked it over with my wife and told her that I'd like to see you, get caught up on each other's lives. I'll give you a call once I land and know for sure what evening I'll be free."

"I look forward to it, Cy. It's been a long time."

"That it has. I'll call you next week."

"Okay. See you soon, Cyclone."

"Goodbye . . . Trisha."

Cy ended the call, not missing the skeptical look that Derrick was casting in his direction. "Cyclone?"

"That's what they called me back in college."

"I don't know, man. I'm not too comfortable with the vibe I'm getting."

"Look, we'll meet for dinner in a very public place, say our good-byes, and go on our merry ways. What can happen?"

"When it comes to the dynamics between a man and a woman . . . anything is possible."

"Duly noted, Pastor."

"I hope so. You and Hope make a great team; in a way y'all remind me of myself and Viv. Don't head to that meeting without donning the full armor."

Cy nodded, understanding the meaning of Derrick's comment. "Put on the whole armor of God, that you may be able to stand against the wiles of the devil."

"For we wrestle not against flesh and blood," Derrick continued. "But against principalities, against powers, against the rulers of the darkness of this world, against wickedness in high places."

"But isn't this the same passage where it talks about standing?"

"That's right. Having done all to stand, then stand therefore, having your loins girt about with truth, and having on the breastplate of righteousness." Derrick gave Cy a long look. "I'd pay *particular* attention to the girding of your loins."

Cy laughed. "No need to worry about that, Dee. The wife is taking care of home."

Derrick nodded, seemingly satisfied. But he still made a mental note to put Cy and Hope on his private prayer list. He wanted to do whatever he could to protect Cy from the adversary's marriage-destroying shenanigans. It wasn't that he didn't trust Cy Taylor; Derrick just knew that the devil was always busy and that next week . . . her name might be Trisha.

18

Watch and Pray

It was another Fourth of July at the Montgomery residence. Poolside was crowded and the atmosphere festive. Along with Frieda, Stacy, Hope, their spouses and children, several members from KCCC were also on hand as well as members of both Derrick's and Vivian's extended family. The catering company had provided all of the holiday favorites: baked beans, coleslaw, potato salad, and everything barbecued that one could imagine. The children played in a makeshift wonderland complete with a bounce house, sandlot, and swings. People clumped in various groups: around the food, the pool, and under two tents that had been erected in the backyard. Before the day was over, more than seventy-five people would have crossed the megaminister's threshold at one point or another. In the words of Ice Cube, it was shaping up to be a good day.

Under one of those tents, Derrick stood to the side talking with Tony. "It's good to see you, man. I miss you and Stacy in the congregation."

"We miss you too."

"How are things going at the Church of New Hope?" CNH was the fast-growing church in Arizona, led by the young and charismatic pastor, Jeremiah Dunn.

"Okay, I guess. I haven't been there much lately."

"That doesn't sound like you. I know you love the Lord and attended Noel's church faithfully before joining your wife at KCCC."

It was true. When he wasn't playing on any given Sunday, Tony Johnson could be found within the pews of Noel Jones's church and later, after meeting Stacy, at KCCC. His countenance hardened as he responded. "Right now, my thoughts are on one thing and one thing only. And that's getting picked up. As a husband, father, and the provider for my family, nothing else is more important than that."

This information did not surprise Derrick. During Sunday's brunch two days ago, Cy had told Derrick that his wife was worried about Tony, and wanted Derrick to speak with him. But Derrick's face was as unreadable as a star poker player. His body language remained casual as well as he asked, "What are you doing about that?"

Tony told him about the planned walk-on with the Sea Lions. "I know I've still got a few years left in me," he finished. "All I need is a chance."

"I hope you get it, man. But just remember . . . football is what you do, not who you are."

Tony frowned. "Have you been talking to Stacy?"

Derrick could almost feel anger and tension palpitating from Tony's body. But he stayed as cool as the watermelon salad that chilled in the patio fridge. "No, I have not had a conversation with your wife. Should I?"

Tony was immediately defensive. "Just what are you asking me, Pastor?"

"I've been reading people a long time, Tony. It's a gift, really, one that has been honed through more than twenty years in ministry: counseling, ministering, supporting the flock. You're hurting, and you're worried. Now, the average person wouldn't recognize it. But I do. And while I've never played professional sports, I've counseled my share of athletes who were coming to the end of their careers. I am aware of the myriad of emotions that come up when faced with retiring from something that they love. It's not easy, man. Heck, I watched my own son go through depression when his injury temporarily kept him off the court. Even though the doctors assured him that he'd play basketball again, the mere thought that that might not happen was not an easy one for him to deal with. So I'm not trying to get in your business, brothah. I just want you to know that I'm here for you, that's all."

Tony held up a hand for a fist pound. Derrick obliged him. "Thanks, Pastor. Everything you said was right. Sorry for snapping."

Derrick noted the set of Tony's jaw; the coldness in his eyes that didn't match the warmth of his voice and knew that before him stood a very troubled man. Another name to be added to his prayer list. "Apology accepted."

"I might take you up on the counseling one of these days and before we leave, I definitely want you to pray with me. If I don't get on with the Sea Lions next week, I'm more than likely out for the season."

Across from the tent where Tony, Derrick, and several others chatted, Vivian, Hope, and Stacy sat sipping sparkling juices and munching on watermelon salad.

"This is so refreshing," Hope said, after finishing a bite of what for her was a first-time treat. "I never would have paired watermelon with onions, and the mint adds a burst of flavor."

"Yes, a church member turned me on to this caterer and I really like them. Of course, I had to soothe the feathers of the church mothers who wanted to cook the meal, but everyone deserves time off, to spend with their family and friends. That and gift cards put a smile back on their faces." As they continued eating, Vivian noticed that Stacy's eyes kept traveling to where Derrick and Tony stood. "You've been quiet, Stacy. Everything all right?"

"Yes," she responded. After another second of staring, she pulled her attention back to the women around her. "I'm just glad that Tony is talking to Pastor."

Vivian felt there was a huge back story to that sentence, but she decided not to press. If and when Stacy decided to open up to her, she'd be there to listen. In the meantime, she made a mental note to add the couple to her and Derrick's prayer list. This thought brought about another—the conversation she'd had with Hope before the Taylors had come to LA. On Sunday, there'd been no time for a private chat, but now was perfect. "Hope, there's something I need to do in the house. Can you help me?" She turned to Stacy. "Do you mind?"

"Not at all. In fact, I think I'll try Frieda again and see if I can reach her."

Vivian nodded. "We'll be right back."

Once inside the spacious Beverly Hills home, Vivian led Hope into her office and closed the door. "That was a ruse so that Stacy wouldn't feel left out; I actually want to discuss what was on your mind the other day when we talked on the phone. Here, let's sit on the love seat."

"Okay," Hope began with a sigh after they were both seated. "Here's the situation." She told Vivian about her concerns regarding Cy's plans to meet Trisha, and underscored the confidence she had in her husband remaining faithful.

Vivian listened mostly, only asking a couple questions as Hope shared this interesting marital turn of events. Afterward, she sat silently a moment, listening for Spirit. "I believe you're doing the right thing in not protesting his meeting her," she said at last. "As you've shared, he's been very forthcoming, even letting you read the e-mails. Cy is a stand-up man, and I think that you can trust him. This Trisha woman? I'm not so sure. When will he be visiting her?"

"Next week."

Vivian nodded. "Then keep the lines of communication very open with your husband, and watch and pray." She looked at Hope, picked up a bit of discomfort in her friend's spirit, enough for her to say again, "Watch and pray."

★　★　★

In another part of Los Angeles, View Park to be exact, one person was watching and another was praying. Frieda Moore-Livingston, who usually had a two-date rule with the Lord—Christmas and Easter—now found herself in an awkward state of communication. *Please don't let her ask about—*

"Frieda, is this a birthmark?" Alice Livingston held her squirming grandson firmly on her lap as she investigated the heart-shaped mark on the toddler's foot. "Funny that I've never noticed it before."

Interestingly enough, it was Frieda's nanny, Cordella, who'd brought the mark to Frieda's attention when little Gabe was around six months old. Then, it was a barely discernible mark just below the ankle, near the outside of the child's right heel. At the time she'd shrugged it off, thinking that it was possibly a fall-induced bruise or mosquito bite. As time passed, the mark had not gone away but had gotten darker, especially in the summertime. By the time Gabe was one year old, the heart-shaped mark was more defined, but still too light to draw much attention, even while the child was being bathed. While Gabriel's mother doted on her grandchild, she'd rarely kept him overnight. Most times, she'd pick him up or Frieda would drop him off, already bathed, dressed, and ready to be spoiled by Alice and her husband, Gabe's grandfather, Mark. Most often they'd take him shopping, followed by time at the beach, park, or occasionally a playdate to get to know his cousins by Gabriel's sister, whom Frieda couldn't stand. The feeling was mutual, which was yet another reason why Frieda questioned whether this holiday gathering with the Livingstons would be treat or torture. At any rate, after a day with the grands he'd return home fat, happy, and ready for bed. Cordella would bathe him and Gabriel's parents would see him next time. Because the retired Livingstons had spent most of June with friends who'd relocated to Jamaica, they hadn't seen Gabe since summer began, and in the meantime the birthmark had darkened even more. Today, against Frieda's better judgment, she'd allowed Alice to change him into the swim trunks she'd purchased so that he could could be taken into the wading area they'd added to their in-ground pool. Big mistake.

Realizing that Alice was still waiting for an answer, she took a sip of champagne and said, "I think that mark is from him scraping against a shrub in the backyard."

Alice eyed Frieda for a long moment before returning her attention to Gabe. "Hmm, I don't think so." She rubbed her manicured fingers against the mark. "This looks permanent."

Fortunately for Frieda, Gabe had had enough of the examination. He squirmed and puckered up for an all-out cry, causing Alice to let him down so that he could join his cousin, a five-year-old stunner with two thick braids, blemish-free skin, and a ready smile who was already wading in the water.

"Hey, Frieda," Everett said from the patio door. Gabriel's sister's husband and her brother-in-law, he was the one member of the family that Frieda genuinely liked. "The concert is getting ready to start."

"Thanks, Everett." Frieda had asked him to let her know when the televised concert starring her good friend's baby daddy came on the air. Darius and Company at Central Park was definitely success on another level. For now she could take her mind off the innocently asked yet loaded question that her mother-in-law had posed. Until recently, she'd been sure that she knew who Gabe's real father was. But the man she'd thought might be Gabe's father, and the one she was almost sure had a similar birthmark...were not the same man.

19

Three's a Crowd

It was a picture-perfect day in New York City's Central Park. Tens of thousands of excited fans had gathered for the free Fourth of July concert starring several artists, including D & C: Darius and Company. Darius, Bo, Darius's publicist, makeup artist, stylist, assistants, and finance manager all occupied a spacious trailer several yards away from the concert's main stage.

A knock on the trailer door announced to Darius that it was showtime. Bo answered it.

"Five minutes, Dee," the man said, before hurriedly moving on to the stage where the rest of the band were already set up. The comedian who entertained the audience between acts was in the final stages of his routine. The makeup artist gave a few final dabs to Darius's forehead while the stylist and her assistants swarmed around him like bees, making sure that his outfit looked shabby chic, and that his bling could be seen.

After a moment, Darius brushed them away. "Let's go, y'all." He took a last look in the mirror, and then headed for the door.

Bo rushed ahead to open it. "You look good."

Darius gave him a pat on the back as he moved purposefully toward the stage. Except for the original mike check, and taking a peek at the opening band two hours ago, he'd purposely not gone back outside. He wanted to experience everything in real time: the atmosphere, the weather, the stage, and the multitude of people stretching as far as the eye could see.

"Wow." Bo rubbed the area between Darius's shoulders, knowing that as calm as his husband seemed on the outside, his insides were churning with a mix of nervousness and excitement. "This is going to be good, baby." He kept his voice calm and even. "You're going to kill it, Dee. Do your thing. I'm right here."

"New York!" the comedian intoned above an already-frenzied crowd. "Are you ready?"

An affirmative rumble was his response.

"I said, Are. You. Ready?"

Again, a massive roar as some in the audience began a rhythmic clap that was soon picked up in row after row.

"That's right. You're already doing it, so continue to put those hands together and welcome one of R and B's brightest stars, a triple threat, an award-winning maestro...D...and...C!"

The Company, an award-winning band that had been with Darius since his Ministry of Music days at KCCC, broke out with the introductory chords of "Power," the first hit song off his latest CD, *Me, Myself, and You.* When the CD dropped at the beginning of the year, "Power" spent an unprecedented fourteen weeks on Billboard's R & B Top Ten. The second release, "Subtle Sexy," came in at number one, while "Power" still occupied the number eight spot, and the song that would serve as the show's finale was officially dropping next week. Darius strolled confidently and with singular focus to the mike. He'd timed the walk to reach it at the exact moment the hook kicked in.

"Power! That thing in you, that thing in me, that
      makes us all what we should be.
Power! Gonna make it, cannot shake it, the destiny
      that through the Spirit just awaits me.
To that place in our soul, the ultimate goal, where
      blessings unfold and ...
Victories untold are more than I can hold. It's...
      Power! Power! Power! Power!"

There was something otherworldly about having more than a hundred thousand people, fists in the air, shouting the title of your hit song. Darius worked every inch of the sixty-foot-long stage, making sure that he acknowledged the fans who were behind him. Every band member showcased the mastery of their instrument: bass and lead guitars, horn section, keyboard, and percussion. It seemed as though nature itself joined in; the rustling trees swayed to the beat and the birds dipped in and out of the branches on cue. Various smells wafted up from the crowd, vying for attention. Weed, sweat, perfume, and scents from the surrounding food courts mingled in the air. Every color of the rainbow was represented, both in the clothes being worn and in the races that gathered. Darius was in his element, looking deceptively cool dressed in low riding jeans, an open black shirt, platinum jewelry, and confidence. It was six feet of sweaty sweet chocolate: strutting, gyrating, crooning, encouraging the masses to believe in life and themselves. Barely two minutes into the concert and Darius had the crowd in the palm of his hand...and what a large, talented palm it was.

As Darius did his thing on the stage, Bo was handling a different type of power all together: the type of power that came with managing one of the country's top R & B artists. While Darius whipped the crowd into a musical frenzy, Bo conferred with Darius's publicist before heading toward the area of the venue where product was being sold. From a discreet location, he observed the salespersons who were handling the sales of D & C merchandise: CDs, DVDs, T-shirts, key chains, flash drives, autographed pics, hats, jewelry, and other collectibles that fans would enjoy. Satisfied with the customer lines and what seemed to be lots of brisk business, he returned backstage and eventually stood in the wings as Darius came to the close of his forty-five-minute performance. There, as the audience matched the R & B star word for word on "Possible," his first break-out hit, Bo saw something. Or more importantly, he saw someone. In the front row. Front and center to be exact. Bo let out a string of expletives. *I have got to find a way to get that dog to stop sniffing around my bone!*

Later, as Paz Demopoulos not only joined them backstage but also for a dinner at an A-list director's house, Bo sat . . . and stewed. The only thing that kept him from going smooth off were memories of how Darius had come running back to him after one of Stacy's rants. Every time that woman had given Darius the blues about choosing Bo over her and her son, she deepened the bond between the two men. So Bo smiled and schmoozed and held conversations with others as if he was really interested in what they had to say. Truth is, if someone had asked him later what he'd talked about while Paz was cozying up next to his husband, Bo wouldn't have been able to say. But there was one thing he did know. . . . At the end of the night, when all the parties had wound down and the paparazzi were gone, it would be him lying in the bed next to superstar Darius Crenshaw. Tomorrow, he decided, he'd think long and hard about a way to deal with the person who dared to try and threaten his marital future. Tonight, he'd concentrate on something else long and hard. Bo had what Paz wanted, plain and simple. He didn't plan on that fact changing any time soon.

20

Healing, Health, and Happiness

"Hey there, Doc."

Gabriel smiled and nodded at the plain yet pleasant nurse behind the desk, who'd worked at the hospital for almost thirty years.

"How'd it go, Dr. Livingston?" The other nurse sitting at the desk had just passed her boards. She'd been on the job less than a month.

"It went well, thank you."

An attractive redhead fell into step beside him. "Good work in there, Doctor."

"Thanks, Amber. I'm very proud of the team's performance today, you included."

Amber blushed. "Thank you. It was touch and go there for a while; first her rapidly falling blood pressure, then the concern of whether we could successfully remove the cancerous cells so close to the veins. . . . I tried to maintain professional distance, but the fact that she has a daughter was never far from my mind."

They reached Gabriel's office. He put a hand on her shoulder. "We're all human, Amber. It's very difficult to stay totally detached from patients, especially someone like Hillary, who has such a positive outlook on life. I thought about her daughter too."

Amber smiled her appreciation of his understanding and after another couple minutes of conversation continued down the hall.

Gabriel entered his office and immediately began the postsurgery paperwork. Usually focused and disciplined, today his mind kept wandering back to Amber, and how well she'd done in the operating room. It wasn't the first time; since joining his team as a perioperative nurse five years ago, he'd quietly observed her stellar knowledge, natural skills, and endless compassion. After she'd gotten comfortable in her position and begun flirting with him, Gabriel had been flattered but uninterested. Aside from a couple file room trysts during residency, he'd stuck hard and fast to his "no nurses" dating rule. Their friendship was just deepening when he'd had "the encounter." That's what he called his meeting with Frieda, the day his world got tilted on his axis after they literally ran into each other at a Beverly Hills mall. She was crass and loud and he was immediately intrigued—a demeanor so unlike anyone in his circle, or anyone he'd ever known.

Frieda had been the aggressor. Had she not taken the lead, it is unlikely that they would have ever seen each other again. Gabriel was quiet, studious (some would say geeky), and while his female friends had told him otherwise, he'd always felt his freckles kept him off the list of handsome hunks. She'd suggested they meet for drinks and when he didn't move fast enough in the intimacy department, had ambushed him in his office one evening and sexed him on the couch. Satisfying to be sure, and a definite spark to his predictable life. But a temporary one. Or so he'd thought. And then came the news that she was pregnant. There was never any question that he'd do the right thing. A signed prenup followed by a destination wedding, and a somewhat shell-shocked Gabriel had gained himself a missus.

Gabriel rose from his desk, walked over to the window that looked out onto a well-landscaped lawn. July had come in with a vengeance, with record-breaking heat, but here, from the climate-controlled confines of his second home, the scene he beheld was a postcard: stark blue sky, fluffy white clouds, swaying palms, and vibrant flowers lining the walkways. *That first year was pretty good,* he thought, as he followed a jet's journey across the sky. Gabriel's thoughts weren't as linear as the plane's flight appeared. They flitted from one incident to the other that had transpired when he'd first married, when he'd actually felt hopeful—thought there might be a chance to soften Frieda's rough edges. He'd tried to establish a friendship between her and his mother, Alice, one of the most refined women he'd ever known. The match wasn't one made in heaven. Alice was cordial because after all, Frieda was her son's wife, the mother of her grandchild, and human. Alice treated stray dogs kindly; she'd do no less to another person. Frieda's discomfort upon meeting his mother had lessened over time, but they'd never developed the camaraderie that Gabriel had hoped. Now, their communication revolved almost solely around Gabe and usually included planned drop-offs, pickups, or sleepover dates.

Gabriel's cell phone rang and as if he'd conjured her up, Alice was on the line. "Hello, Mom."

"Hello, Gabriel. You sound tired."

"I am. Just got out of surgery."

"I hope everything went well."

"It did."

"Thank goodness for that, son. I know we say it often, but your father and I are so proud of you."

"Thank you, Mom."

"Son, I won't keep you. I tried reaching Frieda, but her phone keeps going to voice mail. The ladies of the committee want to know if she's going to participate in the upcoming charity event. We need to know as soon as possible so that if not, we can call in one of the alternates."

"I'm here for forty-eight hours, Mom, but if I can't reach Frieda, I'll make sure our housekeeper passes on your message."

"Your father and I have been married for forty-five years, Gabriel. I believe I can count on one hand the times that I couldn't reach him, and didn't know where he was." Silence. "You know, honey. I can remember the quiet, contemplative little boy who'd sit for hours in his room, reading books or dissecting one thing or another with the biology set we gave you one Christmas. You and

Raymond, remember? You two would have your heads together, studying the organs and trying to determine which ones were affected by the liquid you'd used to end the poor creature's life."

The memory of the experiments he and his best friend concocted brought a smile to Gabriel's face. "Yes, and now Raymond is a force in his own right, as one of the leading researchers at Johns Hopkins."

"When is the last time you visited with him?"

"It's been too long," Gabriel admitted. "Both of our schedules are always so busy and his wife just had another baby not long ago."

"That makes four for them, correct?"

"Yes, fourth and final, according to Ray."

"Little Gabe is such a delight, son. I'm sure he'd welcome a little brother or sister. It's just that . . ."

"What, Mom?"

"Oh, honey, it's really not my place to say. It's just that . . . well, I just thought that . . . imagined your wife would be a different kind of woman, that's all. Someone more like who you've been surrounded with your whole life, someone well educated, from a well-heeled family, perhaps someone in the medical field."

"Honestly, Mom, so did I. But Gabe's arrival changed all that."

"Are you happy, son?"

"I love little Gabe. He's one of the best things that's happened in my life."

Gabriel hadn't answered his mother's question, but long after they'd ended the call, he was still thinking about it, still trying to come to terms with what he knew to be the answer. Because the truth of the matter was that Gabriel wasn't happy. Not at all.

21

That Cake, Cake, Cake!

"You look happy, Ma. Is that me putting the smile on that pretty little face?" Clark ran a finger across Frieda's upturned lips. She'd been at his house all afternoon. Now it was evening. They'd had sex, ate, had sex again, smoked a blunt, taken a shower where they enjoyed yet a third round, and now lazed on the new couch that Frieda had purchased, munching on chips and dip, and drinking shots of tequila.

"Quit it!" Frieda playfully slapped Clark's finger away from her face. Truth was, she was happy, giddy even. Hadn't felt this way in a long time, hadn't felt like she was living in her own skin since becoming Mrs. Gabriel Livingston. She loved the lifestyle, but wanted to enjoy it on her own terms. Like this. Just kicking back and chilling. Not putting on airs or a phony "I'm interested" face, or trying to have a conversation with Gabriel's snooty mother and uptight friends. She missed this life, where she didn't have to be anybody but herself. "Dang, man. Why do you keep flipping through the channels? See what's on TV One." Frieda didn't watch much TV these days, but she'd heard about a show called *Unsung* that was supposed to be very good.

"Who's got the remote, woman? Me no let no woman control me a'tall. Not even the TV. I'm the man, right?"

"Whatever, nucka."

Clark let out a confident chuckle. "I'm *your* man." He continued to scroll the channels, settling closer to Frieda in the process.

"Wait! Who's that?" They'd landed on the Food Network, where a handsome African-American man was smiling into the camera as he pulled barbecued meat out of a countertop smoker. The man, not the meat, is obviously what had gotten Frieda's attention.

"Him? The brothah whose family owns that restaurant off Sepulveda?"

"What restaurant?"

Clark's look was a question mark as he turned to Frieda. "You haven't eaten at Taste of Soul, haven't seen any of their commercials? Everybody's talking about that place. The atmosphere is on point and the food is bangin'." They both listened in silence for a moment. "As a matter of fact," he continued, "his last name is Livingston too. Y'all might be related."

"Hmph, I wouldn't mind being that brother's kissing cousin."

"With your hot nana, you'd be more than that! But seriously though, you should find out whether y'all are related; might be able to get us some free barbecue."

"Where are they from? Do you know?"

"No," he said with a shrug, before changing the channel.

"I don't think they're related to Gabriel. All of his people have a lighter complexion, nothing like that Hershey bar I was looking at. Turn it back!"

"Watch yourself, girl." He reached for her hand, placed it on his crotch. "You've got all of the chocolate you need right here."

Frieda moved her hand and changed the subject. "Clark."

"Hmm?"

"How mad at me would you be if I fired your mother?"

"What's up with you and my moms?"

"She hasn't asked you about us?"

"Yeah, but I said we were just friends."

"Please, boy. Your mom isn't stupid. I've caught her looking at me with this accusatory expression on her face. She knows there's more going on here and she doesn't like it. Worships the ground that Gabriel walks on too. It's just a matter of time before that loyalty has her talking even more out of school than she already has. You know I've warned her about sharing my schedule and whereabouts and if it happens again, if she takes some of my personal business and shares it with my husband, her employment for me is going to have to be a wrap."

"I'll talk to her."

Frieda shook her head. "I don't know if that will be enough."

"Mom is good at what she does, has excellent references, and never has problems finding work. As much as she needs that job, you won't be able to bully her, Frieda. So don't even try."

"Cool. I'll just put old girl into my yesterday. If that happens, we're still good?"

Clark ran a hand through Frieda's short, weave-free cut. "Yeah, Mami. We're good."

Frieda was ecstatic. So a couple minutes later, when two of Clark's friends joined them, she ordered up a few pizzas and sent one of them out for bottles of Dom Pérignon. Her husband would be at the hospital all night, so after calling Cordella and telling her that she was spending the night with a cousin, she settled in for an evening of fun with the boys. She'd worried about firing Cordella and keeping Clark, but now it looked like she would be able to have her cake and eat it too. Only later would she have to wonder whether that particular piece of chocolate was worth it.

22

Friends and Favors

Cy stepped out into the brilliant July sunshine and walked the short distance from the newly restored brownstone he'd just purchased to the restaurant where he'd meet Trisha. He'd dressed casually—jeans, sneakers, button-down black shirt, and no jewelry—but wealth still oozed from his pores. Because of the design of Southern California in general and his neighborhood in particular, people rarely walked to where they wanted to go. In DC, however, while attending school at Howard, he'd been a pro at walking and catching public transportation, interacting with the masses even if by no more than sharing a seat on the train. Taking in the activity around him on his way to the restaurant, including the street vendors selling artwork, jewelry, books, and more, he realized how far he'd gone from this lifestyle . . . and how much he missed it.

During a conversation with Hope, he'd decided on a lunch rather than a dinner meeting. It was one o'clock in the afternoon and the restaurant was bustling. To eat at the Red Rooster had been Trisha's suggestion, and Cy decided he liked it at once. It was open and airy with large picture windows at the front of the room. As his eyes adjusted from the bright sunshine to the room's interior he looked around, stopping as he noted a table where a woman sat alone. Her head was down, face intent as she either texted or typed on her phone. It had been fifteen years, and she looked smaller than he remembered, but there was no doubting that it was Trisha Underwood, the woman who at one time had been the love of his life and the one he thought would occupy the title of wife. He observed her a second or so more, his heart clenching at something indefinable . . . something different about her that he couldn't quite name. *Stop tripping, brothah. Nobody looks the same as they did in college.*

"Hey, Tricky."

Trisha's head came up slowly as she heard this pet name, a smile spreading across her face in the same fashion. "Hey, Cyclone."

She pushed back her chair and stood to give Cy a hug. They embraced and Cy forgot all about the church hug that he was supposed to deliver. Now he knew for sure: she was thinner than when he'd known her, less voluptuous, less cushion as he squeezed her, and it seemed a lanky frame had replaced the curves that used to drive him wild. No matter. This was his little Tricky, the one who'd given him a run for his money when all the other girls were giving him open access. She'd taken the C out of his cocky and matched his attitude stroke for stroke. They'd dated three years, and he'd been crazy about her. And here she was again, in his arms. They stood back to look into each other's eyes, examine each other's faces, and then hugged again.

Finally Cy broke the hug and stepped around to get Trisha's chair. "It's good to see you, Tricky. It's been way too long." He took his seat.

"I know, and I need to apologize about that, about never returning your calls and shutting down completely after . . . what happened."

"Ah, Trisha, I understand why you did that. I hurt you."

"Perhaps, but we'd loved too long and shared too much for me to not have given you the benefit of the doubt or, at the very least, a chance to share your side of the story." Her voice lowered as she continued. "It's one of my biggest regrets."

An awkward silence ensued, into which walked the waiter

with their water and menus. Neither of them knew it about the other, but they were both glad for the reprieve, the temporary diversion to focus on food instead of their complicated past and surprising yet interesting present—the fact that they were here, together, all these years later after that first shared kiss.

Cy browsed the menu. "So you say this place comes highly recommended?"

"I highly recommend it. Been coming here since it opened a few years ago. The owner is a famous chef, Marcus Samuelsson, who regularly appears on the Food Network. He also served as guest chef for Obama's first state dinner."

"Wow, impressive. Can't wait to try his food."

"He's cooked here occasionally, but the executive chef is Michael Barrett. According to the Web site, where I read all of this information, they've worked together for years. The food is really good."

"What do you recommend?"

"I've never had anything here that I didn't like, but my personal favorites are the fried chicken Caesar, the shrimp and dirty rice, and the gravlax."

"Grav who?"

Trisha chuckled. "It's a Scandinavian dish made with cured salmon. Delish."

"Hmm, I've never heard of it, so I think I'll try that."

They continued discussing the menu until Trisha made her selection and the waiter returned to take their order. Once he'd gone the silence returned, a silence filled with the presence of a much-needed conversation that had never taken place.

Cy leaned back in his chair. "How do you like living in Harlem?"

"I love it. Been living here for the past ten years. It's gone through many changes and is really getting a makeover these days. Brownstone prices have skyrocketed. I'm thankful that I bought when I did."

"So you own a brownstone?"

Trisha nodded. "I renovated it so that I live in the top two floors and rent out the bottom."

"That's smart."

"It works for me." Trisha eyed Cy as she took a drink of water. "You haven't changed, Cy."

"Maybe not that you can see, but I've put on a pound or two. Not as fast or as fluid as I used to be. But I work out regularly, try and stay in shape. What about you, Tricky? You're smaller than I remember. Have you been doing Pilates? Or yoga? I know that those types of exercises can burn off all the fat."

A wistful look tinged with sadness darted across Trisha's face before she quickly replaced it with a smile. "No, I can't say that I exercise much these days. I've, uh, had some health issues and have lost weight as a result."

"I'm sorry to hear that. Have you taken care of it? Are you better now?"

"I'm okay. So you're here buying up half of Harlem?"

Cy grinned. "Not quite. A partner and I are acquiring several of the commercial locations and a block of brownstones. Hope and I plan to renovate one for our family so that we can have a place on the East Coast. The rest will be renovated and then sold at a profit."

"Hope—that's your wife's name?"

"Yes."

"Cy, she's a very lucky girl."

"I'm the blessed one, Trisha. Hope is a beautiful woman, inside and out, and a wonderful mother to our children."

"How many children do you have?"

"A set of twins, Camon and Acacia. They're four years old."

"One big happy family."

Cy looked intently at Trisha, tried without success to gauge her feelings as he spoke about his family. "We're very happy," he said at last. "I was taken aback that you'd remained single all these years."

"Like I told you . . . could never find a man to take your place."

"You can't possibly mean that."

"Trust me, I tried. Dated several men, even lived with one for some years. But I could never give him what he deserved—my whole heart, my total commitment. He kept proposing and I kept putting it off. Finally he got fed up and moved on. And rightfully so. He got married within a year of our breakup. But we remained friends. I'm cordial with his wife as well. They have two children and one grandchild."

"Trisha, I don't know what to say."

Trisha shrugged. "There's nothing for you to say, really. I'm the one with so much to share with you, so much that I've wanted to say and never said."

"What we shared was over a long time ago. Your contacting me lets me know that I've been forgiven. For me, that's enough."

"Yes, I've forgiven you, Cy. But that's not enough." Trisha's voice was firm, her expression intense. "I don't have—There are some things I've wanted, no, needed to say to you for a long time and . . . well . . . I didn't want another year to pass without trying to find you, without letting you know what's in my heart."

The waiter brought out their appetizers. Neither Cy nor Trisha picked up their fork.

"When I was growing up," Trisha began as soon as the waiter had left the table, "I watched my father hurt my mother by having affairs. He was and still is a great father and I adore him. But I also made a promise to myself that I would never put up with what my mother did. I had a zero tolerance for infidelity. One time and the man was history. That was my vow to myself since I was sixteen.

"Cy, I've never been so happy as when you and I were together, and for the first and only time in my life I envisioned a happy ever after. I had a confidence, a smugness even, that I'd found what my mom had not—a man who would be faithful, a man who wouldn't mess around on his wife. For three years, you were that man."

"Trisha, I—"

"Shh, I know. But let me finish. I've waited so long." Trisha picked up her fork and nodded to Cy. "Please." He picked up his fork and took a bite of salad that he couldn't even taste. His appetite had lessened as he became emotionally filled with the impact of Trisha's words. "When Jeannetta told me she'd slept with you, she was beaming. She relished providing me with every sordid detail of what had happened, took great pleasure in describing your room—and your anatomy—so that there would be no mistaking that what she said was true. I was hurt, and angry, and very, very proud. So against everything I felt in my heart, I cut you out of my life. The emptiness that ensued as a result was excruciating, almost unbearable at times. But I kept reminding myself of a sixteen-year-old's promise to herself. Zero tolerance. First time and I was out the door. If I knew then what I know now, I'd have understood that sometimes a good man deserves not only a second chance, but a third, fourth, fifth one, that what you have is much more valuable than what you'd lose, and that someone's temporary dalliance can't match a lifetime based on a soul connection. I would have learned that every man shouldn't be sent packing, that some are worth holding on to...no matter what. That's what my mother understood, and that's why this year she and my father will be celebrating fifty years together. She knew, and tried to tell me, that that which didn't kill a relationship made it stronger." Trisha's eyes shone with unshed tears as she looked at Cy. "I wish I would have listened." Again, she picked up her fork, but instead of eating, just moved the greens around.

"For months I beat myself up for what I did to you. It was my fault that our relationship ended. Yes, someone coerced me into doing what I did, but I was a grown man and she wasn't holding a gun to my head. It was an unfortunate decision that changed the course of both our lives. I know it's been a long time in coming but...I'm sorry for what I did to you, Tricky. So very sorry for the hurt I caused, and how that choice affected your life.

"Like I said when we talked by phone, I often thought about you over the years. Every time I did though, I imagined you married to some über-conscious, world-changing dude, yours a strong presence beside him as you conquered the world, possibly with a baby tied to your back. I always knew you were going places, were going to do great things with your life." They were silent a moment. "So you decided against a family. What about your career?"

Trisha explained that she'd most recently been the artistic director of a program for at-risk youth in the heart of Harlem. They talked about that briefly before the conversation meandered back to their past: long-forgotten stories from those college years, catching up on each other's families, news of mutual friends. By the time they'd finished dessert, the heavy air that had existed earlier had lightened and laughter had been a common punctuation mark.

"This was nice, Tricky," Cy said, as he motioned for the bill. "And since I'll be coming up here more often, perhaps we can become friends again. I'd like you to meet Hope. I think the two of you would like each other."

Trisha's smile dimmed somewhat. "I'm sure she's a good woman. You wouldn't have married her otherwise."

"So you're agreeable to meeting her?"

"Perhaps." And once again that look, focused and intense, dark almost black orbs connecting with Cy's equally attentive ones. "But first, Cy, I'd like to ask you a favor. It's a lot to request from a long lost friend, but you granting it would mean absolutely everything."

"Okay." Trisha talked and as Cy listened, he felt his stomach churn.

23

Sounds Like a Plan

Stacy eased back from the computer and stretched in her chair. She'd been online for more than an hour, arranging and rearranging her resume, and looking for innovative ways to use her marketing background to do something she liked. She'd been considering this for a while now, getting back into the workforce. Not only because in the future she and her family might need the money, but also because of a recent, startling revelation: slowly, and almost imperceptibly, she'd become Tony's wife and DJ's mom and in the process lost the old Stacy Gray.

When did you lose yourself, girl? What happened to your having a life? The phone rang. Stacy looked at the ID and was reminded of the first time who she was took a backseat to what she wanted. "Hey, Bo."

"Hey, Stacy."

"What?" For almost as long as they'd known each other, Bo had greeted her as Spacey Stacy. "Something must be wrong." She heard a heavy sigh through the phone.

"I'm so damned tired of people going after my husband."

"Women can be scandalous. But history has proven that you have nothing to worry about." She knew that Bo knew exactly what she was talking about.

"I wish it were a woman, instead of a gorgeous, famous actor with more money than God."

"Ooh. Who is it?"

"Paz the Ass."

"Who?"

"Pascual Demopoulos, known to moviegoers the world over as Paz Demo."

"Shut. Up." Stacy stood and walked into her kitchen. "I just rented his last movie the other week. That man is fine forever."

"Just what I need...somebody who feels the same way Dee does."

"Darius told you that he thought homeboy was fine?"

"He's told me and showed me. That same movie you watched is part of our collection. Darius has watched it no less than five times."

"Oh, Bo," Stacy said, having stood in front of the open refrigerator for a minute before settling on the bottle of flavored water now in her hand. "It sounds like Darius has a harmless crush. I don't think you have anything to—Oh, wait. You said Paz was after Dee?"

"It takes a while to warm up, but eventually that brain of yours remembers how to function."

"Forget you, Bo." She took a drink. "What happened that makes you think he wants your man?"

Bo told her. "Darius thought that by us all hanging out in New York, that I'd chill and be less suspicious. But now knowing that that man is as beautiful in person as he is on screen, I'm freaking the hell out. Darius loves beauty and I can't see him resisting that kind of temptation forever. Hell, if Dee didn't have me all lost and turned out I'd screw the man myself!" Silence, and then, "It's been so good between us these past few years. Guess the good times can't last forever."

Stacy leaned against the couch, her voice just above a whisper. "I know what you mean."

"Girl," Bo replied, drawing the word out as only a sistah could, "you've got to tell me how you know this."

Stacy didn't hesitate. As crazy as the mind of Bo Jenkins was, he was in full supply of common sense. Her girls, Hope and Frieda, were biased. Bo would tell it straight up like it was. "Tony's been tripping too."

"Girl, shut the front door and run out the back! With who?"

"No, not like that. Trying to get another woman is the last thing on his mind right now."

"Well, honey, if it ain't the kitty cat, then what can it be? Brothah man hasn't changed lanes has he?"

"Hardly."

Bo clucked. "Well if it ain't sex, then it must be money."

"It'll be about money soon enough. Right now, it's about Tony's job." She gave him the short version of Tony's attempts to rejoin the NFL and his increasingly erratic mood after each rejection.

"So he didn't get the job with the Sea Lions?"

"We don't know yet. I pray he does though. He's become a different person than the one I married. And while I never begrudged his penchant for the finer things in life, I worry about our future, especially DJ."

"You know Darius is going to make sure that boy wants for nothing."

"I know. But I'm thinking of myself as well. What will I do if Tony and I split?"

"Dang, girl, it's that bad?"

"Not yet. But I'm not trying to wait until things go from bad to worse before I start making plans."

"What kind of plans, other than moving back to LA?"

"Those for sure. You're not the only one who wants out of the heat." Stacy's tone turned serious. "I'm updating my resume."

"What?! Resume as in thinking about getting a nine-to-five? How does Tony feel about that? And how will that work anyway? You know how Dee feels about people he don't know looking after his child. He wasn't too pleased when you let him spend the weekend with your brother, and he's the boy's uncle."

"I don't know how he'd feel about it, because I haven't told him and don't plan to. And I don't want you to tell Darius either. I'm not sure what the future holds, but I know that the way things are doesn't feel good right now. Tony is scared of his career ending, true, but I think he's just as concerned about taking care of his family. Plus, he's so prideful. Whatever job he gets after football will have to have the same type of status that comes with being a pro baller." Stacy was tempted to tell him about the Ponzi scheme and all the money that Tony lost as a result of it, but she'd promised not to tell anyone and so far had kept the promise. Barely.

"Then why doesn't he do like some of those other retired players and become a sportscaster?"

"That's an option, but Tony would much rather work on the field."

"Mommy!"

"Bo, we'll talk more later. DJ just woke up from his nap," Stacy headed toward the stairs. "Thanks for listening and remember to keep this between us."

"My lips are sealed."

"And don't worry about Dee, Bo. At the end of the day, he's a family man and he knows that DJ is crazy about you. He wouldn't want to do anything to jeopardize that."

"I hope you're right, Spacey."

"Bye, Little Bo Peep."

Several hours later, Bo was still thinking about his conversation with Stacy. One part in particular played like a loop inside his head, while fixing dinner, as he and Darius ate and chatted about the day's events and now, while Darius showered and Bo checked his phone. More texts between his husband and Paz. And a phone call too. Bo's jaw clenched as he remembered what had happened last week at the restaurant, when Bo had excused himself to go to the restroom but had instead found a covert spot behind a large potted plant to watch the interactions between Darius and his competition. Paz had wasted no time getting his flirt on, placing a hand on Darius's arm while looking at the R & B superstar as though he were a menu choice. It had taken all of Bo's will (and a few days off his life) for him not to run over and slap the taste out of the handsome, gregarious actor's mouth. In the end the only thing that stopped him was thoughts of Darius, and how much his husband hated a scene. So he'd gone to the bathroom, splashed cold water on his face, and stopped by the bar for a double shot of Courvoisier. After downing it he'd returned to the table and openly flirted with the waiter. That tit-for-tat action had brought about the tense atmosphere Bo had hoped for. The dinner had ended without dessert, he and Darius had argued when they returned to the suite, and the night had ended with explosive makeup sex. Bo thought things had chilled between Darius and Paz. Wrong.

Bo watched dispassionately as Darius walked out of the shower, wearing his favorite lounging outfit—nothing. It had been eight years, but Bo never tired of Darius's eight inches: watching it, holding it, loving it. He loved how it hung neatly over Darius's dual sac, and swayed gently from side to side as Darius crossed the room. Acting like he was reading the latest *LA Gospel* magazine, he continued to surreptitiously eye his lover. Darius's booty was one of God's most amazing designs. It was round and juicy and sat high above big, muscled thighs. He stood at six feet, and his shoulders weren't overly broad, but his muscles were defined and his chest was ripped.

"What?" Darius asked, having caught Bo eyeing him when he glanced in a mirror.

"Nothing."

Darius's smile was lazy and genuine. "That didn't look like a 'nothing' look. That looked like an 'I want some' kind of message."

"I guess I am turned on a little bit," Bo admitted, as Darius joined him in the bed. He showed Darius the magazine's centerfold.

"Kelvin Petersen? Please. You've never liked athletes." Darius took the magazine out of Bo's hands and viewed the photo of the pro basketball player who was also his former pastor's son. On more than one occasion he'd been at Derrick Montgomery's home when Kelvin was present. "Besides"—Darius tapped the page—"this caramel cutie beside him seems to have him on lock."

The two men looked at the picture of the woman who'd claimed the pro baller's heart. Princess Brook was the daughter of Derrick's best friend, King Brook, and a star in her own right. Darius turned the page and they looked at the other pictures that accompanied the article about the reality show called *KP and His Princess,* which now also featured their twin boy and girl. He remembered weekends he'd spent in a Kansas City suburb, playing at Mount Zion Progressive Baptist, her father's church. "Have you ever watched their reality show?"

"No," Bo said, turning the lamp off from his side of the bed. "I've got my own reality situation happening right here."

Darius turned out his light. They both settled beneath the covers and for a while, the only sound heard was their individual breathing.

Finally, Darius broke the silence. "I'm tired, Bo."

Bo turned toward his lover. "I know."

"I haven't taken a vacation in what . . . three, four years?"

"Something like that; since DJ was a baby."

"Remember those days?" Darius said, the smile evident in his voice despite the darkness. "When DJ was in diapers and our days were consumed with just navigating parenthood."

"He's grown so fast." Bo reached out for Darius's hand and squeezed it.

"Sometimes I miss those days, when our schedule wasn't so hectic and he could spend more time in our lives. That's my heart right there."

Bo cuddled next to Darius. "Have you ever thought about having another baby?" He felt Darius stiffen beside him, felt him relax just as quickly.

"Not really. But now that you mention it, having a daughter might be nice."

The conversation drifted after that, to Darius's schedule for the rest of the month, which included traveling to several promo appearances in the south and southeast. They didn't make love, but rather cuddled and simply enjoyed each other's company. But as Bo drifted to sleep he once again thought about his situation, and Stacy's, and decided to try and come up with a plan that just might work for both of them.

24

For Old Time's Sake

Hope looked up from the book she was reading and cocked her head toward the front of the house. *Is that Cy?* Their bedroom was at the back of the house but because of how they had the security system programmed, sounds in one room could be heard in another. Even without the system, she was almost sure Cy was home. She could feel him. A good thing to, since all day she'd had the rare experience of not being able to reach him. Usually if he couldn't talk on the phone he'd send her a text. Aside from when he was out of the country, they'd talked almost every day since they'd met. Hope hadn't even realized how much of a comfort this was until she'd kept getting his voice mail. Breathing a sigh of relief, she bookmarked her spot in the latest Zuri Day release, eased up from the chair in the sitting area of their master suite, and walked toward the front of the house.

After she'd navigated a flight of stairs, walked down the hall, through the great room and combined kitchen/dining area, she was greeted by a sight for sore eyes. "Hey, baby." She opened her arms. Cy walked into her embrace. She rubbed her hands across his back and shoulders as he buried his head in the crook of her neck. They stayed that way for a moment, and then a moment longer. Hope tried to pull back, but when she did, Cy intensified his hold on her. And then she felt it. The wetness. Slight yet quite perceptible . . . A tear, she assumed, that hit her shoulder and rolled down her arm. It was no secret that they hated being away from each other, but tears? This was something new.

Placing her hands on Cy's broad shoulders, Hope forced a bit of distance between them so that she could look in his eyes. "What is it, baby?"

Cy avoided her eyes as he responded, wrapping his arms around her once again and holding her close. "It's good to see you, baby," he replied, his voice raspy with emotion. "I love you so much."

Okay. Something was definitely wrong. Cy went out of town often; last year he'd spent almost a month in South Africa, and even then their reunion hadn't elicited this type of emotion. Hope wrapped her arms around her husband's neck and asked again, "What's wrong?"

Cy held her close for another moment before breaking the embrace and turning toward the stairs. "It's a long story, baby. I'll tell you everything. But first I want to kiss my babies and take a shower. After that, I'll feel more like myself again, and will be ready to talk about New York."

While Cy went to kiss the kids and then take a shower, Hope fixed chamomile tea and once done placed two mugs on a tray along with a couple of spinach popovers. As she entered the room, Cy was coming out of the dressing area, a pair of white linen shorts riding low on his hips.

"I thought you might be hungry," she said, placing the tray on the table in the sitting area.

"Don't really have an appetite, but tea will be nice." Cy joined Hope, sitting in the wingback opposite her. He reached for the tea, took a slow, thoughtful sip, and then another.

Hope nibbled on a popover, trying to be patient and wait for whatever heavy story Cy had to tell her. She instinctively knew it had something to do with his meeting with Trisha. Nothing to do with business would make him act this way. And then out of the blue came a thought that took her breath away, and almost caused her to choke on the bite she'd just taken.

Did he sleep with her?

She thought back to her initial conversation with Vivian about Trisha, and remembered the first lady's words. *Cy is a stand-up man, and I think that you can trust him. This Trisha woman? I'm not so sure.* On the heels of that thought came Frieda's voice ringing in her ears. *Are you crazy? What in the hell does she want?* That's exactly what Hope wanted to know. The only thing that kept her from blurting out the question that Frieda had asked was the restraint suggested by her first lady. That and the memory of the La Jolla Tea Party, when after misinterpreting a series of e-mails between Cy and Millicent, Hope had driven down to the hotel mentioned in the e-mail, finagled her way into the private room where Cy was meeting Millicent's husband, accused him of cheating and within seconds became the poster child for the definition of the word "assume." Hope placed the remainder of the appetizer on the plate and looked at her husband, noting the tightness of his expression. "Cy, just tell me what happened."

"We met for lunch," Cy finally began, wiping strong fingers over tired eyes. "It was like the years fell away when I saw her. Aside from being a bit thinner than in college, she was the same old Trisha."

"How did that make you feel?" Hope prayed that her voice sounded casual.

"Good," Cy instantly replied. "It's like no time had passed. Even though we hadn't seen each other in forever, it didn't take long for the camaraderie we shared to return. We talked about old times and old friends." Cy looked at Hope and then looked away.

"And then what?"

"And then she asked me to do her a favor."

"Okay." Hope willed herself to remain calm, to feel empathy and compassion for a man in pain. It was a Herculean task. When Cy remained quiet, she took a deep breath and then prompted, "What did she ask you?" all the while not sure that she wanted to know.

"She asked if I wanted to walk a bit, for her to show me the neighborhood. I told you that she lives in Harlem, right?"

"You said New York; I don't remember hearing Harlem specifically."

"Perhaps I didn't know that then. During lunch I'd told her about my plans to buy property in Harlem. That's when she told me that she'd lived there for ten years and that because of her love for its history, knew quite a bit about the various neighborhoods, businesses, stuff that research can't tell you."

So what about a tour of Harlem would put you in this horrible mood? Hope dug her fingernails into her palms, determined to wait for Cy to share whatever he wanted in his own time. Even if it killed her, which—with the rate of how long it was taking him to get to the point—it likely could.

"After walking for a while we ended up at her place."

"How convenient," Hope said, before she could stop herself.

"Yes, it was," Cy agreed. "But probably not for the reasons you're thinking. She lives in a brownstone that has been fully restored, near an area that has the same type of acclaimed history as where I'm buying property. Ironically, I'd just met with Joseph the day before, and she knew who I was talking about and pointed out some of the areas he helped redevelop."

"That's the guy who got you interested in Harlem properties, right?"

Cy nodded. "Joseph Holland. He began dealing with Harlem real estate back in the eighties, even wrote a book about it, which Trisha has read. It's called *From Harlem with Love.* Anyway, when I learned where she lived and she offered a tour, I was definitely interested in seeing her space."

"Oh, so going to her house was your idea."

"She asked if I wanted to see the restoration. I said yes and we went there."

Hope turned to face her husband fully. She was out of patience and had to cut to the proverbial chase. "Cy, with what you've just told me, I still don't understand why you're in this dark mood."

Cy looked at Hope and then away. "It's because of what happened afterward, what Trisha told me once we got to her house."

Hope's heart began an erratic beat. Scenarios of what Trisha told him popped around her head like ping-pong balls. *Help her undress? Let them make love? Divorce me and the kids and move to New York?* And then an even crazier thought, taken straight out of a chapter of Vivian Montgomery's life: *Does he have a child who's like around . . . fifteen years old?* "Well, what is it?" Hope hadn't meant to jump off the chair, get in his face and speak through gritted teeth. No, she'd meant to be cool, calm, and collected, to quietly ask what his first love had requested as if she were asking him to pass the butter. But nooooo. She'd had to "go Frieda" and lose her cool. Which is why she was standing over a still-seated Cy with her hands on her hips. "So what was it, Cy? Did Trisha ask you to sleep with her, to have a little nookie for old time's sake?" The look in Cy's eyes should have cooled her ire, but it only fueled it. "Just say it, Cy! What did she ask you or tell you, that has you and me tripping right now?"

Cy looked Hope directly in the eye. "She told me she's dying, Hope. And that one of her last wishes is for us to spend some time together. For old time's sake."

25

The Trisha Temptation

For a moment Hope didn't move, barely breathed. When her brain started working again she walked over to the wingback and sat down. "She's dying?" Cy nodded. "And wants to spend some time with you?" Another nod. Hope leaned back in the seat, anger turning to calm incredulity by the second. "You're kidding, right?"

"Baby," Cy replied, cutting his eyes in her direction, "I wouldn't kid about a thing like this."

"A woman you used to date whom you haven't seen in decades contacts you out of the blue, tells you she's dying, and you believe her?"

"Why wouldn't I believe her?"

"You're much too intelligent to be gullible, babe. And pardon my suspicious nature, but this sounds highly suspect. Wait." Hope leaned forward, narrowed eyes looking off into the distance. "Did she ask you for money?"

"Stop it, Hope." Cy's voice was forceful, his body tense with the delivery. "Trisha isn't that kind of woman. She wouldn't lie about something like this. Besides, as soon as I saw her I felt something wasn't right."

Hope sat back.

Cy tried to relax.

"How so?" Hope twisted the linen napkin she'd placed on the tray, trying to wring some of her anger out along the way.

"She was thinner, and her normally glowing skin had lost some of its glow. But her eyes were bright, her smile was genuine, and like I said, our conversation at the restaurant was like old times. So I dismissed those earlier feelings. Until she told me about her illness. Then everything I'd initially felt made sense."

Silence filled the room as both Hope and Cy nestled into their own thoughts. "So how's this supposed to look?" Hope finally asked, her voice soft and searching. "Her spending time with a man who's married with children?"

Cy sighed heavily while shaking his head. "I don't know, babe."

"What did you tell her?" Hope couldn't help that her voice rose an octave. Considering the conversation she was having, it was the best she could do.

"I was so taken aback by her news that at first I couldn't say anything." Cy quieted, laying his head back against the chair and staring at the ceiling. "I told her how sorry I was to hear about her condition, but being married, didn't know how I could comply with her request. She said she understood, and apologized for even asking. I feel so bad, Hope. The Trisha I remembered was vibrant, full of life and plans and positive expectations. It's just not fair that her life is getting cut short!" Cy stood abruptly and began pacing. He stopped in front of Hope's chair, his look one of quiet desperation. "I don't want her to die, baby."

Hope stared into her husband's eyes, saw his pain . . . and something else. "Are you still in love with her?" On one hand, she appreciated that her husband felt their relationship deep enough to want to confide these feelings in her, as uncomfortable as they were. On the other hand, however, a sistah needed to know.

"You're the only person I'm in love with," he said after a pause, turning away from her to stare out the window. "But I'd be lying if I said I didn't still feel love for her. We were practically inseparable throughout college. I think there's always something special about that first love." Turning to look at her, he leaned against the wall. "Don't you?"

Hope thought about Shawn Edmunds, the handsome musician she'd met at a church function, who'd swept her off her feet, into his bed, and away from her virginity faster than she could say hallelujah. "Mine was different," she answered, a bit surprised that this was the first time she and Cy were discussing this particular topic. Then again, after meeting and falling in love with the man in front of her, she'd not given her past a second thought. "We only dated for six months. My feelings for him were obviously nowhere near the ones you're feeling."

"Hope, I love you. There's no other woman for me. But can you understand how it feels to know that the first woman you ever loved is dying without doing many of the things that she wanted to do?"

"What is she sick with?"

"Some form of cancer. That's the other problem. The doctors say it is some rare strain with which they're not familiar. I feel so helpless. And ready to do whatever I can to make her life a little better."

"Including some one-on-one time?" Seeing the weary look in his eyes, she reached for his hand, took it, and walked them toward the bed. "It's okay, baby. It must be a lot to deal with and I thank you for trusting me enough to share your real feelings."

"Thank you, baby."

They went to bed, made slow soul-wrenching love, and then settled spoon style into each other's arms. He'd been attentive and thorough as always, but as she drifted off to sleep Hope just couldn't shake the feeling that there had been three people in the bed.

At breakfast the next morning, Hope and Cy were joined by the twins. Not the norm since many mornings Cy was up and out before they were ready to meet the world. Their presence had kept the mood lighthearted, and kept both Cy's and Hope's thoughts off what they'd discussed last night. But after kissing Cy good-bye and spending a few hours with the twins before they settled into their routine with Rosie, Hope was consumed by what she'd begun calling in her mind the Trisha Temptation. She definitely needed to talk to someone about it... but who? Or maybe a better question was, who all? Vivian Montgomery was the first person who popped into her head. The first lady of Kingdom Citizens Christian Center had heard just about everything, was a great listener, and a nonjudger. She was also the first person Hope had reached out to when this whole situation had begun.

She walked into the great room and saw the cordless phone that sat on the granite bar separating the space. She picked it up and began to dial. Halfway through the numbers, however, she ended the call. She'd talk to Vivian for sure, but right now she felt she needed another point of view. *Stacy? No, it sounds like she has enough on her plate right now.* Hope knew there was no need to talk to her cousin. Frieda had been very clear about her position on reconnecting with exes. Don't do it. Which was mostly Hope's position too, but seeing what a strain this was on Cy, she was really trying to be understanding. Hope started as the phone rang in her hand. Looking at the ID she smiled. *Thank you, Jesus. Of course!* She quickly pushed the talk button. "Hey, Mama. You're just the person I need to talk to."

Stuck in 91 freeway traffic on his way to Los Angeles, Cy was also in search of an objective listening ear. He'd called Derrick and been told by his assistant that the pastor was in a meeting. Immediately, another name came to mind. He clicked the button on his steering wheel and activated the speakerphone.

"Call Simeon." While waiting for the call to connect, Cy thought about his younger, gregarious, womanizing cousin. The one he loved to death. Growing up they'd been extremely close, and for the most part had maintained the bond through adulthood. But for the past three years, Simeon Taylor had lived in Alaska, working long hours and making big bucks. They hadn't talked as often as Cy would have liked.

"Cousin! What's up, man?!" Simeon's smile almost shone through the car speakers so prevalent was it in his voice.

"You, I see. Wasn't sure I'd catch you. You're becoming as hard to reach as a logger!"

"If you ever see me in a plaid flannel shirt you have permission to hit me with a hard uppercut followed by a jab."

"Man, forget some well-placed boxing moves. I'm going to beat you like I did when we were kids, until you go off crying to your mama ... or mine."

"Whoa! Sounds like you've got a case of selective memory, cousin. But I guess that's what happens when one gets old."

"Oh, I see where this is going. When are you coming to the lower forty-eight, so that we can do our talking on the basketball court?"

"Mid-October, if everything stays on schedule. In fact, I was going to call you later. I might need your help to secure a property in New York."

"New York?"

"Yes. I'm thinking that will be a good place to land after being here for three years. The pace, women, food ... I'll need all of that and plenty of it upon my reentry into society." A pause and then, "Cuz, you still there?"

"Yes." Cy was still there, but his good mood had left him.

"Why do you sound troubled all of a sudden? What's wrong with New York?"

"Nothing's wrong with the city, Sim. But after a recent visit there my life is crazy."

"What happened?"

A brief pause and then, "I saw Trisha."

Simeon didn't try and check his surprise. "Trisha Underwood?"

"The one and only."

"Wow. It's been years since I heard you mention that name. It took you forever to get over that fine sistah breaking your heart."

"Yes, well, it turns out that it took her a while to get over things too."

"She didn't try and get back with you, did she? I mean, with all of your former mutual friends, she's got to know you're married."

"She knows. But she still wants to spend time with me and, because of a very unfortunate situation, I want to spend time with her as well."

"Okay, Cy. You need to tell me what's going on."

Cy did, the whole story, from the first e-mail to the last good-bye and all the talks with Hope.

"You're right. This situation is very unfortunate." Both were silent before Simeon continued. "What are you going to do?"

"I don't know," Cy acknowledged. "But if Trisha died without me doing everything in my power to make her last days better . . . I don't know how I could live with myself."

26

Game. Set. Match?

Gabriel walked out of his dressing room dressed in white: polo shirt, cargo shorts, crew socks, and tennis shoes. Sporting contacts instead of the glasses he preferred gave him a younger look, even as the spray of freckles across his nose was more visible. He crossed over to the bed and looked down upon a still-sleeping Frieda. *What is going on with you, huh, Frieda? What is going on with us?*

He sat on the bed and lightly touched her shoulder. "Frieda." She shook off his hand and burrowed further into the covers. "Frieda," he said a bit more loudly, removing the covers as well.

Frieda's face was in a scowl as she turned over, her sleep-filled eyes squinting against the room's bright light. "What is it, Gabriel?" she asked testily, glancing at the clock. "Why are you waking me up?"

Gabriel bit back a retort, choosing instead to stay focused on his mission. "I thought we might get in a tennis lesson, and play a game or two. It's not often that I have free time and I don't have to be at work for another three hours."

Frieda eyed her husband, noted his freshly shaven face and hooded eyes. Sometimes she really wished she had more feelings for the man. He was...as society labeled them...a good guy: great provider, father, and doctor. If she let him, he'd probably be a good husband too. Problem was...she liked bad boys. "I told you. I don't like doing stuff I'm not good at."

"You're only not good at it because you don't practice. You have natural athletic ability, hon. But more than learning the game, I'd just really like to spend some time with you. We don't do much together anymore, Frieda. We're living more like roommates and less like husband and wife."

"That's because you work all the time!" Frieda exclaimed, immediately taking the offensive.

"You're right," Gabriel readily agreed, not taking the bait. "And I'm going to do something about that."

You are? Aw, hell. Please don't cut into my time with Clark. "What are you going to do?"

"In the fall, we have another doctor and a couple interns coming on board. I'm going to request a reduction in my hours so that I can spend more time with my wife and son." He reached out and rubbed Frieda's exposed arm. "Would you like that?"

"As long as my bank account stays the same."

"Is that what's most important to you? The lifestyle that my hard work affords?"

"I didn't mean it like that."

"How did you mean it?"

"Look," Frieda said, flopping onto her stomach and closing her eyes. "I can't argue without eight hours of sleep. Please turn out the light and close the door on your way out."

For a long moment, Gabriel continued sitting on the bed, gazing at his wife, who he was sure feigned sleep. Snippets of their past four years together wafted across his mind's eye: Disneyland with Gabe; vacations to Hawaii, Fiji, and a Caribbean cruise; strained dinners with his mother; a lone encounter with Frieda's mom. Undoubtedly the best times were those where their son was the center of attention. The vacations were mostly spent apart. Frieda didn't like golf, reading, or water sports such as snorkeling or skiing, and Gabriel didn't like excessive drinking or clubs. Times spent together when at home were even harder to recall. They didn't like the same TV shows or movies, so companionable viewing was a no go. More often than not when they were both home, Gabriel would either be reading in his study, watching TV, or playing on-line chess (another passion for which Frieda held no interest). Frieda, on the other hand, would usually hole up in the master suite talking on the phone, taking long bubble baths in their soaking tub, or sleeping. It was not the type of marriage he'd envisioned, nor the type he wanted.

After retrieving his racket, work scrubs, duffel, and other items for when he left for the office, Gabriel quietly closed the door and sought out the sunshine of his life, Gabriel Jr.

"Good morning, Daddy!" Gabe immediately ran for his father's knees as Gabriel rounded the corner.

Gabriel scooped him up. "Good morning, son."

"You playing tennis?" Gabe reached for the racket.

"Yes. Would you like to join me?"

"Yes!"

"Okay, buddy. Let's go."

Father and son enjoyed a half hour filled with Gabe hitting balls and Gabriel chasing them down. It wasn't the workout he'd envisioned, but the doctor worked up a slight sweat and more than that, enjoyed some quality time with his son. As Gabriel chased his son around the tennis court, Cordella walked to the edge of it bearing a tray of ice cold lemonade. Gabe switched courses and made a beeline for the refreshing-looking brew.

"How'd you know I was thirsty, Cordella?" Gabriel gave the small, plastic cup to Gabe before reaching for the tall glass and taking a long swallow. "This is perfect, absolutely delicious."

"You're welcome, Doctor."

"You take good care of me, Cordella, and excellent care of my son. I appreciate you."

"You are a good man, Doctor. You deserve—" Cordella stopped, turned her spouting mouth into a fine, hard line.

Gabriel's eyes narrowed. "Is there something you'd like to share with me, Cordella?"

"Yes, Doctor," Cordella truthfully answered. "But it is not my place."

"Why don't you let me determine where your place is."

"Not only that, Doctor," Cordella continued, with furtive glances toward the side patio and up to the master suite window that faced the backyard. "But the missus has warned me to mind my own business and not speak to you regarding her . . . activities. I could be fired for speaking out of turn."

Gabriel looked from Cordella to the master suite window and back to the housekeeper. He then looked down to a wide-eyed Gabe, who was drinking in the conversation as intently as he had the lemonade. "I think I should head to the office," he said with a smile, reaching for the towel nearby and wiping his forehead. "When the opportunity arises, please give me a call. And don't worry about the missus, Cordella. It's my money that pays your salary, not hers. Regarding your employment, I'll have the final word."

A little over an hour later, a shocked but not surprised Gabriel Livingston flipped through his electronic Rolodex. Upon finding the number he wanted, he tapped the screen. "Gregory," he said, when the call was answered. "Gabriel Livingston."

"Dr. Livingston! This is a pleasant surprise."

"We're long overdue for a round or two," Gabriel said, referring to the golf games that he and fellow doctor Gregory Morgan often enjoyed. "But this is not a social call."

"All right, then. What can I do for you?"

"You can give me your brother Troy's phone number."

"Sure thing. But if you don't mind me asking, what on earth do you want with my crazy baby brother?"

"Information. And access to some of his connections through his security firm."

"What do you need, Doc?"

Gabriel's jaw hardened as he formed his answer. "A private investigator. ASAP."

27

The Juice

Dr. Gabriel Livingston's contact with a PI was just beginning, but Tony Johnson's hour of time with his PT was coming to an end. Sweat ran down his face and over his body as he finished the last repetition of leg lifts on the weight machine.

"Fifteen," Vince said. The Los Angeles Sea Lions had trainers for the team, but Tony had hired Vince for additional training.

"Argh!"

"Come on, man. Sixteen!"

Tony gritted his teeth, pulled his chin down to his chest, and lifted the one-hundred-pound weight with his lower leg.

"Seventeen. Eighteen. Nineteen. Twenty."

Tony kept going.

"All right, man. That's enough."

After completing twenty-five lifts, Tony let the weights drop with a clang.

Vince raised a brow. "I'm not working you hard enough?"

"You're kicking my ass," Tony replied, reaching for his towel as he rose from the bench. "But where the average player has to go one extra mile, I have to go ten. This is my last shot, dog. I've got to go all out."

"Why don't you let me handle how far you go? I know you feel all powerful"—Vince handed Tony his water bottle as he looked around the weight room—"but don't overdo it because of the . . ." Vince nodded toward the locker that held Tony's belongings— among other things.

"I'm cool, man."

"You say that, and you probably believe it." Vince lowered his voice. "But I gave you a time frame for using, and that time has passed. You're in good shape, man, with natural ability. Let that be enough."

"As soon as I get on the roster, I'll do just that." Tony reached out and gave Vince a soul brother's handshake. "Thanks, man." He turned and headed for the shower.

"Tony!"

He turned around. "Hey, TaShaun."

"Coach wants to see you."

"Cool." Tony walked over to the temporary locker he was using, pulled out a fresh T-shirt, and replaced the sweaty one he now wore. He and Vince exchanged looks. "Think this is it?"

Vince shrugged. "Only one way to find out." He held out his fist for a pound. "I'm pulling for you, man."

Four hours later, Tony placed the key into the lock of his Phoenix abode. "Stacy!" He came around the corner with his hands full. "Baby, where are you?"

"Shh!" Stacy met Tony as he was about to climb the stairs. She took in the large bouquet of flowers and bottle of bubbly Tony held. Hurrying down the stairs and into the open concept dining area, she whispered, "Sorry, baby, but I just got DJ to sleep. He's got a cold and has been cranky all day." She stopped in front of him. Unsure of how he'd react to a hug, she clasped her hands behind her. "I'm so glad to see you. What's all this?" Tony smiled but said nothing. "Does this mean what I think it means? Did you get the job with the Sea Lions?"

"Coach said he wants to sign me to a one-year contract. It's a backup spot, but I'm not worried about that. Once I get on the field I'll claim what's mine!"

Stacy threw her arms around his neck. "Baby, I'm so happy for you!" She rained kisses on his face. "I know how much you've been wanting this, praying it would happen. Does this mean I need to start looking for houses in LA?"

"Unless you want to hang out in this furnace! I know the market's soft, but I want to put the house up for sale as soon as possible. Hopefully it will sell quickly."

"I knew you could do it, baby." Stacy cupped Tony's face, adoration shining in her eyes. "I'm happy for you."

"I knew you would be. That's why I bought you these"—he handed her the flowers—"and this."

"Thank you, baby." She walked over and pulled an empty vase from a cabinet. "But you didn't have to."

"Yes, I did. I've been an A-number-one jerk these past few months, and I'm sorry."

"I forgive you," Stacy readily told him. "I knew the Tony that's been here recently wasn't the one I married. I'm glad to see that the man I love so dearly is back." She nodded at the champagne. "Is that for me too?"

"This is for us." He reached for her hand. "Have you eaten?" Stacy nodded. "I have to be back at work tomorrow. But I wanted to be with you tonight."

Stacy went to the cabinet and pulled out two champagne flutes. Then, wordlessly, they mounted the stairs. Once in the master bedroom, Tony popped the champagne cork and poured. He handed a flute to Stacy. "In this crazy, uncertain world that is pro ball, here's to the only woman I'd want by my side."

"And to the only man with whom I'd want to take this journey."

They drank in each other with their eyes even as they drank the top-shelf champagne. "Um, this is good, baby."

"It tastes all right," Tony replied, his voice deep and husky, his eyes hooded and black with desire. "But I'd rather drink you, instead."

Stacy shivered. *When is the last time Tony looked at me like this?* Only in this moment did it dawn on her that it had been almost a month since she and Tony had made love, probably the longest time without intimacy since they'd married. In this moment she was very aware of how stress and worry had impacted their lives. In this moment, as Tony's hand made a lazy journey up her arm, across her shoulder, and down her front where he sought and found a nipple, she knew that there was nothing worth putting their love on hold. As she wrapped her arms around him and lifted her chin for a kiss, she vowed to never let it happen again.

"I missed you," she whispered, just before Tony's full lips covered hers. He moved his head from side to side, creating a delicious friction before his firm tongue demanded entry between her lips. She complied, and the dueling immediately began—swirling, tasting, teasing—all while hands touched skin and bodies rubbed against each other. But both of them had a problem. Too much clothing between them.

Tony stepped back and made quick work of removing shirt, shorts, boxers, and shoes. After watching him, Stacy reached for the zipper on her jeans and then oh...so...slowly pulled it down. Tony stopped in midsip, taking in her toned, lean body, the way her short, curly hairstyle emphasized her big brown eyes now bright with desire. Without breaking eye contact, she leaned over to push the jeans down her legs. Tony hardened with every inch of bared skin. *I really do love this girl. As soon as I get my spot back, I'm going to give up the juice.* As he continued to watch his wife's impromptu striptease act, he reached for the bottle and refilled their flutes. By now, Stacy stood in nothing but a flimsy thong. Tony's manhood bobbed from side to side as he walked to her. He handed her the glass; they gazed into each other's eyes as they sipped.

"Let me take that," Tony whispered before they'd finished the bubbly, placing both their glasses on the nightstand while backing Stacy up against the bed. He lifted her effortlessly, and placed her in the center of their king-sized paradise. He ran a finger down the center of her body, from her neck to just above her heat, held his hand there while his thumb made light strokes against her nub. Stacy's breath caught in her throat as her body immediately reacted to Tony's touch, her hips grinding upward as she became hotter, wetter. He reached for the flute, poured a bit of the chilled liquid on Stacy's pebbled nipples before sucking first one and then the other into his mouth. She reached for his dick, squeezing, stroking, waiting for it to harden and expand under her ministrations.

"Baby," Stacy panted, squirming as she imagined her husband inside her. "I can't wait. I want you now!"

Tony smiled as he reached between his legs and stroked himself. He hardened, and with one swift move he entered her and began a vigorous thrusting. That lasted about...five seconds. And then he went soft. Movement stopped. But only temporarily because Stacy immediately reached down to lend assistance. Later she'd try and recall another time when Tony had trouble keeping an erection, but for right now she chalked it up to how hard he'd been working and how long they'd gone without sex.

For the next thirty minutes, both Tony and Stacy tried to get his soldier to stand at attention. But his weapon was seriously AWOL. Even her best oral skills were not enough to wake the sleeping penis.

"It's okay," Stacy whispered, once a thoroughly frustrated Tony had swatted her hand away from his stubbornly limp member. He shifted his weight and lowered his body so that his tongue could do what his dick could not—please his wife. And while he did that well enough, as Stacy listened to the soft sounds of Tony's breathing, she began to wonder if his erratic mood of the past few months had been solely because of his concerns about work...or something, no, make that some*one* else.

28

Back to Malibu

Several hundred miles from Phoenix, in the tony California beach community of Malibu, someone else was working on a relationship. When not on set, Paz normally paid little attention to his appearance. But he checked his image while passing his den's mirror-covered wall, giving his hair a quick tousle on the way to the front door.

"Dee!" He stepped back so that Darius could enter the large foyer.

"Hey, man." The men hugged. Darius looked around, nodding his approval. "This place is nice. I forgot how nice the drive is up from Los Angeles."

"I know, right? It's why we put up with all of the inconveniences: traffic, isolation, wildfires. For what's out back." Paz placed his hand on Darius's shoulder, his turquoise blue eyes boring deeply into chocolate brown ones. "I'm really glad you came." He placed a kiss on Darius's cheek. A woodsy smell with a hint of citrus wafted from his body. His hand left Darius's shoulder and traveled down his back, offering a casual tap on the R & B crooner's taut rump before stepping away. "You look good."

"Where is everybody?" Darius took in the man who was slightly taller than he, equally well built, his body being showed off to perfection covered in swim trunks alone. The smooth olive skin was even darker than when he'd last seen him weeks ago, during the Fourth of July concert in Central Park. *The concert.* A perfect image of Bo's scowling face flashed across Darius's mind. But it was quickly replaced by the image of the model-perfect man in front of him. Paz was good people, an A-list star, and someone who made Darius feel good. Not only that, but the chemistry was undeniable. Darius tried hard not to think of this right now. He was here to meet an award-winning producer about possibly scoring the movie in which Paz had already agreed to star. The world mainly knew Darius as a singer, but those close to him knew that he also loved composing music. Writing movie scores would be a wonderful next level for his career and with Quincy Jones being one of his idols, it would bring him one step closer to mirroring a career he admired from afar.

They walked through a large, open-concept space that was bright and airy. The view was stunning: a large deck framing an infinity pool with a stretch of private beach between it and the vast Pacific Ocean. A dozen or so people milled around the deck while two couples—the guys in swim trunks, the women in thong bikinis—played volleyball on the strip of beach below. Stepping out on the deck, Darius immediately recognized one of the guests as the man who'd costarred with Paz in his latest movie, a reality-TV star, and behind the grill, a face he recognized from Bo's marathon watching of the Food Channel. Paz introduced him to a couple people on the way to the infinity pool, where a white-haired man lounged on a large tube.

"Gary, there's someone I want you to meet."

Gary slowly spun around, shielding his eyes from the sun as he looked up. A slow smile of recognition spread across his face. "Darius Crenshaw!"

"Darius," Paz began, "this is Gary Weiss. Gary, this is the music producer for our next movie."

Gary climbed out of the infinity pool and soon the two men were seated and Darius was getting schooled on the operation of the Hollywood machine. Gary was cocky and irreverent, with an encyclopedic knowledge of the industry. Darius liked him right away.

"Paz says you have some instrumentals?"

Darius nodded. "I put together a couple pieces with this project in mind."

"I'd like to take a listen and..." Gary's words died as he became distracted by a sight beyond Darius's shoulder. "That Paz is a Greek god. I'm as straight as an arrow, but I swear I'd do him in a heartbeat."

Darius looked over his shoulder. Heart stopped. Dick jumped. Paz and the couples who'd been playing beach volleyball were now cavorting naked on the private strip of beach, rushing into the ocean and riding the waves back to shore. Even from a distance, Darius could see that Paz's flaccid member was swinging down by his well-sculpted thighs. He turned to dive into the water and his ass was just as taut and round as Darius had imagined. *Get it together, man,* he admonished himself. *You'll be drooling in a minute.* He abruptly turned back to Gary to find a curious pair of gray eyes looking at him. Taking a moment to recollect himself, he reached into his pocket and pulled out a flash drive. "You were saying that you wanted to hear some of my music?"

Gary smiled, a knowing "I can keep a secret" sort of smile. "I do," he said around the grin. "When it comes to this movie, you might be a perfect fit."

"Here're a few cuts. You've got my number. After you take a listen, I'd love for us to talk again." Darius stood and extended his hand.

Gary stood as he shook it. "You leaving?"

"Yeah, my flight leaves in a couple hours."

"I thought you were local."

"I've got a place here but lately have been spending most of my time in Phoenix."

"Well, I'm glad I met you, Darius. I'll take a listen and be in touch."

"Cool." Darius spoke to a couple of the guests on his way out, trying very hard not to appear to be doing exactly what he was trying to do: beat a hasty retreat. He couldn't imagine how he ever thought he could have a casual visit with the man whose torrid texts exchanged on the prepaid phone he'd purchased had kept him so sizzling hot. He'd done what he came here to do. In the future, he'd make sure that he and Paz met in a place where the demigod couldn't run around naked. *That body . . . damn!* Picking up his pace, Darius had reached the front door when a hand clamped down on his shoulder.

Darius would know that scent anywhere. He turned around.

Paz's blue eyes bore into his. "Leaving without so much as a good-bye to the host?"

"I was going to call you." Darius knew his reply was lame, but it was the best he could do.

"Talking on the phone is one thing," Paz replied, licking his lips as he lessened the distance between the two men. "Interacting in person is another."

"Paz, I—"

His excuse was cut short by the feel of a set of firm, smooth lips on his soft, cushy ones; the scent of fresh air and warm sun emanating from a hard body; the fact that the tongue gently pressing its way into Darius's mouth didn't belong to his husband; the fact that he didn't want the kiss to end. He felt his hand on Paz's back, pressing him closer, and wondered how it got there. He felt Paz's response, a low, soft moan as he tilted his head to deepen the kiss, a hand sliding down from Darius's back to his backside, pushing them closer together. Darius's physical response—a hardening, an involuntary grinding, and a wave of heat rising from his core and causing his heart to constrict. His heart. *Remember, man? The one that belongs to Bo?*

Darius stepped back, placing a defensive hand up as he did so. "I can't do this," he panted, noting the hurt and intense desire in Paz's eyes before turning quickly away. "I'm married."

"I know." Paz ran a hand through tousled black hair. "I also know that I love you." Silence enveloped the two men as the sounds of the party, the ones that had faded into silence during their brief romantic exchange, returned. Paz noted that someone was calling his name. "I'm sorry if I upset you," he said, his voice low and hurried, his accent pronounced. "But I won't apologize for loving you, Darius." He stepped forward for another quick peck on Darius's lips. "Call before you leave town," he whispered, and then walked back to his guests.

Darius watched Paz's sculpted body as he walked away: broad shoulders, narrow waist, hard buns, and long legs. His lips still buzzing from the kiss, he turned and walked outside to the SUV he'd rented. During the scenic, winding drive down Pacific Coast Highway, Paz occupied every corner of his thoughts. Determined to divert this focus, Darius phoned his minister and good friend Derrick Montgomery. When Derrick's wife, Vivian, informed Darius that her husband was out of town, Darius called a couple members of his band. His drummer's wife had just lost a family member, counting him out for Friday night drinks. His horn player's phone went to voice mail. Twice. Deciding against hitting the clubs, Darius finally headed back to his hotel room, planning to try and catch an earlier flight out.

He did all of those things: arrived at the Four Seasons, checked flights, packed his bags, and left the hotel.

And then he went back to Malibu.

29

Family Affairs

Cordella stood in front of her stove stirring a pot of chicken, onions, garlic, and tomatoes, and given the fact that she'd been cooking since the age of nine, the worry lines on her face had nothing to do with whether the chirmole would thicken properly or her roti bread would taste good. No, after what she'd done two days ago, she was wondering how long she'd have money to put food on the table. Gabriel had assured her that her job was secure, but Cordella knew better than to take Frieda lightly. She'd worked for women like her before: without conscience and calculating, and married to the money instead of the man. In fact, it was going up against such a woman that got her fired from her last job. *But this isn't the same. Mr. Livingston is not like Mr. Worth.* When she'd told the sixty-two-year-old Mr. Worth about his thirty-seven-year-old wife's romps with the pool guy, he'd thanked her by giving her a nod and a severance check. She'd made a vow then to never *ever* again get involved in her employer's shenanigans. *So what are you doing here again, girl?* "Doing the right thing, that's what!" Cordella mumbled under her breath, angrily jerking open the oven and removing the warm, soft bread. For this staunchly religious woman, it was the Christian thing to do. "God don't like ugly and neither do I!"

"Ma, what you talking 'bout?" Clark strolled into the compact kitchen and hugged his mother from behind. When talking among each other, their lyrical island accent became even more pronounced. "You go crazy talking to yourself now?"

Cordella tried to swat his hand with the large stirring spoon as he reached around her for a piece of roti. "I go crazy with sinners like you, placing your business where it don't belong!"

"C'mon now, Ma!" Clark raised his hands in mock surrender. "Sinners need love too. And we need to eat!" Again, Clark reached for the roti bread. "I'm hungry!"

"So it's true. You're sleeping with her."

"No." The look that scampered across Clark's face told her otherwise, reminding Cordella of the time when she found the candy that then six-year-old Clark said he didn't steal hidden under his mattress.

"What's done in darkness comes to light," she warned.

"Ma, we're just friends. She asked me about a computer program and I came over to help her with it. That's all."

"You aren't a computer programmer and have no business being friends with a married woman. I'm not playing with you, son." The ladle now served as a pointer as Cordella's eyes narrowed. "Your relationship with that woman is not right." A warm feeling swept over Cordella, something that often happened when situations were being seen with her third eye. There was more wrong with Frieda's marriage than the cavorting happening with her son. She couldn't put her finger on it, but she was sure of it. Mr. Livingston was a good man. Whatever shenanigans Mrs. Livingston was up to—and she'd bet her rosary of her childhood faith that there were some—the doctor didn't deserve them. And whatever those shenanigans, she didn't want them to involve her son. "I don't want you to talk to that woman," she finished. "And don't come over to my workplace again."

Later that evening, Cordella sat in front of her television, thankful that her daughter and two grandchildren were still at the county fair, and that Clark was spending the night with his cousin. Peace and quiet was rare in the Pratt household, even rarer these days in Cordella's spirit. First there was her daughter, Shelly, and her two grandchildren. They'd been back in her household for over a year and while she loved them, she was also frustrated. Like Clark, Shelly had left the faith of her childhood and—as much as Cordella had warned her against it—was making the same mistakes that she'd made. "That's why you're struggling, Shelly," she whispered, having been unable to stop the habit that began being raised as an only child by a doting yet strict grandmother—talking to herself. "You're going down the same path that I did, the one I told you led to hard times and plenty tears." She looked beyond the muted television, tuned to a talk show that she rarely watched, and into the eyes of her daughter's father, an older gentlemen Cordella had known since childhood, who married her when she was seventeen and died of leukemia shortly after Shelly was born. Like Gabriel, Peyton was a good man, a provider, a no-nonsense man who lived by the word of God. True, she had not loved him, but at such a young age, what would she know of that? He was kind, and gentle, and though he'd been gone almost thirty years, she still missed him every day. The smile on her face shifted as she thought about another man, the man whose spitting image she saw almost every day. As he grew older, the striking resemblance caused her to almost hate her son, and even now their uncannily similar personalities and dispositions created an intense resentment. Clark's father was a player too, with no moral compass to direct him back to the small yet comfortable Long Island home that Peyton had left Cordella in his will—the home she lost when Clark's father used it as collateral for a gambling debt—right before he ran off with the mother of Clark's half-sister, the one who to this day he'd never met. She'd fled all the way across the country to try and escape the pain that betrayal caused. She had left her children with an aunt in Queens until she'd landed a job as the house manager for a wealthy European family. Eventually she secured enough money for a one-bedroom apartment in Inglewood and bus fare for her children and a cousin who'd escorted and then lived with them until Shelly was old enough to watch herself and her younger brother while Cordella worked.

"Those were hard years," Cordella said, with a casual glance toward the television. Her brow creased as she saw an older, well-dressed woman talking to a woman who was several decades younger. The older woman looked to be in her seventies, was wearing a hat that fifty-eight-year-old Cordella would wear in a heartbeat (she always was an old soul—most people who saw her thought she was older). Somehow the woman had a look that made you think you could trust her on sight. Cordella reached for the remote and unmuted the sound.

". . . the older women to teach the younger ones," the woman wearing the hat was saying. "My family has been involved in this conference for many years. I was honored when your mother-in-law, Mrs. Montgomery, invited me to teach a session."

"What's the name of your session, Gram—oops." The woman chuckled as she looked into the camera before returning her attention to the elder sistah. "I mean, Mama Max." Again, she turned to the camera. "No matter how much the prompter says Mrs. Brook or Mama Max, y'all, she's been Gram for all of my twenty-plus years." The woman shrugged. "So forgive me, and bear with me." Turning once more to the older woman, she continued. "Mama Max, what will you be teaching us at this year's Sanctity of Sisterhood Summit, themed The Woman I Am?"

The woman called Mama Max sat back. "Well . . . they say that experience is the best teacher. But I say learning from somebody else's mistakes is easier. So I'm calling my session 'My Error, Your Education.' I want y'all young women to learn from some of the women in the Bible, women on TV, women in your neighborhood, or even in your home. I want to try and help some of my sisters learn and to avoid diving head first into pain when they can go around it. And I want to see the younger generation of women start acting like they've got some sense, stop showing their privates in public and wearing in broad open daylight what I wouldn't even dare try on behind closed doors." She leaned toward the host. "Truth is some of those clothes look so tight I probably couldn't get them past my knees, but that's beside the point!"

The host laughed. The guest's eyes twinkled. Cordella turned up the volume. *Now that's a lady with some sense.*

"Thank you so much, Mrs. Maxine Brook, for joining me today." The host turned from her guest and looked directly into the camera. Cordella felt a twinge, as though the pretty young woman was looking directly at her.

"Please join me, my grandmother, and hundreds of other worthy women for the Sanctity of Sisterhood's autumn event. Again, the theme is The Woman I Am and will be hosted by one of Los Angeles's fine first ladies, Vivian Montgomery, and somebody you may have heard of...the award-winning television host, Carla Chapman. And speaking of Carla, she'll take back the reins of her show on Monday. I've had a fantastic time guest hosting this week, and remember, you can see me Wednesday nights on Bravo. *KP and His Princess* airs at nine p.m. Eastern, eight p.m. Central. Until then, I'm Princess Petersen wishing you a great weekend. Bye, everybody."

Cordella walked from the living room into her daughter's bedroom, where the laptop was stored. Upon hearing the name Carla Chapman her enthusiasm had waned a bit. Everyone in the country had heard about her scandal, how she'd cheated on her pastor husband and was now married to the man with whom she'd had the affair. It was one of the reasons Cordella didn't like those highfalutin megachurches, why after going from Catholicism to Christianity she'd been more than happy to make her church home at the Lord Jesus Christ Presbyterian Church in south Los Angeles. A small and close-knit congregation whose pastor seemed old enough to have known Kunta Kinte. This was fine with Cordella. If the plumbing wasn't working there were no worries about trying to plug up drains. Stopping when she reached Shelly and the kids' bedroom, she hesitated. *Do I really want to invite Shelly to listen to a bunch of rich, designer-wearing women who were probably more concerned with wearing the right style than getting folks saved?* But then she thought about the godly older woman who was going to be at the event. "What was her name? Mama something-or-other." Cordella turned on the computer and clicked on a search engine. She was determined to find out more.

And she did. By the time Shelly and her children returned home Cordella had not only reviewed the SOS Web site and the conference coming to LA, she'd registered both her daughter and herself to attend. Maxine Brook was the name of the older woman she'd seen on television, the woman whose spirit somewhat reminded Cordella of the grandmother who'd raised her. *My Error, Your Education,* Cordella thought as she turned back the covers and climbed into bed. And then something happened that caused Cordella to freeze—half lying down and half sitting up. Her employer's wife's face swam into her consciousness. "There's no way someone like Mrs. Livingston would darken a church door," she mumbled, having regained her movement and settling beneath the sheet. "But she's still Your child, Lord, and somebody's daughter. So while I try and help mine, please send somebody to help her."

30

Freaks and Peeks

Frieda was hoping someone would help her all right. That's why she'd gotten up bright and early, gathered what she needed for this appointment, and been out of the house before eight a.m. Now here she sat, about a half block from her destination, a nondescript brick building just off Wilshire Boulevard in West Los Angeles. She pulled her Lexus SUV into the CVS parking lot and after quickly donning a shoulder-length wig, head scarf, and oversized shades, clicked the lock, looked around, and hurried toward OGT, the Office for Genetic Testing. One thing she appreciated about this particular setup was that the DNA tests could be performed in complete confidentiality and anonymity. She'd provide the samples; they'd tell her if they were a match. Twenty-four hours. That's how long she had to wait to decide her next course of action regarding Gabriel, Clark, and that nosy-ass Cordella. One day and she'd know what she needed to do, and where she needed to go.

Frieda entered the office and punched the buzzer, as she'd been instructed during her inquiry calls.

"Hello!" said a cheery voice through the intercom. "Is this Mrs. Maguire?"

"Uh, yes." Had the situation not been so serious, Frieda would have laughed. Not only did she feel like a bad imitation of Jackie O, but when they'd requested her name for the appointment, she'd said the first thing that came into her head. The name came to mind because at that very moment Tom Cruise had been talking to Cuba Gooding Jr. on her television screen, professing his love for black people and yelling about dollar bills.

"Come right in, Mrs. Maguire."

Frieda heard the door to the inner office click, pushed it open, and stepped inside.

Fifteen minutes later she was back in her car: scarf gone, wig off, oversized shades replaced with more sensible D & Gs. The small plastic bag containing Gabriel's hair had been left at the center. "Damn, I'm glad that's over," she said aloud, starting her car and blasting Rihanna as she prepared to head east on Wilshire Boulevard on her way to La Brea Avenue. She was rocking out with her girl, ready to smoke a blunt and then have Clark help relieve her tension. Her hands-free beeped. She looked at the caller ID: Gabriel. No way was she answering that call. She knew what it was about. The inner-city assistance planning luncheon happening today. The one his mother had invited her to. The one she'd miss because she needed some charity herself—about nine thick inches worth, to be exact. Thinking about what awaited her in the hood, Frieda eased out of the parking lot and hit speed dial. She'd talked to Clark last night and told him she'd call when she was on her way. She wanted to make sure he was at his cousin's house. As amped up as she was feeling, she wouldn't mind if the cousin was there too. She'd always wanted to get her freak on where three wasn't a crowd. Maybe today would be that day. Her, Clark, and that fine-ass Spencer. The thought turned her on so much that she punched the gas and ran her car through the yellow light.

While Frieda was dreaming of a ménage à trois, private investigator Wagner was taking notes . . . and pictures. Sure that her car was well down the street, he got out of his black Honda, walked the short distance to the tan brick building, and went inside.

A plume of smoke rose above Clark's head as he blew out a hit of marijuana or, as he called it, the mighty gunja. He wasn't a

Rasta, but like many of his peers he smoked these "special cigarettes" every single day. Following the "puff, puff, pass" rule, he took another long drag and passed the blunt over to his cousin. "Here, Spence," he managed to utter, while holding the smoke in his chest.

Spencer took the joint, his head bobbing to the latest Ziggy Marley release. He took a hit off the blunt, closed his eyes as he released the smoke, and then took another hit. "Can't believe your girl," he eked out, passing the cigarette back to Clark.

"I knew that bitch was a freak." Clark frowned, even as his manhood twitched at the recent memory of him and Frieda engaging in wild, loud sex, made all the more titillating by the fact that his cousin had been within earshot. "You can't trust a woman like that. She acted like she was joking, but if I'd allowed it she would have done us both."

"Wow." Spencer shook his head. "I didn't know that you were feeling her like this, man, all possessive like she's your woman and shit."

Clark's eyes slid in Spencer's direction. "Well, she is. I've got that woman doing whatever I tell her. She'll even leave her husband if I want her too."

"Word?"

"Yeah," Clark said, though he honestly didn't believe it. Frieda was married to the doctor's dollar bills and truth be told, Clark's lifestyle had also improved courtesy of Mr. M.D. "She'll do anything for me."

"What about Auntie Cordella? I thought she was riding you about hanging out with her employer."

Clark shook his head. "Moms is trippin' for real. I just hope she doesn't do something stupid and mess up this mad game I've got going here. She got fired from her last job for doing the same bullshit she's threatening to do now."

"She's planning to tell on you and your girl?"

"Man, I don't know what she's going to do. I told her to chill on that fixation, that me and Frieda together was all in her head.

But Frieda said she's still acting funny and now . . . so is her husband."

"Dang, Frieda is gangsta; she don't like people in her business. Auntie Cordella probably acting all judgmental too? I know homegirl is probably not too happy about that."

Clark rose from the couch, stretched his six-foot-plus frame and walked toward the window. "If Ma ever decides to act on her suspicions, I have a feeling that my girl Frieda is getting ready to be unhappy about a lot of things."

31

And You Must Be...

"Hope, focus! Concentrate on your abs!" Yvette clapped her hands for emphasis, letting her uninvolved client know that she meant business. They'd been in the workout room at Hope's home for thirty minutes. Yvette felt that only half that time had truly been productive.

"Maybe I should end this for today," Hope said, reaching for her water and uncapping the bottle. "My mind is just not here."

Yvette's face showed concerned. "This isn't like you, Hope. You're one of the most positive, always upbeat people I know. What's the matter? Are you feeling all right?"

"Physically, I'm fine." Without warning, she felt her eyes moisten and quickly batted away the threat of tears. Ever since a woman named Trisha Underwood had gotten all up in her marital business, she'd been moody and on edge. It hadn't helped that Cy was out of town more these days, seriously interrupting her flow of love. *It's a good thing my baby is coming home tonight.* "But I've got a lot on my mind." She took off her weight bands, a signal that their session was over. "Sorry to waste your time, girl. Give Millicent my extra minutes."

"Your neighbor won't be using extra minutes any time soon."

The tone in Yvette's voice immediately got Hope's attention. "What's going on with Millicent?"

"Hmm . . . Maybe she should be the one to tell you."

"Don't tell me she and Jack are divorcing."

"No, nothing like that."

"Is it Sarah? Thomas? Or Jackson?"

"No, their children are fine." Yvette took the towel from around her neck and placed it in the duffel bag along with the weights. "Don't tell her I told you and act surprised at the news." A pause and then, "They're having another baby."

"Really?"

"Yes," Yvette said with a nod, smiling at the incredulity in Hope's voice. "Sarah, Thomas, and Jackson are getting ready to have a little brother or sister."

"Oh." It was the last type of news Hope expected and she didn't know why hearing it made her feel bad. "That's . . . interesting."

Little did she know, but "interesting" had just begun.

Cy eased into the backseat of the town car, aching with weariness and more than a little ready to see his wife and kids. The trip to South Africa had been a challenge from start to finish: from losing the contractors his company thought they'd secured for the village rebuilding project to his flight home being canceled just moments before they were scheduled to board. He was tired, hungry, and horny . . . and not necessarily in that order. After a brief chat with the driver, he raised the partition and pulled out his phone. His first thoughts were of Hope, wanting to call her and to hear her voice. But his wife hadn't been too talkative these days; an outward manifestation of the inner turmoil his seeing Trisha had obviously caused. He knew she tried to be understanding but every now and then her frustration would bubble to the surface. *Can you blame her?* No, Cy could not. He had to admit that given the circumstances, Hope had been more than patient. *How would you feel if the tables were turned?* He'd asked himself the question a thousand times and still didn't have the answer. After a series of talks with her mother, Pat, Hope had come to Cy determined to trust him and see what was happening from his point of view. Their lives had returned to a slightly different yet peaceful kind of normal, and he'd tried to be as sensitive as possible, not emphasizing his dealings with Trisha, but not wanting to hide them either. And then there was the other conversation, the one where Hope had all but accused him of—Cy looked out the window, observing without really seeing the passing scenery as he remembered.

Cy walked into the kitchen to find Hope juicing vegetables for what she called his morning health drink. "I talked to Trisha today."

"What else is new?" Hope mumbled as carrots churned in the juicer chute.

"What did you say, baby?"

"I said . . . what'd she say to you?" She placed another carrot into the chute.

Cy moved closer so that he could be heard over the noise. "This is a good week—no nausea, better energy. She almost sounded like her old self."

"How nice."

Which caused Cy to look at her—really look at his wife. He placed a hand on hers, preventing her from stuffing another noise-inducing vegetable into the chute. "What's the matter, Hope?"

"What's the matter, Hope?" she mimicked, as if channeling her four year-old child. Turning around, she leaned against the counter and crossed her arms. "Oh, I don't know, Cy. Maybe it's just a little much for a wife to have her husband come bouncing into the room all chipper because his 'first love' "—she said with air quotes—"is sounding more like her old self. Maybe she's wanting you to visit her in New York, so you can help her feel even more like her old self!"

What the hell? Cy did a quick calculation before he spoke. *When was your last period?* Cy spoke in a deceptively calm manner. Where was Hope's compassion, her concern for a human being? "Would you prefer that I not say anything, that I not discuss with my wife how I'm feeling about someone I used to care about?" No answer. "I'm telling you, Hope, because I thought you'd rejoice in the fact that someone who's dying is having a good day for a change. Referring to Trisha's old self is remembering someone who was healthy, vibrant—okay, maybe I shouldn't have said that—someone who wasn't wondering whether the next breath she took would be her last."

"Oh, please." Hope turned back around and added cabbage and celery to the juicer before throwing over her shoulder, "You're being a bit dramatic, don't you think?"

"And you're being a bit selfish, don't *you* think?" He began walking out of the kitchen.

"Wait, Cy, your drink."

He stopped abruptly and turned around. "You drink it. So *you* can stay healthy."

The two didn't talk that day, a rarity as their lives were generally peppered with frequent, quick phone calls, often just to ask a question or to let one know that the other was thinking about them. By the time Cy returned home they had both cooled off. Cy had also talked to his cousin who told Cy to look at the situation from Hope's point of view. Which led to the question he'd been asking himself since: how would he handle it if it were her first love wanting her near? It also led to a second question. *Is this right, what I'm doing?* And a third. And fourth. *How can I leave Trisha at what may be the end of her life? How can I just turn away?* He'd entered the house not knowing what kind of reception he'd get. Hope had met him with open arms. They'd apologized to each other and sealed their "I'm sorry" with a night of making love. The next day they'd had a heart-to-heart about it. He'd agreed to only discuss Trisha on a need-to-know basis, and Hope had agreed to trust Cy's faithfulness. For a while, the Taylor household had returned to a kind of normal. But even with her name rarely spoken, the situation with Trisha was often still the elephant in the room.

★ ★ ★

Cy's phone vibrated. He didn't recognize the number, but the 212 area code told him it was New York. Immediately, he thought of Trisha and hoped it wasn't some hospital calling with bad news. "Hello?"

"Hey, man. What's poppin'?"

"Sim?"

"Ha! Thought that number would throw you off. I bought a new cell phone and thought I'd get a new number to help me acclimate to my new zip code."

"So you bought the brownstone?"

"No, I decided on the loft in Tribeca."

"Good choice, but I'm a bit surprised."

"I know, all of the renovations. But the contractor you recommended has assured me that he can have the work done in six weeks."

"That sounds reasonable. So what are you doing there now?"

"I'm—Oh, wait a minute, Cy. This is my new business partner calling. I'll call you back."

Cy reached La Jolla, tipped the driver, and was soon walking through his front door to a lovely sight. "Hope!"

Hope, who'd been sitting in the living room surfing the net, was in his arms in an instant. "I missed you," she said, after a prolonged kiss that said the same thing. She stepped back. "You look exhausted, baby. I can see dark circles under your eyes."

"This trip was a bitch, babe," he said, taking her hand as he walked toward the stairs and their master suite. "Delays in construction, material delivery and—Never mind. I'd rather not even talk about that right now. The twins asleep?"

"Yes, thankfully. Acacia caught a cold and now that she's getting better I think Camon has it. They both kept me up almost all of last night."

"So I guess I won't wake them up for a little fun time with father."

"Not unless you want to make their mother very unhappy."

They reached the bedroom. He turned to her and once again,

pulled her into his arms. "I definitely don't want to do that," he cooed, his voice low and dripping with desire. "Because as soon as I shower off the tiredness from this trip, I'm going to show you just what I've been thinking about while I've been gone." He started a slow grind against her, letting his arms fall until her booty was perfectly cupped in his hands. He squeezed one set of cheeks while kissing the other. Feeling himself begin to harden, he broke their embrace and began undressing. He set his cell phone, keys, and items from his pants pocket on the nightstand and then added his slacks to the shirt draped across the bed. "I got a call from Simeon," he said from the en suite bath as he finished undressing.

"Oh, yeah?" Hope had already showered and after taking Cy's clothes to the hamper in their dressing room, climbed into the center of their custom-made bed. "What did he want?"

"He's moving to New York."

"Really, when?"

"When the renovation on his loft is finished. In fact, he's there now."

"Has he found a job there?"

"I don't know. He got a call in the middle of our conversation. He's supposed to call me back." Hope heard Cy turn on the shower. She reached for a catalog, idly browsing the selection of underwear and lingerie. Seeing a set that she thought sexy and knew Cy would love, she eased off the bed to retrieve her iPad and place the order. While across the room, Cy's phone rang. At first she didn't give it a second thought, but then remembering what he'd said about Simeon calling, she hurried over to catch the call. It stopped ringing in her hand.

Darn it. Hope hit the screen and saw the missed call. *212.* Hope hit redial, excited to talk to her cousin-in-law. Even though they hadn't socialized often during her and Cy's six years of marriage, she absolutely adored Simeon. He was smart and gorgeous and kept her laughing. At one time she'd thought about him for her cousin, Frieda. Too bad that didn't work out. Simeon was one of the good ones.

The voice answering on the other end abruptly brought her out of her reverie. "Well, if it isn't my handsome cyclone! Are you back in the states?"

"This isn't your *handsome cyclone*," Hope said, with the type of calm that's found in the eye of the storm. "It's his wife, Hope." Silence. "You must be Trisha."

32

Get Here When You Can

Trisha closed her eyes against the reality of the moment. She had pushed all the strength she had into the chipper greeting that she'd meant for Cy's ears. It had become her practice, trying to sound upbeat when they talked, when in reality she was anything but. The truth of the matter was that her health wasn't getting better, but worse. The last round of treatments that her doctor had devised weren't working and short of the intense and debilitating rounds of chemo and radiation that he'd recommended, options that guaranteed her only a few more months at best, Trisha's end was rapidly approaching. She tried to keep these facts hidden from Cy because she didn't want to worry him and she wanted the time he'd agreed to spend with her to be filled with living life, not thoughts of death. Given her prognosis, his next few visits needed to happen sooner rather than later. She wanted to see him as soon as possible, in hopes of spending as much time with him as she could. That's why she'd called.

After she recovered from the spasm of pain in her abdomen, Trisha responded. "Hello, Hope."

Hope's chuckle was hollow and insincere. "Not as enthusiastic to talk to me, I see. But then again, I can understand that. It's a bit awkward to speak to the wife of the man with whom you're flirting."

"It was innocent, Hope, a pet name I used to call him. But you're right. It's inappropriate. I apologize."

Well, damn. Hearing the sincerity in her voice, mixed with something else, took some of the wind out of Hope's angry sails. "Why are you calling?"

Because time is running out. "Because I wanted to find out when Cy might be visiting New York. I need to see him." The pain in Trisha's heart brought on the pain in her stomach, a fact that was reflected in the breathiness of the last sentence.

One minute cooing and the next sounding ready to die? Is this woman faking? Are both me and Cy being played? "Oh, so now we're trying to sound sick. Where's that sexy sounding voice you used just a minute ago?"

"A front," Trisha managed as she endured another stab of pain. "I know what kind of man Cy is, Hope, and don't want him to worry. But woman to woman, and just between us, I don't think I'm going to last much longer. I've decided not to endure the pain of chemo and radiation. I know this is incredibly selfish of me, but this is why I wanted to spend time with Cy. If I weren't dying, it's a request I'd never consider. But I'm only asking for a couple days, or weeks, Hope. Then you guys will have each other for the rest of your lives."

The honesty in her statement left Hope speechless, which is why she stood silent, clutching the phone, as a towel-clad Cy walked out of the bathroom, noted that Hope was on his phone. That was unusual; she didn't normally answer his cell. And then he remembered his earlier comment. "Is that Simeon?" he asked, as he crossed the room to where she stood.

"No," Hope answered, handing him the phone. "It's Trisha."

Cy locked eyes with Hope as she handed him the phone and started to walk away. He placed a hand on her arm, stopping her, and then put the call on speaker. "Hey, Tricky!"

"Hey, Cy."

At the sound of her voice, Cy glanced at Hope. "How are you, Trisha?"

"Oh, as I was telling Hope, a little tired tonight. But what I didn't get to do is apologize to her for coming into your lives the way that I did. I knew you were married when I contacted you, Cy, and probably should have done this at the beginning, talked to her, made sure that she was okay with my talking to you. It was selfish of me and if I were in her shoes I'd be angry too. I'd like to tell her that I'm sorry."

"You just did," Cy replied. The look he gave Hope was hard to read. "You're on speaker."

"I appreciate your saying that, Trisha, and while I've tried to put myself in your place, I'm glad that you realize how this is from my side. I'm sorry for what's happening to you. I know that being able to have closure at a time like this, to leave . . . to not have regrets . . . is important. Cy is rightfully concerned about you, and wants to do whatever he can to make things better right now. I believe that that's the right thing to do."

This time when Hope looked at Cy there was no mistaking the look in his eyes—adoration . . . and love.

"So, Trisha, you're doing okay?" Cy nodded as Hope gestured toward the door, then watched as she left the room. He walked to the suite's sitting area, but paced instead of sitting down. "I can hear the tiredness in your voice."

"Yes, Cy, I'm very tired. And I received some news today that wasn't the best." Trisha relayed what she'd told Hope about the chemo. "I was hoping that work would be bringing you here soon," she finished. "And that perhaps you could spend some time with me?"

"I'll make it happen," Cy said without hesitation. "In fact, there's somebody else who'd love to see you."

"Hope. Of course you'd bring her. I guess it would be too much to ask to spend that time with you alone."

"I wasn't talking about my wife. I was talking about my cousin."

"Simeon?!"

Cy laughed. "The one and only."

From the moment they'd met, Simeon and Trisha had formed a mutual admiration society. More than once she'd threatened to hook up with Simeon if she ever broke up with Cy. When the breakup happened, however, Trisha had disappeared from Simeon's life as completely as she had from Cy's, and like Cy until recently, Simeon hadn't seen Trisha in a very long time.

"Have you told him about...my illness?"

"I did."

"Wow, Simeon. Just saying his name brings back so many wonderful memories. I'd love to see him again." There was silence, as both Cy and Trisha thought of the time surrounding those memories and, given Cy's marital status, some thoughts were more appropriate than others. Trisha's interruption of these thoughts was well timed. "Where is he living now? Wait, don't tell me he's married with children."

"If I did, it would be a lie. Up until a month ago, he was living in Alaska."

"Stop it! You've got to be kidding."

"No." Cy told Trisha about Simeon's job. "But as we speak, he's in New York."

"Living here?"

"He will be in about six weeks. I had an emergency happen with a project in South Africa, so an associate has been working on the businesses in New York. Things are crazy right now, but I'll definitely be there when he gets moved in."

"I wish you could come sooner." Trisha's voice was soft, plaintive.

"Why?"

"Um...not feeling well."

Cy's heartbeat increased. "When would you like me to try and come up?"

"As soon as possible, Cy," was Trisha's immediate response. "I need to see you, to spend time with you as soon as you can."

33

For Always

Bo and Darius had just enjoyed a simple yet delicious dinner of salad, baked potatoes, ears of corn, and perfectly done steaks straight off the grill. It was a rare week when Darius's schedule was light, void of rehearsals, meetings, or travel, and he and Bo had been taking full advantage. Last night they'd enjoyed front-row seats at a Jay-Z and Beyoncé concert and two days before that they'd treated themselves to twenty-four hours at Canyon Ranch, a luxury spa just two hours from Phoenix where they enjoyed mud baths, steam baths, and couple massages in a gay-friendly atmosphere. The food had been stellar and while they'd passed on the hiking trails, Bo had admired Darius's taut backside when the physically fit producer/musician/singer/R & B star scaled the climbing wall. They'd laughed and loved and watched shooting stars while floating in a natural pool. Darius remembered all of the reasons why Bo was the love of his life and Bo almost forgot the reason Darius was being so attentive.

Unfortunately, the ringing phone on the granite-countered bar separating the kitchen and the living/dining space was a constant reminder. The fool who fancied himself madly in love with Darius had been calling all day.

Darius, who was helping Bo put away the food, walked over to the phone, checked the caller ID, then casually strolled back over to the dishwasher.

"You might as well answer it," Bo said, after noting how Darius tried to keep his nonchalant expression. Emphasis on *tried*. "You know you want to."

"How do you figure? I told you at the beginning of the week. This is our time. Business can wait."

"Oh, you're still trying to sell me that fairy tale that Paz's calls to you are all about that movie project? Do you have some ocean-front property in Nogales that you want to sell me too?" The words were harsh, softened only by the kiss Bo placed near Darius's neck as he pinched his butt.

"Ha, ha. If you ever decide to get out of management you might check into becoming a comedian."

"No, thank you. One of us on stage is enough in this family." Bo placed the remaining salad into the refrigerator and reached for the sliced strawberries marinating in a sugary juice. "You want dessert now?"

Darius slowly turned around, his brown eyes twinkling as he licked his lips. "I'm sure you did your Aunt Gladean proud, baby, so I'd love some of that strawberry shortcake you made from scratch." He walked over to Bo, and gave his face an affectionate caress. "I'd love it even more in the bedroom. And don't forget the whipped cream."

Bo preened like a peacock in full heat. "You're such a bad boy. It's why I love you."

"I think I'm going to take a quick shower. See you in a few?"

"You got it, lover."

In the master suite, just inside the bathroom, Darius talked on the home's cordless phone. "I told you, P. I've been spending time with Bo. Quality time, with no distractions." A pause while he obviously listened to what Paz had to say. "That's just it. I didn't talk to anybody! We went to a day spa; I didn't even have my telephone."

Bo rounded the corner to the bedroom, immediately aware that instead of water running it was Darius's voice that he heard.

"It's not something I take lightly, believe me. I haven't been able to get you out of my mind."

And then something else, said very lowly, at almost a whisper. Bo would have done a cat burglar proud, so quiet was he as he placed the sweet-laden tray on the cedar bench at the foot of the bed before tiptoeing over to the wall that separated him from his betrayer. His movements were especially noteworthy, considering they happened with his heart on the floor.

Darius's voice took on a pleading quality. "Don't do that. Listen to me, baby. I didn't take what happened lightly. Please believe that. This isn't easy. You knew from the start that I was married." Bo's heartbeat escalated to...oh...about fifteen-hundred beats per minute, way beyond what should have caused a heart attack. All of the doubts and fears that had gathered in the past couple months returned full force, accompanied by pain. A picture of their spontaneous Canadian wedding flashed before him as he continued to listen, those magical nights when they relished the feel of freshly fallen snow, exchanged uniquely designed wedding rings, drank pricey champagne before a crackling fire, and made love in every room of the luxuriously appointed suite. *This muthafucka told me he was taking a shower. Didn't know that meant showering Mr. Holly-weird with bullshit.* In his mind Bo was strong and secure, using his ready sarcasm to mask the emotional shifting happening as a result of his worst fears being verbally confirmed. But in reality, Bo felt as though he'd been punched in the gut by Mike Tyson, Evander Holyfield, and an in-his-prime Muhammad Ali...all at once.

Suddenly, Darius felt uneasy. "Look," he whispered, "I've got to go."

Silence as Bo imagined Paz pleading for Darius to...what? *Meet him somewhere? Leave the marriage? And just what had happened that Darius did not take lightly?* Bo didn't know, but he planned to find out. In the seconds it took for Darius to end the call, Bo's hurt had turned to anger. He stood ramrod straight, arms crossed, face set in stone that rivaled the boys on Mount Rushmore.

"Look, I said I would, all right? Just stop calling me." Darius ended the call and turned with a huff. "Oh, hey, baby."

"Hey, baby, hell! I heard you, muthafucka!"

"It was nothing."

"So why was nothing being discussed in the bathroom?" Bo's voice escalated along with his blood pressure. "All on the down low and shit!"

"This is why—because I knew you'd get upset!" Darius's volume increased as well.

Probably not the best move as evidenced by the split second it took Bo to get within microinches of his face. "Which do you think would make me more upset, Dee? You talking to that asshole or you doing it behind my back? You're fucking him!"

"I told you I'm not," Darius retorted, figuring that technically this was true. He took a step back.

"You're lying!" Bo took a step forward.

"Bo, calm down!" Steps back.

"Calm down? You want me to calm down?" Steps forward. "I walk in here all ready to make love to my husband, only to find him on the phone with his lover? And I'm supposed to calm the hell down? Or beat you the hell up? Which one sounds more appropriate right about now?"

The clenched fists at Bo's side signaled that he was more inclined to do the latter.

Darius's back was against the wall, in more ways than one. He took a deep breath, silently cursing himself for giving in to his desire to hear Paz's voice. "Baby, can we just talk about this?"

After a tension-filled moment, Bo stepped back and again crossed his arms over a slightly heaving chest. "Okay, talk. I'm listening."

"I needed to talk to him about the project."

"Bullshit."

"No, it's not."

"Paz is acting in the movie; you're writing the score. What does one have to do with the other?"

Darius walked over to the toilet, put down the lid and sat down. "You're not going to like it."

"Just tell me!"

"We're collaborating." He forced himself to meet Bo's incredulous gaze. "It was an executive decision. I guess Paz gave them a CD of his work; some poems he'd written and set to music. They like his voice." He shrugged. "Thought it would be good PR for us to work on the title track for the sound track."

Bo stormed out of the bathroom.

"Bo, wait!" Darius followed him into the bedroom. "Bo, please . . ." He reached out to grab Bo's arm.

"Don't touch me!" His look was one of pure disdain. "There's no telling where your hands have been."

"C'mon, Bo . . . it's not even like that. I was going to tell you."

"When? When the song came on the damn radio?"

Darius laughed. Bo scowled. Darius raised his hands in surrender. "Okay, I'm sorry." He sat on the bed. "Will you sit down? Please." Instead of sitting on the bed next to Darius, Bo perched on the bench at the end of it. He sat sideways, not looking at Darius but straight ahead, placing Darius in his peripheral vision. "I'll admit that I flirt around with Paz." Bo snorted. "I probably shouldn't do it. Guess you could say I'm a bit starstruck." Silence. "You don't have anything to worry about, Bo."

"But I do worry." Bo's voice was soft, tenuous. "People are always throwing themselves at you. Men, women, hell, even the neighbor's dog has fallen in love." He looked at Darius now, his eyes bright with unshed tears. "This is the first time that you've flirted back."

"Oh, baby." Darius moved to the end of the bed and wrapped his arms around Bo. This time there was no resistance. "I love you."

"Me too, Dee." Sniff. "You're my world."

"And you're mine." They sat silently a moment, Bo feeling Darius's breath on the side of his face, Darius feeling Bo's heartbeat return to normal. "Our fifth anniversary is coming up."

"I know."

"Might be nice to spend it in Canada."

Bo smiled. "At the Fairmont Le Manoir Richelieu?"

"That's one of my favorite places."

"Why?"

Darius kissed Bo's temple. "You know why."

Darius kissed Bo again, moving from his temple to his cheek and when he'd coaxed Bo into facing him, his mouth. Soon clothes were removed and strawberries and cream were spread on the places that Bo had envisioned. The lovemaking was awesome, as always. Darius was extra-attentive and in a rare move was on the receiving end of love's penetration. They went to sleep wrapped in each other's arms. And as they did so, Bo's last thought was on making sure that he was always wrapped in Darius's arms . . . where he belonged.

34

The Million-Dollar Question

"Hey, brother!" At the sound of her big brother's voice, Stacy's heart soared.

"Hey, lil' sis. It's about time you answered your phone. We were getting ready to put out an APB!"

"I'm sorry, Brent. I have been missing in action."

"What's going on with you?"

That was the million-dollar question, and the reason why Stacy hadn't called the brother who'd practically raised her. He could read her like a national best seller and her latest life chapters weren't ones she wanted him to peruse. From the time their father died, when Stacy was only ten years old, Brent, who was the oldest of her four brothers, became the undisputed head of household. He'd teased her mercilessly, shooed her away when his friends came over, and basically lorded over her as though he were God. In turn, Stacy adored him.

When Stacy turned sixteen and began dating, Brent was worse than the LAPD. He insisted on meeting all of her boyfriends and she didn't know what he said to them after his standard, "let me hollah at you for a minute," but she'd never been treated with anything less than the utmost respect from these dates. After his marriage and the birth of his first child, Brent wasn't as hands-on as before. By then, however, Stacy had come into adulthood and after growing up with four rambunctious brothers, was more than able to hold her own.

Stacy didn't introduce Brent to her first husband, Darius, until after they were married. But that's not why Brent never liked him. According to him it was because Darius never fully looked him in the eye. "Don't trust that dude," had been Brent's first, middle, and last impression.

Tony was different. Brent had liked him right away. Along with a love for sports they shared a love for business and golf. In fact, all the brothers liked Tony. When it came to the Gray family, he'd fit right in. Which is why the ups and downs Tony and Stacy had recently experienced were all the more troubling, and made it all the more necessary to keep her brother out of the messy marital loop.

"What's been going on with me?" Stacy repeated in a playful manner. "Well, brother, you'll be happy to know that involves my looking for real estate in Calabasas."

"Seriously, Stacy? Y'all are moving back to Cali?"

"That's the plan. As we speak, Tony is working out for the Sea Lions."

"Well, that's just great. I know how much you've wanted to move back here."

"You know it. There are parts of Arizona that are simply stunning, but California will always be home."

"Your niece and nephew will be glad to hear that you'll be living closer."

"Ah, how are my little bedbugs?"

"Growing like weeds. How is DJ?"

"Five going on fifteen. He fancies himself having a girlfriend."

"My man! Sounds like I need to school my nephew on a thing or two."

"He'll be delighted. Nothing thrills him better than a visit with his favorite uncle."

"Don't let our brothers hear that."

"Naw, we'll just keep it between us." A beep sounded in Stacy's ear. She looked at the caller ID. "Brent, hold on a minute." She clicked over. "Hey, Little Bo Peep."

"Stacy, are you busy?"

"No," Stacy replied, noting that once again her usual moniker, Spacey, was noticeably absent. "Just talking to my brother. You okay?"

"No, but I will be. I'm going to make sure of that. Can I come over?"

"Sure."

"Good, I'll see you in fifteen."

Stacy shifted back over to her brother and after agreeing to give him a heads-up regarding her LA visit, and to try and get him four tickets to the first game, she ended the call and made DJ's lunch. In a rare move, she bypassed the dining room table and let her son eat his chicken nuggets and fries while watching his favorite cartoon. Darius would definitely have something to say about it if he knew that the TV was serving as babysitter, but what he didn't know wouldn't hurt him. Stacy got the feeling that whatever it was that Bo had to tell her, she'd need to have her wits about her.

Just moments after getting DJ settled, her doorbell rang. That he pulled out a large bottle of cognac shortly after their hug was her first indicator that this was not going to be an ordinary visit. She had a flashback to the first time she saw Bo totally imbibe—in a cozily warm cabin in Big Bear where a recently exposed secret of a three-way love affair had caused quite a chill.

"Where's DJ?" he shouted, barely inside the door.

"Uncle Bo!" DJ ran into the room and gave Bo a high-five. "Where's Daddy?"

"Working, little man. When are you going to your job?"

"Uncle Bo," DJ laughed, "I don't work."

"With the amount of food you eat, you should."

"Speaking of which," Stacy interrupted, "are you finished with your lunch?" DJ shook his head. "Then go back into there and finish eating."

"Uncle Bo, can we play videos later?"

"We'll see, DJ. Right now, I need to talk to your mama."

DJ walked back into the game room, and after retrieving a glass and ice for Bo's afternoon drink, Stacy joined him in the living room. Once they were alone, she wasted no time assuaging her curiosity. "Okay, Bo Peep. What has you chugging liquor in the middle of the day?"

Bo fixed her with a look. "I'll give you three guesses and the first two don't count."

Stacy didn't have to guess. There was only one thing, or more accurately one person, who could put Bo Jenkins Crenshaw in this kind of mood. "What's going on with you and Dee?"

Bo tossed back the cognac and refilled his glass. "I think I'm going to lose him."

"Trust me, when it comes to losing Darius I know what that feels like." Bo smiled at the inference of the time when he and Stacy battled for Darius's love. "And it doesn't feel like what I see between y'all."

"Yeah, well, that's because you haven't seen the crowd in our bedroom."

"Excuse me?"

"Darius is in denial, but he's in love with Paz the Ass."

"He's still tripping on that actor?"

"Yes."

"How do you know?"

Bo gave her a look. "Trust me, I do." His normally jovial countenance turned sad. "I think Darius is in lust with him," he whispered, followed by a generous gulp of Courvoisier.

"Maybe, but I don't think you have anything to worry about."

"For real, Stacy? You really believe that?"

"When it comes to knowing how much Darius loves you, trust me, I know. I'm the one he left so he could be with you, remember?"

"As crazy as your ass was, how can I forget?"

"Me? If anybody was crazy it was Darius. How'd he think he

was going to get away with taking both of us on vacation—at the same time?"

"Ha! That Big Bear situation was a mess with a capitol M."

"Him thinking he could go between cabins, giving me a kiss and you a hug."

"He thought you wouldn't notice him tipping out in the middle of the night."

"That's because he never bothered to find out whether or not I was a light sleeper. I knew as soon as he left the bed, heard him trying to slip into sweats and tennis shoes and ease the keys off the table. Felt the whoosh of cold air when the door opened and the click when it closed."

"And then you came storming over to my cabin yelling like a banshee." Bo's humor had returned and he now laughed at the memory.

"I was on what was supposed to be a romantic getaway with my fiancé. Oh, and I was pregnant. Forgive me for being just a little upset."

"A little? Girl, you came at me like Joseline did Stevie. You wanted to beat. My. Ass."

"I'll admit it. I wanted to clear a path of snow with your narrow behind."

"Ha!" Bo poured another glass of liquor and motioned to Stacy. She held up her soda. "No, thank you, I'm good. DJ," she yelled so that he could hear from the other room, "are you finished eating?"

"Yes. I'm watching TV!"

"Okay."

"You're lucky to have DJ," Bo said, his mood once again swinging from happy to sad.

"He's a good kid," Stacy admitted.

"Not only that, but Darius loves him. And because you have his son, he'll always be a part of your life."

"Yes, I guess that's one way to look at it."

"Those are the times I feel most complete—when DJ is over

and we're sharing family time. Me cooking, him and Dee in the other room watching TV or playing a game. Then later when we're watching some crazy Disney movie and later, when DJ falls asleep in between us on the couch. Those are the times that Darius is settled and calm; I know that it makes him feel complete too."

"There's nothing that says family like a child in the home."

"I feel that way exactly," Bo said, placing down his glass and turning to Stacy with a serious look. "Which is why I have to ask you something, and why I want you to hear me out before you throw me out."

"With the crazy way your mind thinks, Bo, I can't make any promises."

"I'll just have to take my chances then. See, I've thought of a plan that can alleviate both our fears—yours about financial security and mine about marital security." He took a deep breath and continued. "If I talked Darius into paying you a million dollars... would you have a baby for me? One that Darius and I can raise as our own?"

35

You Want Me to Do What?

"Y ou want me to do what?" Stacy hadn't had a touch of alcohol, but she could have sworn she was drunk.

"I know it sounds crazy."

"You think?"

"But I've given this a lot of thought. Darius loves DJ, loves kids. Just recently we had a conversation about it, and he admitted that he'd love to expand our family."

"And he said he wanted to expand it with me as surrogate?"

"No, the conversation didn't get that far. But you know how private Darius is, and with his public profile, you know how untrusting he is of people."

"Yeah, but famous people use surrogates, and others adopt."

"Darius wouldn't do that," Bo quickly retorted, shaking his head. "He wouldn't want to go through that process. Plus, he loves the fact that he can look into DJ's face and see himself. Stacy, he would love to have another biological baby."

Stacy met Bo's intense stare. "You're really serious about this, aren't you?"

"Yes."

"Wow, Bo. I don't know what to say, except . . . are you fricking crazy?! Have you forgotten that I'm married? And even if I weren't, I don't know that I could carry a child for nine months, give birth, and then turn the baby over to y'all without a backward glance. Actually, even just saying that out loud lets me know that I couldn't. I couldn't have a child out there somewhere with my DNA and not have anything to do with it."

"That's just it, Stacy. It wouldn't have to be that way. This child would be DJ's biological sister, and you'd be Aunt Stacy. We could handle it as an open adoption, with you seeing the child as often as you'd like. The only difference is that he or she would grow up in our home, instead of yours."

Stacy looked at Bo with creased brow. "You've really thought about this, haven't you?"

"I've thought about saving my marriage, Stacy. I've thought about keeping my man."

"Bo, stop drinking. Alcohol is clouding your judgment. Darius is not going to leave you."

Bo threw back the last of his drink. "He'd better not," he said, his tone low, his eyes narrowed. "Because Bo Jenkins Crenshaw wouldn't take that shit lightly. He wouldn't like that move at all."

Hours after Bo left, Stacy was still reeling from their conversation. *He wants me to have a baby? For him and Darius? True, we've learned how to coexist, but . . . did he actually let those words come out of his mouth?* Shaking her head, she walked to the computer, decided to check her e-mails as a way to get her mind off the madness. Aside from the normal spam, there were e-mails from two potential employers that she'd sent resumes. One was from Globally Green, a company that served as an online networking community between environmentally friendly companies and consumers. This marketing position appealed to Stacy because she'd work from home. Tony didn't even need to know she had a job!

She opened the e-mail. Her heart sank. It was a "thanks but no thanks" rejection letter that she deleted without finishing. She clicked on the other job-related e-mail and deleted it too. They'd requested an interview, but the job was in Phoenix. Stacy hoped that by the end of the week it would be confirmed that Tony was a Sea Lion and she'd be relocating back to LA.

Her phone rang. Looking at the caller ID, she said to herself, "Maybe this is my answer now." She placed the call on speaker. "Hey, baby!"

"Hey, baby girl! You found our house yet?" The enthusiasm in his voice jumped through the phone and almost slapped her in the face.

"I've got a couple serious contenders." Stacy tried to rein in her joy. She didn't want to celebrate prematurely. "Why, should I step up my search?"

"Damn right! You're talking to an official Sea Lion, baby!" Tony whooped for emphasis. "I just signed the contract."

"Yes!" Stacy joined in the celebration, dancing around the room. "Congratulations, baby."

DJ came running into the room. "What is it, Mommy?"

"Daddy got a job, baby. He's going to play football in Los Angeles!"

"Sea Lions!" DJ exclaimed. He too joined in the dance.

"Tony, I'm so happy for you. So happy for us!"

"Me too, baby. I know the stress and pressure of this whole situation has made me less than an ideal husband lately. I want you to know that I'm sorry, Stace. For everything. I love you, baby. Thanks for always believing in me."

His words caused tears, happy ones. With one phone call, and one announcement, Stacy's world had gotten brighter and all of her problems had gone away. Even a one-year contract would be enough for them to pay down their debts and allow for a bit of a savings account. Maybe Tony would even take her advice and hire a financial planner. Mismanaging finances was a common mistake among professional athletes. Maybe it wasn't too late to turn their finances around and secure their future!

She and Tony talked for half an hour and it was by far the best, least stressful, most upbeat conversation that they'd had in months.

She got off the phone and immediately called the realtor, followed by her travel agent. In two weeks, Tony would be playing in a preseason game. If all went the way she'd hoped, the family would be relocated by the time that happened and the Johnsons could be ready for a new, more peaceful chapter in their lives.

36

Mama's Baby, Daddy's Maybe

Stacy wasn't the only one looking for peace. So was Frieda Livingston.

"It's not his baby." She was talking to Hope, had finally gotten up the nerve to call her after wrestling with the truth solo for over a week.

"Oh my God, Frieda," Hope said, balancing a load of laundry with the phone cocked under her ear. "Hold on." This kind of news could not be dealt with while multitasking. She placed the load in the washer and walked from the laundry room to the combination library/theater room where she shut the door before resuming the convo. "Okay, sorry about that. I'm back. Now . . . are you sure?"

"Don't ask dumb-ass questions," Frieda barked. "Bitch, do you think I would have called you if I wasn't sure of this shit?"

Hope forced herself not to respond to her cousin's outburst. She knew it wasn't personal. She also knew she wasn't going to be too many more bitches, no matter how upset her cousin was. She sat down in one of the custom-made recliners and began fiddling with the controls built into the chair's arm. "Did you just find out?"

"No, I got the results about a week ago."

"And you're just now calling me? Why have you been trying to handle this by yourself?"

"I think I was in shock the first two, three days. Then a couple days ago, I made a list of all the dudes I was messing with around the time that Gabe was conceived. And before you can ask me, it's none of your damn business how long that list is."

Both women laughed.

"Then I called Gorgio; told him he might be a baby daddy."

"How did that go over?"

"Old Gorgio boy surprised me. Considering that he's now engaged to Blondie, he took it rather calmly. I told him that I needed a DNA sample and he overnighted me some of his hair."

"Looking at Gabe, do you think Gorgio's the father?"

"I'm hoping he's the father. At first I wanted it to be Shabach's baby—"

"Shabach?! Please . . ."

"Yeah, I know. He's a ho and an asshole, but one with paper. If Gabriel divorced me and he's the father, I can sue him for child support and keep it movin'. But more than anything, me and Gee are friends, so if he's my son's father and I can keep this secret, at least I'll know that he won't trip on letting Gabriel continue to raise him as his son."

"Whoa, back up. You're not planning to tell Gabriel?"

"Girl, that ocean air has you losing your mind. Why in the hell would I tell my husband that the child he adores isn't his blood? He's Gabe's father in every sense of the word and I have absolutely no intention of rocking that boat. Not at all."

Even though she didn't get a good feeling about this revelation, Hope held her peace. Perhaps Frieda was right, and not saying anything to Gabriel was for the best. Their marriage was already shaky. Little Gabe was the one thing that they had in common. In Hope's mind, that little boy was the tiny thread that was keeping that family together. "What if Shabach is Gabe's father. How do you think he'll react?"

She heard Frieda sigh. Her short stint with Darius's former nemesis and America's gospel hip-hop darling had ended as fast and furiously as it had begun. "I know how; tracked down his number and called him last night. He tried to get all indignant, saying there was no way that he could be the father. I told him that as many times as me and him rolled raw, he was as good a candidate as anybody."

"What did he say to that?"

"He finally agreed to send me some hair. Knowing his ass, though, that sample might end up coming from anybody's comb. That man is making millions and still acting cheap. But I don't have time to worry about him. I have a couple more guys that I want to talk to before I go back to the lab. And then there's the matter of seducing Gabriel as much as possible."

"Oh," Hope teased. "Do I hear a little more love for the doctor seeping into your voice?"

"More like you hear Mami securing her future. Gabriel's mother has never liked me. And with what happened a few months back, if she gets wind of my marital problems, she may get ideas." Frieda shared with Hope about Alice noticing the birthmark. "If she finds out that Gabe isn't her natural grandson, she'd be the first one trying to push my ass out the door. I need to get pregnant with an insurance marker—the sooner, the better."

"Frieda...Never mind." Hope knew that trying to talk her crazy cousin out of this madness would simply be wasted breath. "Let me know if you need me to drive up there for emotional support. I might not always agree with you, cousin, but you know I've got your back."

"Yeah, I know," Frieda said, her voice devoid of its usual sarcasm. "I appreciate it. I know I come off as all hard and whatnot, but I don't want to go through this shit by myself—for real."

Across town, another conversation was about to take place.

"Dr. Livingston."

"Hello, Dr. Livingston. This is Amy calling from the Office for Genetic Testing. You wanted me to call you as soon as we received the results of the DNA you sent us."

Gabriel leaned back in his chair, not as weary from the three-hour surgery he'd just performed as he was from expending the energy that trying to save his marriage had required. When it came to Frieda, he felt he'd done everything possible to bring them closer together, to try and make this sham of a marriage into a real one. His parents had been married almost half a century. There were very few people in his circle who'd gotten divorced. If not for his son, their unity may not have been as much of an issue. But he'd grown up in a two-parent family, in a household filled with love and laughter. He wanted that for Gabe. A stable, loving family was the very least of what his son deserved.

"Dr. Livingston?"

"Uh, yes, Amy, I'm here. What are the results?"

"Well, they're conclusive. And they show that within a one-hundred-million to one probability...the two strands of DNA presented are not a match."

Gabriel's eyes flew open. No matter how much his intuition (and his mother) had suggested otherwise, Gabriel had clung to the belief that Gabriel, Jr. was his biological son. "I'm sorry. What did you say?"

A slight hesitation and then Amy responded. "Between the two samples that were tested, there is zero possibility of a biological match."

Gabriel didn't remember ending the call. Later, he wouldn't be able to recount the moments, or hours, after receiving the information that the boy he raised, the one he loved and adored, was not his biological child. The next moment he remembered, with absolute clarity, was the one when he picked up the phone and made a pivotal call—one that began the process of the dissolution of his marriage.

37

Life After

It was seven p.m. and Frieda was excited and a bit apprehensive at the same time. She couldn't remember when she'd last spent almost a whole day alone with her son, not only playing and spending time with him, but cooking his meals and then doing the cleanup. But after the conversation with Hope about the DNA results, she'd determined that there was no time to lose when it came to putting her plan into action. First she'd called Gabriel's office and found out his schedule for the day so she'd know what time to expect him home. Then she gave the chef, housemaid, and Cordella the day off, with pay (after Cordella had bathed and dressed Gabe and the housemaid had finished the morning dishes and the laundry). Once they were gone, she piled Gabe into the car and headed for the upscale grocery not far from their home. Though it had been a couple years since she'd done so, Frieda used to get around a kitchen without a map and in those early days before they married, had fixed Gabriel a dinner or two. She remembered how much he seemed to enjoy her effort, how he'd praised how good the food tasted. But following their nuptials and upon return from their honeymoon, one of the first things she'd done was to hire Tito, a chef with more than ten years' experience in private homes. Gabriel had questioned her about it, but didn't complain about the extra expense. Come to think of it, short of his desire for them to spend more time together and do more things as a family, he didn't complain about much at all. *Hope is right. I'm married to a good man yet still out chasing dick. I need to do more than get pregnant; I need to try and be a good wife . . . for a change.* Frieda felt that the fact that she hadn't seen Clark in two days was proof that the change had already begun.

After leaving the grocer with four perfectly thick pork cutlets, mixed vegetables, and wild rice, she'd driven to Le Pain Quotidien for a loaf of their one-of-a-kind five-grain bread, to Marie Callender's on Wilshire Boulevard for Gabriel's favorite double-cream blueberry pie, and then on to BevMo's for two bottles of Moët & Chandon. By the time she returned home, Gabe had thankfully fallen asleep, so she took that time to shower, taking extra pains with her douche and rubbing a specially designed honey-milk mixture into skin already made soft by regular mud baths and skin peels. Afterward, she'd massaged patchouli-scented shea butter into her skin before donning a robe and heading to the kitchen.

Once there she'd made quick work of reproducing the pecan-crusted pork cutlet recipe that she'd found online. She'd chopped the vegetables and after placing them in an acid-bath to prevent discoloration had gone to a now-awakened Gabe and washed him up before dressing him in a navy-colored short set, complete with mini gold chain and black Ralph Lauren sandals. At six-fifteen she'd put on the rice and then gone to change into a sheer bra and thong set from Victoria's Secret and a simple, royal-blue silk mini-dress from the same store. She'd gone back into the kitchen, placed the vegetables into the steamer, and quickly set the table. Just before seven, she'd searched the home iPod for Gabriel's files and soon the sounds of Dexter Gordon's tenor sax poured into the candlelit atmosphere. She slipped into a pair of blue satin Sergio Rossi sandals adorned with Swarovski crystals. She dabbed on perfume recently purchased from Nordstrom and, after throwing back two shots of Don Julio to calm her nerves, sat playing with Gabe—something that she surprisingly enjoyed—and waited for her man.

At seven minutes past seven, Frieda pushed the button that

opened the garage door. "Come on, Gabe. Let's go greet Daddy. When you see him, run up and give him a hug, okay?"

Gabe jumped down from the couch and clapped his hands together. "Okay!" he said eagerly, already rushing toward the side door that led to the garage.

"Okay, chick," Frieda said, wishing she'd drank a third shot to calm the roiling nerves in her stomach. "Time to go and be the perfect wifey."

Almost before he entered the house, he felt a different atmosphere. *What is it?* Gabriel's brows furrowed as he tried to place his finger on what seemed different when he pulled up the drive. Then it hit him. No extra cars in the driveway. On a normal day there'd be at least three: Tito's, Cordella's, and the newest housemaid's, who'd just been hired two months ago. Gabriel's scowl deepened. *What has Frieda gone and done this time?* After pulling into the garage he sat in the car, motionless, trying to rein in the barrage of emotions that had gripped him almost to the point of paralysis since hearing the news.

A one-hundred-million to one probability. The two strands of DNA presented are not a match.

He placed his head in his hands, the headache that he'd eased with a prescription-strength aspirin threatening to return full force. *There is zero possibility of a biological match.* Gabriel gripped the wheel, worked to control his escalating temper by taking deep breaths. He'd never been a violent man, rarely been angry to the point of raised voice. But a part of him wanted to strangle Frieda, quiet every sarcastic comment or well-planned lie that could come out of the mouth that knew how to please him below the belt. The other part of him was hurt, wondering whom he'd married and how he'd gotten to this place. From the time he'd bumped into her at the Beverly Mall, literally knocking her down, to when she'd invited him to buy her a drink, to when he'd found himself walking her down the aisle with a barely showing baby bump, his normally placid, predictable world had been turned upside down.

He couldn't recall the exact moment he fell in love with Frieda Moore. But it was earlier today, at 4:45 p.m. to be exact, when he fell out. If not for the admonishments of his attorney to conceal that he knew the truth until they were ready to take action, he'd go straight into the house and throw Frieda out on her lying, cheating rump!

After preparing himself for the inevitable, he exited the car and stepped inside the hallway that passed the laundry room on the way to the kitchen. As soon as he turned the corner, he saw his son.

"Daddy!"

No matter his state of mind or how tired he was, Gabe could always brighten his mood. Even now, given what he knew, his eyes lit up at the sight of his son running toward him with arms spread wide. Gabriel knelt down and scooped the child up in his arms. "Hello, son. How's my boy today?"

"I had fun with Mommy, Daddy. We went riding, and got your pie, and then we played games. She said I was real good and I beat her, Daddy. I beat her!"

"You are good, Gabe. How many times have I told you that?"

Gabe laughed. "A lot!"

They continued down the corridor, with Gabe wrapped in his father's arms as Gabriel thought, *Cordella must be sick.*

They rounded the corner. Gabriel stopped short, the smile on his face doing a slow fade. How many times had he imagined what now stood before him: his sexy wife standing there with a smile, waiting to greet him after a hard day's work. For more than three years to be exact. And how many times had it happened? This was the first.

"Hey, baby." Frieda's normally confidently sarcastic voice was soft, tentative. "It took you a while to get out of the car."

"Long day," Gabriel replied, kissing his son on the temple before setting him down. He noticed the pots on the stove. "Where's Tito?"

"I gave the help the day off."

Gabriel's eyes narrowed. "You cooked?"

Frieda's laugh was a bit too loud to be natural. "I deserved that one, baby." She took a seductive step toward him and when he didn't back up or show any other sign of distaste, she took another. "I've been slipping on my wifely duties and I plan to change that . . . starting today."

Gabriel worked hard to keep a casual veneer in place. "What brought this on?" *Besides a DNA test showing that I'm not Gabe's biological father, something you might already know.*

"I talked to Hope," Frieda answered truthfully. "You know that girl is the modern-day Suzy Homemaker. She told me about the dinner she was preparing for Cy. I tried to remember the last time I'd made dinner for you, and felt guilty. So . . . I decided to let the help have the day off, took Gabe shopping with me for some of your favorite things, and then I came home and made dinner. Which is ready, by the way." She took a final step, placing her pert nipples against his chest. She reached down and blatantly grabbed his sex. She began to massage his flaccid member. "I hope you're hungry."

Gabriel batted her hand away. "Did you forget our son is in the room?"

"Did you forget how we got that son?"

It took a Herculean effort, but Gabriel let that loaded question pass right on by. He took time to collect himself by walking over to the stove and lifting up the pot. "Smells good," he said, after sniffing the spicy rice. "What meat did you cook?"

"If you'll wash up for dinner and take your place at the table, I'll show you." She tilted her head and kissed him on the lips. "And later," she whispered, "there's something else that I want to eat."

Gabriel turned and left the room without responding. Any other time, he would have been hot and further hardened by Frieda's antics. She'd always been able to turn him on. But tonight, every verbal flirt made him nauseous, every batted eyelash made his fists clench. Still, he kept his focus, went upstairs and changed his clothes and within ten minutes was back downstairs sitting at the table and playing with the welcomed diversion otherwise known as his son. By the time he'd arrived, she'd set their plates on the table, having chopped up Gabe's meat and vegetables into small, bite-sized pieces and adding a sweet and sour sauce to his meat and rice.

Gabriel looked at the perfectly done chop and vibrant vegetables and for a split second, wondered if they might be poisoned. But after watching his son take a few bites, and unobtrusively examining his meal for any suspicious-looking ingredient, and almost laughing out loud at his own paranoia, he took a healthy bite. "This is good, Mrs. Livingston. I can't remember the last time this happened—dinner at the table with the three of us."

"It's a shame, isn't it? I guess before it just seemed more convenient for Gabe that he eat with Cordella and give us some quality time to spend alone." Gabriel gave her a patient look. "That is, on those days when I was home for dinner." She placed down her fork. "Look, Gabriel, I've messed up. All right? I've acted like a spoiled bitch, and I'm sorry. But I'm going to do better, baby, starting today." She reached out and placed her hand over his. "Okay?"

Gabriel moved his hand, looked at Gabe, the only reason that his smile was genuine. "Do you like the food that Mommy fixed?"

Gabe enthusiastically nodded his head, picking up the meat with his fingers and popping it in his mouth like nuggets. "Uh-huh."

"What was that?" Gabriel asked.

"I mean yes," Gabe corrected, before being mostly successful at getting the rice and vegetables on his spoon and into his mouth.

They shared small talk with Gabe for a moment before Frieda turned her attention to Gabriel. "So how was your day, Gabriel?"

"Interesting."

"Really? How so?"

Gabriel bit down on his tongue so hard he almost drew blood. He'd never been good at lying, had never perfected the poker face. But his attorney was right. If he tipped his hand tonight, told her what he knew, and that he planned to divorce her, she could make his life a living hell. No, he'd bide his time so that by the time he delivered his legal jab, she'd have no choice but to behave. He took a couple more bites, shrugging as he chewed before answering her question. "A couple surgeries that yielded surprises once we cut the patients open. But they were both successful."

"Is Amber still chasing you?"

"You're still concerned about her?"

"Naw, but I know how bit—" Gabriel cut Frieda a hard look. He'd chided her many times about cursing in front of their son. "Uh, women can be when it comes to successful men like you. She never liked me, always had her nose in the air when I visited you at the hospital." Frieda took a bite of the pork cutlet, silently congratulating herself on a job well done. "The feeling is mutual."

"You don't have to worry about Amber. She'd never sleep with a married man." *Which is more than I can say about what you would do as a married woman.*

"I talked to Alice today and told her I'd host the next committee luncheon."

"First this homemade dinner and now cozying up to my mom? All this after a conversation with Hope?"

"Guess she finally got through to me. So when your mother called, I volunteered our house."

At the thought of the conversation he'd eventually have to have with his mother, Gabriel's heart clenched. Yet Frieda's statement was enough to steer their discussion toward calmer waters, punctuated by Gabe's errant and funny comments. Dinner ended, and Frieda suggested that they put Gabe to bed and then have dessert in the master suite. Gabriel countered that he'd like to eat his pie with his son. Frieda acquiesced, and after they'd finished and tucked Gabe into bed, she reached for Gabriel's hand as they walked to the bedroom. "This was nice," she whispered.

"Yes, it was." He walked into the master suite's dressing room and, after gathering clothes from it and toiletries from the bathroom, started for the door.

"Gabriel," Frieda said as she watched him get ready to walk out of the love lair she'd created, "where are you going?"

"It's been a long day, Frieda. I appreciate the family time but want to enjoy an uninterrupted night's sleep."

Please . . . Frieda all but slithered over to the man she'd had wrapped around her finger from the time she'd cursed him out. *Soon as I wrap my mouth around his mediocre manhood, it will be all over.* "Are you sure?" she cooed, wrapping her arms around his shoulders. "I'm still a little hungry, and you're what I want to taste." Not only had Frieda missed her two-to-three times a week Clark sexing, but she'd calculated that there was a very good chance that she was ovulating right now. She had every intention of getting Gabriel's seed inside her. Tonight.

Gabriel had other plans, as evidenced by his next words and actions. "Good night, Frieda," he said with a chaste kiss on the tip of her nose. "I'm looking forward to a good night's sleep. Alone. I have a meeting first thing in the morning, so I'll see you tomorrow night."

Frieda was more than surprised . . . she was pissed! After slamming the master suite door and calling Gabriel everything but a child of God, she climbed into their king-sized bed, wondering what the hell had happened. Whatever it was, she had no intention of being ignored. She called Clark, and less than thirty minutes after playing the devoted wife, was on her way to the jungle, and some serious dickage.

And Gabriel? He heard her leave, swallowed pride and pain, and called the private investigator. "You know where she's headed," he said with a sigh. And then, to his utter amazement, he slept until morning and Cordella's arrival. It wouldn't be easy, he decided, but the past twenty-four hours had showed him that if he could survive a night without her, then he could survive a life without her. The quicker he dissolved this sham of a marriage, the quicker he could put this pain behind him.

38

Choices

She said she wasn't going to do it, had sworn the last time was the last time. Yet not long after the promise to herself and the romantic dinner with Gabriel, Frieda found herself pulling up to Clark's apartment —about an hour after Cordella had arrived to take care of Gabe and thirty minutes after Gabriel had left the house.

Clark opened the door before she could knock, with a smug smile on his face. "Thought you weren't going to come back here," he fairly sang in his lyrical Jamaican.

"I thought I wasn't either," Frieda said. "You know you've got me hooked on that good dick."

Clark nodded solemnly. "I know." He reached for Frieda's hand and led them to the sofa. "Whatchu' know good?"

"Nothing that we can't talk about later," Frieda said, reaching for Clark's belt buckle.

"Whatchu looking for down dere?" Clark embellished his accent, knowing how doing so turned Frieda on.

"You know what."

"Then come on here, girl," Clark replied as he pulled Frieda's top over her head. "Let Papi give you what you came for."

Two hours later, Frieda walked out of Clark's apartment and headed to her car. Two men approached her as she neared it. One was tall and blond; the other short, with salt-and-pepper hair and a paunch.

"Mrs. Livingston," Blondie addressed her, coming across the street.

Frieda's heart sped up when she heard her name. *Who are these muthafuckas and how do they know who I am?* She ignored them, popping the lock with her remote and opening the door.

"Mrs. Livingston," he said again, placing his hand on the open door in a way that suggested he had no intention of letting her close it.

"Look, muthafucka, I don't know you. And you definitely don't know me. So if you don't want me calling the police I suggest you take your hand off my door and go on about your business."

Paunch sidled up next to Blondie. "You are our business, Mrs. Livingston," he said. "This"—he nodded toward Blondie—"is Detective Wagner. He's been following you for several weeks, at your husband's request. My name is Jerry Baumeister, your husband's attorney. Now, what he's asked us to do is a bit unorthodox, but he felt it would be the easiest way to handle this . . . unfortunate situation."

Frieda's mind raced, their words ping-ponging inside her head. She'd be the first one to tell you that she wasn't the brightest bulb in the stadium, but the fact that these men had shown up at her lover's place, at her husband's request, was most definitely not a good look. *This is why he's acted so strangely lately. He knows about Clark!* She tried to remain calm, keep her wits about her. *I can handle Gabriel. I just need to lose Tom and Jerry.* "Look, I don't know what you think you've discovered, but I've just left my cousin's house and am on my way to a lunch date with my husband." She tried to close the door, but Blondie's hold was a no-can-do. "If you'll excuse me."

Jerry pulled a manila envelope from behind his back. "We know about your cousin, Mrs. Livingston, otherwise known as your lover, Clark Pratt. We have irrefutable proof that you two have been intimate."

"Proof? Please, catching me on this block doesn't prove nothing. And Clark would never cooperate with you bitches. Your tactics don't scare me."

"Clark doesn't know about the evidence we've collected. But your husband has more than been made aware. We're not here to argue. We're here to fulfill Dr. Livingston's wishes. Inside the folder, you'll find copies of everything we've collected...along with the address and a key to your new residence."

"My what!" Her mind said stay calm, but her hands said open the damn envelope. Hands won. She fairly snatched it out of Jerry's hand.

"You'll also find the documents dissolving your marriage, citing adultery and irreconcilable differences. Lastly, you'll find the papers of the doctor's intention to gain full custody of Gabriel Jr., contesting that your reckless behavior makes you an unfit mother."

Frieda entered her car and sat stunned, methodically turning the pages in front of her. "There is no way that I'll not go to that house and get my child."

"If you cooperate the doctor is prepared to give you a generous alimony payment, one that quite frankly we don't think you deserve."

Frieda's head jerked up. "Who gives a damn what you think I deserve? Who in the hell do y'all think you are?"

"He's the attorney who's trying to right a grave injustice," Detective Wagner replied. "I'm the detective who's been following you for over a month and recording every sordid detail."

At the same time Frieda's marriage was unraveling, Hope was trying to find a way to keep hers together. It had been five days since Cy left for New York, and in that time she'd experienced every emotion under the sun. One minute she was wishing Trisha would simply disappear and the next she was asking forgiveness for her lack of compassion. She didn't wish the woman dead, at least, but that had less to do with Christian charity and more to do with the words of her mother, Pat. "You'd better let that man do what he can," she'd warned, when Hope had been toying with the idea of giving Cy an ultimatum. "If she dies, you want him to be at peace, child. You can't compete with a ghost." These words were what had Hope up and on the computer first thing, as she'd been for the past four days, finding out more about adenocarcinoma—the latest diagnosis—than she ever thought she'd know. She was stumbling through words she didn't recognize and jargon she didn't understand when she had an "aha" moment. *Gabriel! Of course.* "I can't believe I didn't think of that before," she said, while reaching for the phone. Frieda's husband was one of the top oncologists in the country. *He might even be able to help Trisha.* Almost as soon as she thought that, she thought about Trisha moving to California, almost in their backyard, and considered not making the call. *You can't compete with a ghost, child.* She dialed her cousin.

"You are not going to believe this shit!"

Hope looked at the phone to make sure she'd dialed the right number. It sounded like whoever answered was crying, and this was something that street-strong Frieda Livingston did not do. "Frieda?"

"I have really fucked up this time, cuz. I've messed up everything!"

Okay, Frieda was definitely crying. Hope could only form one thought. *Who died?*

"Frieda, take a breath and tell me what happened." More crying. "Frieda, you're scaring me. Is Gabe okay? Is it your husband? Was there an accident? Frieda, calm down and talk to me, please."

"He knows everything, Hope. About Clark, and the fact that Gabe isn't his. He's filing for divorce. He's going to try and take my son. He kicked me out." Frieda began crying again.

Oh. My. God. Hope said a quick prayer, even as she stood and began pacing the room. The reason why she'd called Frieda had been totally forgotten. "Okay, start at the beginning, Frieda, and tell me everything."

Between sniffles and generous sips of Moscato, Frieda did just that. "I swore I wasn't going to go over there again," she finished. "That I was going to leave Clark alone. Maybe if I had, Gabriel wouldn't have done this. He probably said, 'If she goes over there one more time . . .' and I did!"

For a moment, Hope was at a loss for words. "Don't cry," wasn't practical, and "It will be all right," sounded like a straight-out lie. "I'm sorry," she finally said sincerely, wishing she were there to hug her cousin. *She could really use one right now.* "Where are you staying?" Frieda told her. "Give me a few minutes. I'm going to call Rosie and see if she can come over early, even spend the night if necessary."

"Why? My fucked-up situation is not your problem."

"Don't talk crazy. We're family. You need me and best believe I'm going to be there for you. Just as soon as I can get her over here, I'm on my way."

39

The Bigger They Are

Everything about the new home of the Los Angeles Sea Lions was impressive: the size, the octagonal shape, the sleek, colorful seating, state-of-the-art sound system, strategically placed food courts boasting everything from popcorn to sushi and lobster to Kobe beef, and the suites that companies and a few rich patrons purchased for well into the six figures. Inside one of these luxuriously appointed rooms was where thirty or so people mixed and mingled, some inside the room, watching the first minutes of the first quarter of the preseason game from the television screens, and others outside in their private block of seats. Hope encouraged Cy to join his associates outside while she tried yet again to reach Frieda. "I knew we should have gone by there and picked her up," she mumbled, after getting voice mail yet again. But knowing how important this game was to Tony and by extension, Stacy, Hope had been certain that Frieda would be there. Although, truthfully, she understood why her cousin was a no-show. The past week had been horrible, and that was putting it mildly. The Frieda that Hope had encountered when she arrived in LA was not a woman she'd recognized. Her cousin had been distraught, inconsolable, and had broken down and cried in Hope's arms. "I've ruined the best thing that happened to me," Frieda had wailed. "He won't even take my calls." Hope had spent the night and then demanded Frieda come stay in La Jolla for a couple days. After long talks on the patio followed by long walks on the beach, Hope had felt Frieda rational enough to not do something crazy and hadn't protested when Frieda hired a car to go home. *And now I'm getting voice mail.* Hope's worry returned. She sent Frieda a text, looking up just as Stacy entered the room.

"Hey, girl," Stacy said, giving Hope a hug.

"Hey, Mrs. Johnson," Hope said, taking in Stacy's immaculate appearance. The designer pantsuit she wore, equal parts sexy and classy, was tailored to perfection, her custom sandals rocked, and her short cut was ridiculously whipped. "You look like a model!"

"Thank you, Hope. With the buzzards flying around the paychecks you know I had to represent. This is nice." She looked around Cy's company suite, nodding as she did so. "Y'all almost have a better view than the wives." Taking in the group outside their windows, she added, "Where's Frieda? In the restroom?"

"She hasn't shown up yet and I can't reach her on the phone."

"You think she's all right?" Frieda had broken the news to Stacy during her stay at Hope's house.

"I hope so."

"Do you think we should go over there?"

"Let me worry about Frieda. This is your hubby's big moment. If I haven't heard from her by the end of the game, Cy and I will swing by her condo. Come on, let's go outside and try and enjoy ourselves. I want to be sure and not miss when Big Tony takes the field!"

The two ladies joined Cy outside and soon they were caught up in the excitement of preseason football. The fact that there'd been a drought of football in Los Angeles was apparent by the packed stadium that sat sixty-thousand plus. It didn't hurt that they were playing an old nemesis, the Broncos. But it probably wouldn't have mattered if they were playing Mickey Mouse and company. Angelenos were ready to have a good time. They were ready for some football!

"Hello, Stacy." Cy rose to greet his wife's friend with a kiss on the cheek. He moved aside so that they could sit in his row. "You're looking good."

"Thanks, Cy. I appreciate it. Thanks for coming to support Tony."

"You know I'd be here. He's my brother, and I'm a fan."

"Really?" Hope said. "I thought basketball was your passion."

"Baby, basketball is my game, but sports is my passion."

"Ha! Fair enough."

Hope grabbed Stacy's arm. "I'm so happy for you, girl," she said, her voice low enough for a conversation just between them. "I know how hard you prayed for this moment, for your man to get back to what he loves, back in the game. I'm so glad God answered your prayer."

"Me too," Stacy said, her eyes shining with excitement. "Me too."

Down on the field, Tony prowled the sidelines like a caged tiger, watching the line and the men he'd guard once in the game. He'd trained hard for this moment and knew he was ready. "Come on, man! Go get it, baby. Yeah!" He pounded a fist into his palm, his eyes glued to the field. A couple guys came up to him, gave him a pat. They knew how important the night was to him, how special it was to be back on the field. They also knew that his spot on the roster wasn't totally assured, that the coaches were still trying out combinations to see who would work together the best. Two minutes into the second quarter, Tony got his shot. "Johnson!" He nodded, put on his helmet, and trotted out on the field.

"There he is. He's going in!" Stacy shook Hope's shoulder, not even trying to hide her excitement. She was happy and nervous at the same time. *God, please take care of my baby.* The ball was snapped, the runner moved forward, and Tony made one helluva tackle. A few plays later, he made another one that prevented a Bronco touchdown. The half ended and he was still in the lineup, looking great. After halftime, Tony's supporters were all happy to see him trot back on the field. He lined up for the first play of the second half, eyed his target and as soon as the ball was handed off dove in for the tackle. The timing was perfect. The tackle was clean. But when everyone came out of the pileup, Stacy saw that Tony was still lying on the field, holding his knee. Oh. No.

40

Game On

Bo sat out by the pool nursing a drink that he didn't even want. The only reason that he'd stopped at the bar and gotten it is because he was bored as hell. Darius didn't even like football. Why he'd decided to accept Kelvin Petersen's invitation to the viewing party at his house was beyond him. *And he'd been so adamant about it!* Sure, Darius and Kelvin knew each other from LA and Kelvin's father, Derrick Montgomery's, church, but hell, just barely. They'd interacted a bit when Darius was minister of music at KCCC but that was usually casual conversations during dinners at the pastor's house. *What is he, homesick?* If he'd known that was the case, he would have sought out Kelvin much more during the two years that they'd lived here, invited him over, given him tickets to shows. Now it didn't seem to matter; he and Darius were moving back to Los Angeles. Oh, well.

"Let me go find Princess," Bo mumbled to himself as he got up from the stool at the poolside bar. "Maybe she can tell me some juicy gossip that will make my visit worthwhile." He walked into the house and was surprised to see quite a few more people than were there when he went outside. *Dang, I wasn't gone that long. Was I?* He weaved his way through the people in the room by the pool and headed toward the theater at the back of the house, one of the places where the football game was on and where the diehards were watching it. *Maybe it's halftime and somebody good is performing.* As he passed the dining room, he saw Princess amid a group of excited females.

"He is gorgeous," one was saying as he stepped into the group.

"Oh, thank you," he answered, without missing a beat. "I know I am, but I appreciate your saying so."

The women looked around; some laughing, others obviously not knowing what to think. "Everybody, this is a friend from Los Angeles, Bo Jenkins. He's Darius Crenshaw's partner and manager."

"Wife," Bo corrected, as he shook the ladies' hands. "Nice to meet y'all. I was just playing. It was probably my handsome husband that you were talking about."

"Close, but not quite," the sistah with the short locks said. "You'd have to go a little taller and a lot lighter." The women laughed. "Paz D.," she explained. "That's who we're talking about."

"Oh, please," Bo said, disdain written all over his face. "That's a face that is overrated."

"There are probably, oh, a billion women who disagree with you," a cute little redhead responded. She looked at the woman beside her. "Have you seen a more gorgeous body cross a room?"

Bo ridged, immediately on full alert. "Cross what room?"

"The one we're standing in," Redhead said. "I took one look at that butt and almost died!" She gave a fake swoon that sent the group laughing.

Bo? Not so much. "Uh, excuse me." He turned and made a beeline to the theater. There were about twenty people, mostly men, watching the game in animated fashion. Something had them really focused. Bo vaguely heard them discussing an injury, but he couldn't digest that information for looking for his man. He walked over to where Kelvin lounged in a theater chair. "You seen Darius?"

Kelvin looked around. "He was in here a minute ago. He might have gone to get something to eat. Check the dining room."

The last statement was said to Bo's back as he was already heading out of the theater and back into the main part of the house. Various scenarios were coming to his mind, none of them good. The Petersen house was big, but he made his way to one side of the double staircase and began to climb. On his way he remembered how much Darius liked to get his freak on in strange places, how they'd be at a party and he and Bo would—*No! He wouldn't do that to me. He . . . there's no way.* Still, Bo's footsteps quickened as he neared a hall of rooms. He reached the first door and opened it without hesitation. Empty. Bo let out the breath he didn't know he was holding. His heart slowed a little as he reached the next door. Empty again. *Bo, you're tripping. Those girls might be lying. Paz is probably not even here.* Rationality returned as Bo checked one room after another. Darius wouldn't have invited Paz to a party that they'd driven to together. "Boy, you are something else," he whispered to himself as he retraced his steps.

He was almost to the flight of stairs when he heard a voice, a man's voice, low and muffled. *I thought I checked that room.* He crept to the door, put his ear against the wood. There it was, the sound he heard. No, more like a moan. And then another one, the same but different. *Two men? Aw, hell, no.* He tried the knob, but the door was locked. But considering that he was ninety-nine point nine percent sure of who was on the other side, it would take more than that to keep him out, especially since this was one of those push locks and not the kind requiring a key. He fairly ran down the hall to the bathroom he'd passed and opened the vanity's top drawer. *Bingo!* He grabbed a bobby pin and then, as an afterthought, grabbed something else out of the drawer before marching back down to the door. The grunting had gotten louder. Bo was so angry he probably could have broken the door down even though it was solid wood. Pushing the pin inside the hole, he turned the knob. The door swung open, revealing the hard, round butt he loved so much. For a few seconds he stood stunned, disbelieving. And then Paz called Darius's name, and jolted Bo out of immobility.

"You son of a bitch," he hissed, running to the ass hovering over another one and striking.

"Ow, shit!" Darius yelled. He jumped off a naked Paz, whose eyes widened when he saw the scissors dripping blood in Bo's hand.

"You hurt him!" Paz said, lunging for Bo.

"I'm not done, muthafucka!" Bo lunged again and sliced Paz in the chest.

"Bo, stop!" Darius grabbed Bo. "Get out of here," he shouted to Paz, while wrestling Bo for the scissors being held in a viselike grip.

"Let me go. I'm going to kill him. Let me go!"

"Calm down, Bo," Darius said between clenched teeth. "You're making a scene!"

"You. Think. I. Give. A. Damn?" Bo panted, trying to break loose from Darius's grasp just as they heard footsteps hurrying up the stairs.

"Aw, hell," Darius muttered, looking down at his state of nakedness and, now that the shock of being caught was wearing off, feeling a major pain in the ass—no pun intended.

"What's going o—Oh, no!" Princess hurried inside the room with Kelvin's best friend, Brandon, hot on her trail. She closed the door against looky-loos while Brandon walked over to where worldwide wrestling was still taking place.

"Guys! Guys! Break it up." With Darius squeezing Bo's wrist, Brandon managed to pry Princess's stainless steel cosmetic scissors out of his hand. "Stop, or I'm going to have to call the police." Bo continued to squirm, but he was clearly exhausted. "Seriously, y'all need to chill on this shit." When it appeared that the fight was over, Brandon turned to Princess. "Go get Kelvin."

Princess left the room. Brandon noticed the drops of blood dotting the floor. He followed the trail up to Darius's hand, the one that held his buttocks while the other one covered his junk.

"Damn, man. What happened?"

"Don't worry about what happened," Darius hissed. "Just get out of here so I can get dressed. I need to make an exit without being seen."

41

Lights Out

For four glorious weeks, they'd been happy. Stacy had put their Phoenix house on the market, had found them a place in LA. Tony was back working and pretty much acting like his old self. He'd even gotten hard a couple times, and rocked her world. Sure, he'd been curt and distracted, but Stacy could understand. There'd been a lot on his mind. He'd promised her that once he got a few games under his belt, he'd be way more relaxed. She hadn't understood exactly how playing football would enhance his sexual function, still didn't, but... okay. Whatever was going on, it had looked like the worse was behind them. And now this: Tony reinjured and cut from the team. *Lord, didn't you hear me when I prayed? Why didn't You protect my husband? Why didn't You keep him from getting hurt?*

"What's the matter, Mommy?"

Stacy hadn't even realized that she'd gone deep into her own thoughts, hadn't even been aware that she wasn't alone. "Mommy's just thinking," she said to her curious and astute son.

"You were thinking *hard!*"

She managed a slight smile. "Yes, baby, I was. Now come on, let's get your pajamas on. It's time for lights out."

As Stacy walked from DJ's room to the master suite, she pondered whom she'd encounter in the room. Since his injury, Tony had gone from being Jekyll one minute to Hyde the next. She didn't know what to say to him because for the most part, just like before, whatever came out was wrong. She'd almost suggested that he move into the guest room. *Heck, if things keep going the way they are . . . I'll move in there!* Entering the room, she saw Tony hobbling on one leg, trying to walk without his crutch.

"Honey, don't!" She ran to his side. "The doctor told you to be careful and not try to walk on it for three weeks!"

"Oh, so you think you know more than me?" Tony looked at her with sheer hostility in his eyes.

"That's not what I'm saying," Stacy spat back, tired of his petulant attitude. "It's what the doctor said."

"Get away from me, Stacy."

"Whatever, asshole," she said, turning around. She'd had it with his mood swings; was done babying his ungrateful ass. "I'm not the enemy."

But you would have thought she was. Because next thing you knew there was a fist upside her head and a face eating carpet.

Stacy's reaction was instinctive, honed from growing up as the only girl in a house with four brothers, one who'd held her own in many a wrestling match. She reached up and grabbed the foot that Tony had planned to use to step over her or stomp her with—she didn't take the time to figure out which.

Like his, her move was unexpected. "Argh!" Tony cried as he found himself off balance, his injured knee twisting as he tried to regain his footing. "Damn!" He hit the floor and grabbed his knee.

Seeing Tony's pain, Stacy momentarily forgot about her own. "Tony!" She scrambled over to where he lay writhing on the floor.

Bad move.

As soon as she got within arm's reach, he grabbed her and rolled them over until he was on top.

"Tony, don't!"

Slap. "You fucked up my knee!"

"You hit me!" Stacy screamed, writhing beneath him to try and rid herself of the over two-hundred-pound human boulder holding her down. Tony grabbed her hair and glared. "Stop it,

Tony! Get"—she maneuvered her hand between her stomach and his flesh—"off." Twisting slightly, she was able to create a bit more room between them, enough to slide her hand down farther and execute the move Brent had taught her when she was thirteen years old. "Me!" She grabbed nuts and dick and squeezed in a way that would give "bust a nut" a brand new meaning.

"Oooowww!" This word was delivered several octaves higher than Tony's normal speaking voice and lasted almost as long as the note Whitney held ending the "Star-Spangled Banner."

Stacy didn't stick around long enough to admire her handiwork. Shear adrenaline and pure instinct caused her to leap from the floor, dash from the room, and run down the hallway to where DJ slept. She burst into his room, turned on the light. "Come on, baby," she whispered, knowing that the crippling blow she'd dealt Tony would only last so long. "We've got to go."

"Mommy, wha—"

Hearing a sound, Stacy scooped up her sleepy, confused child in her arms and ran for the steps, taking them so fast that she stumbled, almost causing mother and son to fall down the stairs.

"Ow, Mommy. You go too fast!"

"I'm sorry, baby, but—" *Thump. Thump.* Stacy knew that sound: crutches hitting hardwood floor. She looked up just in time to see Tony try and maneuver the top stair. "Come on, DJ!"

"Stacy, wait a minute!" Tony grabbed the handrail with his free hand and between that and the crutch was making pretty good time down the stairway. "Stacy, you'd better not leave this house!"

Reaching the kitchen, Stacy snatched up keys, purse, and cell phone, thankful that she'd left them there earlier that evening, and raced to the garage. She didn't have time to strap in DJ. Rather, she opened the passenger door, dumped him inside the car, rushed around to the driver's side, and yanked the door open. Her heart beating faster than a hummingbird's wings, she was in shock, on autopilot, pressing the garage door opener and starting the car at the same time. The door had barely cleared the hood of her SUV when she backed out of the garage, just in time to see Tony hobbling across the yard. Obviously, he'd made it down the stairs and out the front door in a last ditch effort to do God only knew what. Stacy hit the door lock and floored the gas, fishtailing to the point that she took out three types of shrubbery lining the drive.

The shrill of DJ's voice brought Stacy out of the survival fog she'd been in since Tony had slapped her so hard her teeth had rattled. Three streets away from the house she pulled over, took deep calming breaths, and finally loosened the death grip that the steering wheel had endured. Her hands were shaking.

"Mommy, what's the matter? Why are we running away?" Stacy turned and looked at DJ. He gasped. "What happened to your face?"

Instinctively, Stacy's hands went to the stinging sensation where Tony had slapped/hit/punched her and the throbbing ache in her jaw. She pulled down the sun visor and flipped open the mirror. Clenching her teeth against the pain, she forced herself to remain calm as she took in Tony's handiwork. A clear imprint of his hand was on her left cheek, and her right jaw was clearly swelling. *What do I tell him? Tony and I had a fight? Yes, he hit me?* "Mommy's okay," she finally answered, wanting to keep DJ as shielded as possible, at least for now. Headlights in her rearview mirror caused Stacy's heart to almost leap into her throat. *Oh my God! It's Tony!* Shaky hands put the car in gear as she prepared to race across town to the first shelter of safety that had come to her mind. As the car passed, she let out a sigh, thankful that the large black car she'd seen wasn't Tony's customized Range Rover. She reached for her phone and found the name she searched for, praying that they were in town and that someone was home.

"Hey, Spacy Stacy."

"Bo, I need to come over. Are y'all at home?"

"I'm not living with that cheating muthafucka."

In light of Stacy's drama, she'd completely forgotten about what had gone down with Bo and Darius the previous weekend. "Oh. Right. Where are you?"

"At the Biltmore, about to get even deeper in that two-timing asshole's wallet by taking a *bath* in some Dom Pérignon!"

"Could you put that bath on hold for a minute, and pop a cork? I need to get there as soon as possible. And I need a drink."

"You know where the hotel is?"

"I think so, but give me the address anyway." Bo gave her that and his room number. "Okay, thanks. I'll see you soon."

"Girl, what is wrong with you? You're talking like you've got doodoo in your mouth."

Stacy smiled despite her pain. Someone like Bo was exactly who she needed right now, to help her decide what her next move would be. "I'll tell you when I get there."

Just talking with Bo calmed Stacy and she was able to regain some presence of mind. "Come on, little man," she said, opening her car door, "let's get you into the car seat before I get a ticket."

She made it over to Bo's hotel in a relatively stable state, despite the fact that Tony had called. Twice. After the second call she'd turned off her ringer.

42

That MF'er!

Twenty minutes later, she turned on to Thunderbird Trail and followed it to the hotel's driveway, bypassing the valet option she'd normally use and heading for the hotel's covered self-parking. She reached for a pair of sunglasses that were kept in the glove compartment and put them on.

"Why do you have sunglasses on, Mommy? It's dark!"

Stacy opened her door and went around to help DJ out of his car seat. "Because Mommy is cool, that's why." After retrieving a pair of DJ's sandals from the trunk that had thankfully been forgotten and left there in a backpack, she took her son's hand and walked to the garage elevator.

Surreptitiously eyeing the lobby as she entered, she kept her head down and headed for the elevators. Fortunately, no one else entered and they were quickly whisked to the floor housing the suite number Bo had given her. She knocked on the door, and waited.

"Girl, get on in—" Bo's mouth dropped.

"I had an accident," Stacy said quickly, before Bo could get his mind and mouth working again. She hurried into the room, turning to give him a look and a quick nod toward her son as she did so. "I fell."

"Oh." Bo went from oh-my-God to no-big-deal in a heartbeat. "Did you trip over your own two feet?"

"We almost fell down the stairs," D.J. offered.

The adults' eyes met, volumes communicated in the look. "Listen, Bo. I woke Darius up from a sound sleep. Can he lie in your bed for a little while?"

"I'm not sleepy anymore." DJ walked over to the couch and plopped on it. "I want to watch TV with Uncle Bo."

"You heard what your mother said." Bo walked over to where DJ sat and reached for his hand. "Come on. If you go to sleep now you can get up early and head to the pool with me. And that's after we have your favorite pancakes with strawberry jam."

"Okay!" He jumped off the couch and took Bo's hand.

"I'll be right back," Bo said. Within minutes, he returned to the room. Stacy had dropped the strong-woman-mommy facade and now held her face, in obvious pain. "What the hell happened?" Bo hissed, looking over his shoulder to make sure the door was tightly closed.

"Tony," Stacy said, tears finally forming and running down her face. "He hit me."

"That muthafucka." Bo knelt in front of Stacy and pulled her hands away from her face. "Damn, girl. I can still see his hand imprint. He slapped the shit out of you! And your jaw? Look, we need to get you to the hospital. It might be broken." Bo was already up and looking for his keys.

"No, Bo, wait. Just let me think for a minute. I have to figure out how I want to handle this."

He whirled around. "What's there to think about? Muthafucka hits you. Muthafucka goes to jail. End of story." Walking over to the table in the dining room area, he threw down his keys and picked up his cell phone. "It's about to be nine-one-one up in this bitch."

"Bo, please!" Stacy said, her voice rising before remembering that her son slept not fifteen feet away. "Please," she again whispered. "Just come sit down and help me . . . think."

Bo walked over to the bar, bypassing the champagne that chilled in a bucket and reaching for the bottle of Courvoisier. He poured two shots, threw one back, and refilled the glass, then brought the two over to the couch. "Drink this straight down," he commanded. "It will help calm your nerves."

She obeyed his instruction and, not being much of a drinker of hard liquor, began to cough as the liquid burned her throat. Bo immediately ran back to the bar to pour her a glass of water. He gave it to her, sat on the couch, and with compassion and anger in his eyes, watched her carefully drink a couple swallows as best she could considering part of her lips were swollen. Again, he jumped up. This time it was to retrieve the phone he'd left on the bar and walk over to Stacy. "We need to get some ice on that jaw. But first, get up and come stand in the light."

"Wait, Bo. Just let me sit for a minute, get it together."

"Uh-uh. I have to do this right now."

"Do what?"

"Take these pictures. I want to get them while that mutha-fucka's handprint is still on your face and your jaw is poked out like Dizzy Gillespie playing a bent trumpet." Stacy nodded. However she decided to handle this situation, getting pictures as evidence was a good idea. After taking more than a dozen pictures, Bo seemed satisfied that he'd properly documented Tony's abuse. "Okay, Spacey," he said softly, walking over to the bar and placing ice cubes in a towel. He placed the ice-filled towel in her hand, guided it up to her jaw and sat beside her. "Now, tell me what happened."

Stacy recounted the argument. "When I called him an asshole, it's like he snapped," she finished. "I didn't even see the hit coming. And then I reacted by grabbing his foot and making him fall. That really pissed him off. He accused me of messing up a knee that was already jacked up and got a look in his eyes that I have never seen before. It really was like I was looking at another person. I've been tiptoeing around his uptight ass for months, navigating his errant behavior, treating him with kid gloves. Tonight, I just wasn't in the mood."

"I can't believe he put his hands on you! Yeah, he's a big muthafucka, but I never would have pegged him as the type."

"The Tony I married isn't the type. But this man tonight? He hit me like it wasn't the first time he'd beat a woman down."

"You know you have to file a police report."

Stacy nodded. "I know. I just have to handle this the right way. Once I tell them who assaulted me, there's a good chance it will be all over the news. And if my brothers see how I'm looking right now, there's going to be trouble. I'm not trying to see one of them catch a murder case. At the very least they'd be arrested for some serious felonious assault, and I just can't let that happen. So I need to keep this under wraps until this imprint goes away and the swelling goes down. By the time I tell my brothers, I have to look . . . okay."

Bo nodded slowly, understanding Stacy's dilemma. He'd never met her brothers, but knew from previous conversations that they were not to be messed with. "Okay, here's what we're going to do. You are going to call Darius and let him know that we're bringing over DJ."

"Right now I'm not sure I want Darius to know about this either. He can be as hotheaded as my brothers, and while he wouldn't do the deed himself, he'd hire some thug and I'd still have a man's murder on my conscience. Although at this point, I'm thinking," she said as a fresh stab of pain shot through her jaw, "that's exactly what Tony Johnson deserves."

They were both silent a moment. "What do you want to do?" Bo asked softly, wiping a tear away from Stacy's cheek.

A wisp of a smile scampered across Stacy's face. She was remembering another time and another place when Bo had come to her rescue, and had taken care of her like a mother hen. "Can I stay here with you?" she asked. "Tony won't know to look for me here, and honestly, I can use some of that TLC that you're so good at. Probably just two, three days, a week at most and I'll be ready to make my next move."

"Sugar, you can stay here as long as you'd like. In fact, tomorrow I'll have us moved to the Presidential Suite. It has two bedrooms."

"No, Bo, that's not necessary."

"It most certainly is. I'm just looking for ways to spend money; you being here is doing me a favor."

Someone knocked on the door. Stacy froze. Bo calmed her fear with a wave of his manicured hand. "Don't worry, Stacy, that's probably just my champagne order." He opened the door and two Biltmore employees entered pulling a dolly that was loaded with boxes. After they'd placed them where Bo had directed, they accepted his tip and left.

For the first time since fist met flesh, Stacy thought of something other than Tony. "There is champagne in all of these boxes?"

Bo nodded.

"Dang, Bo. You'll never drink all of this stuff!"

"Did you think I was kidding about the bath, sistah? I'm getting ready to bathe in some bubbly."

"Sounds sticky."

"It feels delicious. Don't knock it till you try it. In fact, I'll place another order tomorrow so you can experience the bliss."

Considering the fact that Stacy had just left home with nothing but the money and cards in her purse and the clothes on her back, she thought that expense might serve better in her purse than in a bathtub, and told this to Bo. "I have no idea how I'm going to make it. I just know I'm not going back there."

"Don't worry, Stacy. You're the mother of Darius's son. Mr. R and B will take care of you."

43

Mr. R&B

Darius was so deep in thought that he jumped when the phone rang. He hurriedly reached for it, hoping, praying, that it was who he wanted it to be. Seeing an unfamiliar number, he frowned, pressed the silencer and tossed the phone back on the couch. A minute later, his message indicator beeped. Whoever it was had left a message. Darius accessed his voice mail and pressed speaker: "Darius, this is Tony. I'm looking for Stacy and DJ, and thought they might be over there. Uh, if you see her, you don't have to tell her that I called. I'll try her cell phone again."

Darius played the recording twice, immediately intrigued. To hear him tell it, Tony couldn't stand his "faggot ass." *And now he's calling her ex-husband for his wife's whereabouts?* He promptly ignored Tony's suggestion to keep his inquiry a secret and dialed Stacy's number. When her phone went to voice mail, he called Bo. Their unlikely friendship was genuine and knowing that Stacy's one good local friend had moved to Dallas when her husband got traded last year, there was a good chance that, considering it was late and she had her son with her, Stacy was with Bo.

"Bo, it's me. I know you're probably looking at the phone and frowning right now, but for once, I'm not calling to apologize. Again. I'm not calling to beg you to come back home either, even though I miss you like crazy. I'm calling because Tony just left me a message looking for Stacy. And since he can't stand us, you know how crazy receiving that call is. So if Stacy is there with you, please let her know that he called. Okay? I love you, baby."

Darius ended the call and followed it up with a quick text: **Don't delete the message from me. It's about Tony.** Then he sent a text to Stacy's phone: **Your boy just called here looking for you and DJ. Is everything okay? Please call me. You know I'll worry.**

Now fairly certain that he'd hear back from one of them shortly, he returned to his journey down memory lane. He'd spent much of the last hour thinking about Bo and all of the good times they'd had. His mind meandered all the way back to the beginning, to the party in West Hollywood where he'd first spotted Bo, wearing a loud, leopard print shirt, tight black leather pants, and a cocky attitude. Darius was on the serious down low at the time—already a popular face in the church community and well known on the revival and conference circuit as a much sought-after musician. He spent most of the evening pointedly trying to ignore Bo, and flirting with a girl who interested him about as much as Miss Piggy. The next day, if asked, he wouldn't have been able to tell you her hair or eye color, or name for that matter. His mind's eye had been filled with leopards, leather, and Bo's lips, which had never stopped moving. Clearly, Bo was popular and the life of the party.

Toward the end of the evening, Bo cornered him out by the pool. "Since you're waiting for me to make the first move, here it is. Bo Jenkins." He'd held out his hand.

"Darius Crenshaw," he'd responded, adding a bit of bass to his voice and raising up to his full six feet. He added another foot of space between them, just in case someone was watching.

Bo simply smirked. "I see that clothes and shoes aren't the only things you're keeping in the closet," he'd murmured, giving Darius the once-over. "I left my card under the sink in the guest bathroom by the front door. If you're interested, call the number. Soon."

Darius had prided himself on waiting a full thirty minutes before going to the bathroom and finding Bo's card stuck exactly

where he said it would be. He was further impressed that he managed to wait a full three days before he called him, just to prove
that he could do so. That first call lasted an hour; their first "meeting" lasted all night. They'd pretty much been inseparable since
then, which was why Darius's heart hurt way more than his ban-
daged rear end.

Just thinking of the puncture to his right butt cheek made
Darius aware of the gauze still over the spot. He'd gone to his private doctor where several stitches, a shot, some medicinal lotion,
and a prescription for pain pills had made him almost as good as
new. But the only thing that would make him totally whole again
was Bo, back in the house and Darius's arms, where he belonged.
As if on cue, the phone rang. But it wasn't his husband.

"Hey, Stacy."

"Hey, Darius."

Darius sat up. "What's the matter with you? You sound funny."

"I'm kind of groggy—drunk a couple shots of Bo's liquor."

"You drank Courvoisier?"

"It's been a long night."

"And an interesting one, if Tony calling me is any indication."

"Yes. We had an argument and I left the house."

"Why didn't you come over here?" Suddenly, Darius was quite
jealous that she'd chosen Bo's company over his.

"Because I knew that's exactly where Tony would think I was
and I didn't want to take the chance of being there if he came
over."

"What do you mean 'take the chance'? What happened over
there, Stacy?"

"Nothing for you to worry about. It was a bad argument and
we were both very upset. I'm going to stay with Bo a few days so
we can both calm down and I can . . . figure things out."

Darius listened to what Stacy told him, and pondered all of
what she could possibly be leaving out. "I'm off for two days before flying to LA. I can keep DJ if you want."

"Thanks, Dee. I'll probably take you up on that."

"You'll always matter to me, Stacy. If you need anything, money or whatever, just let me know."

"I did leave the house rather quickly so . . . I'll probably take you up on that too."

"Are you sure you're all right?" The more they talked, the less he believed her.

"I'm okay. Just sleepy."

"What's the room number? If you'd like, I can come get him now."

"Hold on a minute." A mumbled conversation told him that Stacy had placed her hand over the speaker and was talking to Bo. "It's late and he's already in bed," she said. "You can come get him tomorrow. I might not be here," she hurriedly added, "but Bo will meet you in the lobby when you come to pick him up."

Darius hung up the phone and experienced his first genuine smile since Bo left the house a week ago. In less than twenty-four hours, he was going to see his baby. In the lobby, and probably for just a few minutes, but he was going to see him, to look in his eyes and let Bo see all of the hurt, sadness, and love that was there. *And then he'll come back to me,* Darius thought, rising from the couch and heading to the bed that still carried the scent of Bo's cologne. *My baby will see me and come back home. He's got to.*

44

The Eleventh Commandment

Frieda crossed Fifth Street and continued up Santa Monica Boulevard. Even though Santa Monica was where she now lived, it had been a while since she'd been to this part of the small city, had stopped on a whim after driving around just to get out of the house. She'd walked along the waterfront for a while, but still wasn't ready to go back to her empty condo. What she really wanted to do was go home, to the one she shared with Gabriel. But he'd continued to refuse her calls, and the one time she'd dared venture into her old neighborhood it was only to discover that not only had the locks been changed, but the staff had obviously been instructed to not let her in. "Please leave, Mrs. Livingston," Tito had pleaded when she caught him driving up from a trip to the butcher. "Doctor Livingston made us sign papers that we would not let you in. It could cost us our jobs!"

This embarrassment had made Frieda decide to fight fire with fire. She'd gone home, made some calls, and since she couldn't get an appointment with Gloria Allred or Judge Toler, her first choices, she'd called the law firm that an attorney from the Cochran Firm had recommended, someone who lived in Los Angeles and was used to fighting battles where child custody and big cash were involved. Getting that ball rolling had not only exhausted her, it had also not brought her the satisfaction that she thought it might. The truth of the matter was that Gabriel was a much better parent than she was, and where her son was concerned, probably a better fit. How could she nurture a child the way Gabriel did when she'd never been nurtured herself? Wanting the answer to that question is what put Frieda on a plane headed to Kansas City four days ago. What had her in a taxi heading to Fifty-ninth and Swope Parkway, where her mother now lived. It was what had her knocking on the door at seven o'clock on a Tuesday night. Her mother was there with two of her grandchildren. They were watching a movie on TV.

"Frieda?" Sharon opened the door after looking through the peephole. "What are you doing here?"

"Hi, Mama." Frieda entered the house and gave her mother a hug. She looked around, glad to see that the place was clean and the furniture that Frieda had purchased for her the previous Christmas still looked good. "Where is everybody?" Along with a couple cousins who'd practically lived in their house growing up, Frieda had a half brother. He'd grown up with his father and step-mother. They weren't close. But since he'd gotten married and turned his wife into a baby-making machine and his mother into a grandmother, he'd come around more often. Sharon often babysat. When Gabriel had to work and Frieda had spent last Thanksgiving here with the family, she'd discovered she and her half brother ac-tually had things in common. And Gabe had loved playing with his bad-ass kids.

"Jesse done got him a woman, girl. One with a house and a job."

"What? My cousin has finally found a sponsor?"

"Having that thirty-year-old leech out of my house? You say sponsor; I say savior."

"Ha!"

"Yes, and she seems like a nice girl too. Works over there at Research Hospital. Has a daughter, ten years old."

"Is Jesse working?"

"Is sugar salty? That fool ain't working on nothing but that pus—" Sharon looked down to see her six-year-old granddaughter looking at her mouth hard enough to count teeth. "He's still unemployed," she finished, reaching for the little girl. "Come up here, girl. And stop acting so nosy!" She hugged the child to her, nuzzled the baby's neck until the girl squirmed with laughter.

"Quit it, Nana!"

They continued playing, and Frieda looked on. She searched her memory, trying to find one involving her that resembled the scene before her. Couldn't find it. Sharon played with the child a bit longer and then shooed her into the other room. Y'all go into my room and watch the TV in there. I want to catch up with Frieda."

"Okay, girl. What's going on with you?"

"What do you mean?" Frieda asked, knowing exactly what Sharon meant.

"You haven't come home unannounced in five years, ever since you moved to California. You barely even come home at all. We had to beg you to spend last Thanksgiving with us. And where is your son?"

That was a question Frieda didn't want to answer, a mine field she didn't plan on stepping into. "He's spending time with his grandparents," she lied. "And Gabriel's doing back-to-back shifts. I started missing my family," she continued with a shrug, lies turning into truths. "So I jumped on a plane."

"It must be good to have it like that—just up and travel when you want to." Sharon looked hard at Frieda. "It's good to see you, though. You look like you've lost a little weight. But I like your hair. You look good."

"I keep inviting you out to LA. My stylist could do your hair."

"Naw, girl." Sharon picked up a *Jet* magazine and started flipping through the pages. "Too many earthquakes."

"You must be getting soft in your old age," Frieda said into the quiet room.

Sharon looked up from the magazine. "What do you mean?"

"I don't remember you ever playing with us like that."

"Like what?"

"The way you were playing with Yancy."

"Hell, working two jobs, trying to hang on to whichever boyfriend-of-the-month that was in the house . . . didn't have time."

Well, you're nothing if not honest, is what Frieda thought. "I guess not," is what she said. "I wish you had." Her voice was soft, reflective, as she continued. "It would have made me feel like you loved me more. Sometimes . . . I didn't feel that."

"Love? You didn't feel loved? Did you feel those clothes on your back, shoes on your feet, and food in your stomach? Did you feel those Christmas presents that I couldn't afford, or that money I gave you so you could do field trips and amusement park outings?"

"I'm sorry, Mama. I didn't mean to sound ungrateful. I just never had a moment like that with you, that's all, one like I just saw with you and Yancy."

"I did the best I could with y'all," Sharon said, after a moment. "Taking care of both you and your aunt's kids after she got on crack. It wasn't easy. But I did the best I could."

In a purely reflexive moment, Frieda stood, walked over to the couch where her mother sat. "I appreciate what you did for me, Mama." Then she placed her head on her mother's shoulder and slowly, eventually, felt her mother's arms around her—holding her, hugging her—feeling that which the young child, the teenaged child, never had.

When she left her mother's house two days later, it was with some reading material for the plane. "It's really good," Sharon had said, when handing Iyanla Vanzant's *Peace from Broken Pieces* to Frieda. "Jesse's girlfriend belongs to a book club there at Research. She read it and suggested it to me. It's helped me a lot. I think you'll like it too."

Frieda began reading the prologue on Friday at 10:45 p.m., while waiting to board her plane. She pretty much read nonstop, reading the last page at around five o'clock on Sunday morning. On Monday, she'd looked up the organization mentioned on the book's sleeve and two days later had had her first telephone conference with a life coach from Inner Visions Institute. Two days ago, on Friday, she'd called her attorney, told her to hold up on whatever she was doing pertaining to the divorce and the custody battle and to wait to hear from her. Just two sessions in and it had become clear: for Frieda to be good for anybody else, to really and truly love anybody else, including her son, she had to first learn how to really and truly love herself.

What had transpired in the last two weeks is what Frieda thought of as she walked past a couple shops and then saw a large box of books in front of a third shop. She was just about to walk past it as well when something caught her eye. She entered the store, a seeming hodgepodge of books, trinkets, statues, and the like. "What kind of store is this?" she asked the surfer-looking young man behind the counter.

"New age," he answered casually.

"What does that mean?"

"Different religious and spiritual aids," he answered, coming around the counter to join her over by the case of statues where she stood. "Here you have Judaism," he said, pointing to the Star of David, "and over here is Hindu." They walked to the next shelf. "Here are the Christian symbols—"

"Yeah, I've seen the cross before," Frieda interrupted. "What are these?"

"Those are Tibetan singing bowls." The worker demonstrated how it worked.

"Hmm. Well, I don't think there's anything in here for me." She headed toward the door and was almost out of the shop when she saw a plaque on the side wall. The words "know yourself" seemed to jump out at her. She walked over and read the words out loud:

> *You should know yourself*
> *And uphold yourself*
> *And let unconditional love*
> *Be the only kind that you show yourself.*

Reading these words felt good, so much so that she read them again. They sounded like words her counselor would say as she encouraged Frieda to search inside for the love she wanted. "It's in there," her counselor had told her. "I promise you that." Perhaps it was. Because something inside her shifted, as though the words actually created a hole and then slipped into her heart.

"How much is this?" she asked the cashier. He told her. She bought it, and left downtown Santa Monica feeling something that she hadn't felt since the investigators met her on the street outside Clark's house, maybe even before then, maybe in her entire life. Frieda Moore Livingston felt that no matter what happened, no matter how all of the drama she was dealing with turned out, she was going to survive. Frieda thought—no, *knew*—that she was going to be okay.

45

Everything Is Possible

"**B**aby, look at this." It was a rare weekday when Cy was work-ing from home instead of the office. He'd been out of town so much lately that Hope had joined him in his home office, sitting on the couch surfing the Web while he crunched numbers on his latest project. Now, she walked over to where her husband sat and showed him the page featuring a Nigerian doctor being touted for having upped the survival rates for his cancer patients by over forty percent.

"That's something," Cy murmured, taking Hope's iPad and reading the article. " 'Using a combination of Western, Chinese, and alternative medicines that include new age techniques,' " he read, " 'Doctor Kendrick Ad–Zee–Kiwi . . .' " He looked at Hope. "Is that how you pronounce it?" She shrugged. He continued. " 'Doctor Adzikiwe's patients are experiencing longer life spans and others are seemingly being completely cured of the disease. The medical community is understandably cautious, but cancer patients from all over the world are now flocking to Australia in hopes that this doctor has found their cure.' " He continued read-ing and when he was finished, he looked up with a gleam in his eye. "Are you thinking what I'm thinking?" he asked her.

"Absolutely," Hope said, with a nod.

"I love you, baby." Cy kissed Hope even as he reached for his phone. "Let's call Trisha." He turned his chair so that she could sit on his lap as he placed the call.

Hope sat, silently thanking her mother for the umpteenth time for saying the words that changed everything, the words that had inspired Hope to rethink how she was handling Trisha's illness and her husband's involvement in said illness. "Baby, you can't compete with a ghost." Hope had shared these words with Vivian, who'd readily agreed with Pat, and added, "If you keep him from Trisha and she dies, God forbid, then he'll never forgive himself and you'll never live down your resistance." When Cy returned home from work that very evening, they'd had a long talk. Hope had apologized for being insensitive and Cy had apologized for not being as understanding of her feelings as he should have been. The past three weeks hadn't been without moments of discomfort, but the difference was where before Hope would keep whatever she'd felt to herself, she now shared it with Cy. Immediately. As soon as it came up. Before the negative thoughts could send her on a mental tangent.

"Trisha, it's me and Hope."

"Hi, Trisha."

"Hey, guys. What's going on?"

"How are you feeling?" Cy asked.

"I'm okay. A little tired, but other than that . . . not too bad."

"Do you feel up to making a trip to Australia?" Cy asked. Silence. "Trisha?"

"What's in Australia?"

"Maybe a cure for your disease." Cy read the article he'd found on Doctor Adzikiwe. "Hope and I thought it sounded like it was worth a try."

"I appreciate that, y'all. I really do. But I've already talked with my insurance company about alternative treatments. They're not covered. And even if they were, I wouldn't be able to afford the airfare and hotel stay such a journey would require. Just thinking of trying to do that causes me stress, and I'm supposed to stay calm." She tried to laugh, but it sounded forced at best.

"That's the good news," Hope said. "We want to do this for you, Trisha. We want to take care of all of the expenses—the trip, the treatment, everything—and make that our gift to you."

A longer silence this time.

"Trisha, you still here?" Cy asked.

"I don't know what to say," she finally replied.

Cy chuckled. "Hopefully, you'll say yes!"

She finally did so, reluctantly, but from that moment everything moved at lightning speed. The following day, Hope and Trisha were on a conference call for hours with Doctor Adzikiwe's office. A week later, after releases were signed, records transferred, and prescriptions filled, Cy was at the airport in New York with Trisha. Hope was there laughing, talking, and praying with them before seeing them off. The week before, when Cy had suggested she accompany them, she'd said, "You go on; I'll stay with the kids."

Later, she'd come to learn how much that gesture had meant to him and that because she trusted him, he loved her deeply, and so much more.

46

Break Up to Make Up

"Bo, let me in!" Darius growled, his voice low yet forceful as he stood outside the door to his husband's Biltmore suite. It had cost him a lot of money to get the cleaning lady to reveal Bo's exact suite number and after a month without sex and—aside from five minutes in the lobby during the DJ exchange seeing his soul mate—he had no intentions of being denied. "I mean it. I'm not going to go away until you open this door!"

"Well, I'm not going to open it," Bo said from the other side. "And if you don't leave, I'm going to call security."

"Fine, because I've sold the house and moved out all our things. I guess I'll just put your shit in storage and let you try and find where that is. Good-bye!" Darius moved out of sight from the peephole that he was sure Bo watched him from.

The door flew open behind him. "Don't you touch my—" Too late, Bo realized the ruse and stepped back inside the suite. But not fast enough to close the door before Darius got inside.

"I knew that would get you," Darius said, as pleased with himself as he was with the sight for sore eyes that stood before him. Even if said sight resembled a thundercloud before a hurricane. "It hurts to know you care more about your clothes than you do your husband."

"Husband? Nucka, you need to choke on that word."

"How many times do I have to tell you, Bo. How many ways? I'm sorry!"

"I'm sick of your sorries," Bo chided. But the way Bo was devouring him with his eyes, Darius could tell that his wife was glad to see him too.

"So what are you going to do? Divorce me?"

Bo crossed his arms. "Been thinking about it."

Darius walked over to the couch, sat down, and rested his arms across the back of it. "I miss you, baby. It's been a month. A lot has happened and I need to share it with you."

"Why don't you share it with the man I caught you sharing your dick with?" Darius sighed. "Uh-huh...I thought so."

"The realtor has been showing the house while you've been away," Darius said, deciding to ignore Bo's outburst and focus on something more important, like their future together. "She thinks we might have an offer by the end of the week." A pause and then, "I'm moving back to LA, boo." His voice softened. "I can't imagine being there without you with me." Bo snorted. "The other night, I was reminiscing about us, about the night we met...our first date. We went to the Patti LaBelle concert, remember? Her, Babyface...and who else?" Bo shrugged as though he didn't remember. But his eyes twinkled. "We sipped your beloved Courvoisier all night and you refused to come to the house unless I stopped by IHOP for the Grand Slam breakfast that you ate too fast and then promptly threw up in my car!" No comment, but Bo slid his eyes in Darius's direction before sitting at the dining room table. All ears.

"I took care of you that night," Darius continued. "Remember? Bought you 7Up and crackers, bathed you, tucked you into my bed. I lay there watching you sleep, for a long time, noting your curly eyelashes that fluttered when you breathed, and how you have a tiny mole on the left side of your mouth. I couldn't resist, and I kissed it. And then your lips. You swatted me away like an annoying fly—"

"Yeah, and I should probably swat your ass away again—"

"Before turning on your side, curling up almost into a fetal position and then sleeping like a baby. I think that's when I fell in love with you, watching you sleep. And then you woke up the next afternoon and fixed one of the best breakfasts that I'd ever eaten—that omelet with the spinach and mushrooms that you topped with orange slices. I thought that was so crazy, but it was so good. You know, that's how I feel about you. You're so crazy, but you make me feel so good. If I could, baby, I'd take back those five, ten minutes that I was alone with Paz." Bo tensed at the name, but remained silent. "I never should have gone up those stairs. Hell, never should have gone to the party."

Bo stared straight ahead. "So you knew he'd be there."

"Yes. I knew. I thought I could handle it. I thought flirting with him was"—Darius shrugged—"fun, different."

"Fun, hell. You had a full-blown crush on him."

"I did."

"And now?"

"After what it may cost me, I'll be all right with never seeing him again."

"Yeah, well, since y'all are getting ready to do a movie together . . . good luck with that."

"I walked away from it, Bo."

For the first time since he entered, Bo looked directly at Darius. "What do you mean?"

"What I said. I'm not going to score the film. I told Paz that I'd made a terrible mistake, and that I was prepared to do whatever it took to rectify it."

"You'd give up something like that for me? Something that could provide you with an even bigger crossover audience, take you to yet another level?"

Darius stood, walked over to the dining room where Bo sat. "I can get another movie," he whispered. "But I can't get another you."

That did it. Bo was out of the chair and in Darius's arms in an instant. "I'm sorry I hurt you, baby." Darius rained kisses on Bo's face, his hands roaming over the body whose absence had caused him sleepless nights. "So sorry. Will you forgive me?"

"You cut me deep, Dee," Bo said, his eyes wet.

"Me? You were the one with the scissors. And my ass has a gash to prove it!"

"You know what I mean," Bo said with a laugh. "You hurt me to my heart."

"I'll make it up to you. Will you forgive me?"

Bo reached around and cupped Darius's butt. "I'll think about it."

"Will you think about it while you're living back with me, coming home, like . . . right now?"

Bo looked around the room. "I don't know. I'm growing used to room service and folks turning down my bed and putting chocolate treats on my pillow."

"I'll be your chocolate treat," Darius said, rubbing himself against Bo. Bo reached back, and could feel Darius's quickly hardening erection. "It missed you," he said, nibbling against Bo's ear. "We can spend the night here, baby. I want you so badly." Darius began unbuckling his pants. "Did you miss me?"

"Maybe a little."

"Then come get a little taste." He pulled himself out of his pants, hard and ready.

"Uh, that would be a negative. We've got to take a shower first."

Darius's brows creased. Bo loved to perform oral sex, had never turned him down. "I took a shower before I came here."

"Did you use Clorox?"

"Huh?"

"Pine-Sol. Lysol. Boric acid. Lye? 'Cause that's probably what it's going to take to wash that muthafucka's stank off the dick that belongs to me."

"Ha! Baby, do you want to wash it off or burn it up?"

"I'll wash it tonight. But if you ever cheat on me again, I'm going to set that stick on fire. And I'm not playing."

Darius followed Bo into the shower, where every part of his eight-inch shaft was washed, first with a washcloth and then with Bo's tongue. The makeup sex was at first tender, then explosive, and lasted well into the night, until both men were fully satiated and Bo rolled over into the fetal position, falling into a deep sleep, the way he'd done on their first date.

47

A Reminder

"Good morning, brother." Stacy stood in the kitchen of the condo she was renting temporarily, placing her phone on speaker while waiting for her tea water to boil.

"Good morning," Brent said. "How are you?"

"The same as I've been the last few hundred times you've asked me. I'm fine, Brent, really."

"Has he called?"

"No, and he isn't answering my calls either."

"There's a reason."

"Which you refuse to tell me."

"Stacy . . ."

"Brent. You're my brother and my protector, and I love you for it. And I know that it's killing you not to put a foot in Tony's behind for what he did to me. But—"

"But what?"

Stacy paused as the kettle whistled and she turned off the heat. "I've forgiven him."

For seconds, the sound of water being poured over tea bags was the only thing to be heard.

"Please tell me that I didn't hear what I think I heard."

"You heard correctly. I forgave him, Brent. It was the Christian thing to do. But," she hurried on, over Brent's objection, "that doesn't mean that I've forgotten what he did. I'm not saying that I'll get back with Tony."

"Sounds like you're not saying that you won't either."

"Honestly, besides taking it one day at a time? I don't know what I'll do. I'm in counseling with the pastor's wife at our church, and that's helping a lot." Stacy knew that Tony was also in counseling, both with her counselor's husband, Derrick Montgomery, and also with a licensed professional whose expertise was in rehabilitation from steroid use and anger management. But she didn't think Brent would appreciate these facts, so she kept them to herself.

"Here you are asking me all of these questions, but you still won't tell me what happened when you guys confronted Tony." A friend of Stacy's had been at the restaurant when Brent and the other three brothers had "encouraged" Tony to step outside for a conversation.

"He lived to tell about it. That's all you need to know."

"I wish you guys had kept out of it, let me handle it."

"Couldn't do that, baby girl. Wasn't no way a brothah was going to put his hands on our sister and there not be a discussion. Be glad that that's all it was."

"Look, it's my life, Brent. I have a right to know how you're affecting it."

"I'll tell you this much. I told Tony that to get to you, he'd have to go through me. Which means if he wants to talk to you, wants to so much as *look* at my baby sis, he's going to have to prove to me that he's changed, that he's got his head on straight and that what happened was a one-time occurrence. If he does all that then he may be able to *look* at you in my presence. And then we'll go from there."

The conversation shifted to other family matters, including the upcoming Labor Day picnic they planned to have at the beach, Stacy's nieces and nephews, and whether or not Serena would win another US Open.

"She's like a fine wine, getting better with age," Brent was saying as Stacy's doorbell rang.

"I know that's right." Stacy walked to the door and broke into a big smile when she saw who was waiting for her. "Brother, I've got to go."

"Okay, sis. But don't get Tony in trouble. Stay away from him."

"Mind your business."

"You are my business."

"Bye, Brent."

"Bye."

Stacy threw open the door. "Little Bo Peep!" she said, throwing her arms around him.

"Spacey Stacy," he said, as they rocked back and forth in a dramatic hug. "Girl, you so crazy," he said when they parted. It was the first time they'd seen each other since Bo and Darius's reconciliation and both their relocations. There was a lot to catch up on.

"I just made tea. Do you want some? And before you ask, no, I don't have any cognac."

"I wasn't going to ask, heifah. Tea will be fine, thank you very much." He followed her into the kitchen. "Where's DJ?"

"Over to his uncle's house, bonding with his cousins."

"Ooh, I bet he's glad to be back in LA."

"No more than me."

"Or me."

"So when did y'all get back from the tour?"

"It was over a couple days ago, but we spent some time in New York with my family."

Stacy placed the tea on the island in front of Bo. "Sounds like you guys are back on track."

Bo tried hard not to smile. Failed. "We're doing all right."

"Is 'all right' what has you turning red from the neck up?"

"Girl, I ain't blushing. Get out of here."

"Whatever. You're preening like a peacock."

"Hell, I can't even front. You know that man knows how to pump a penis."

"Yes," Stacy deadpanned. "I remember."

"Ooh, sounds like somebody is overdue for some pumping.

What's going on with you and crazy man?" He blew on his tea and waited expectantly.

"Nothing. My brothers have him on lock; he hasn't called, won't return mine."

"You say that like it's a bad thing."

"You sound as bad as my brothers. I'm not saying I'll get back with him. But he's my husband, the man I was married to for three years. I haven't seen him or said a word to him since that night. I want to talk to him, find out what happened to make him snap like that . . . for my own healing."

"I thought you said he left you messages about taking steroids."

"He did but . . . I don't know . . . I just need to talk to him. That's all."

"What conversation is there to have with someone who left an imprint on your face?"

"I guess the same kind to have with the man who stuck his junk in somebody else's trunk."

"Whoa!" Bo sat back in the chair. "I guess I deserved that. I shouldn't be judging how bad one thing is over another. Wrong is wrong."

"Exactly." She joined Bo and sat at the island. "He wants us to do couples counseling."

"How do you know this?"

"He told me in an e-mail."

"I don't know, Stace," Bo said, slowly shaking his head. "I just don't know."

"Me either." They were silent, sipping their tea and listening to strains of classic George Benson. "What about you? How was it getting back with Darius after . . . all that happened?"

"Strange. But good. In some ways it's better than it's ever been. But I probably shouldn't tell you that."

"Oh my goodness! I totally forgot about what you did—stabbing him in the butt with some scissors. Bo, that was some straight-up ghetto madness."

"It was what it was and is what it is."

"So . . . did it heal okay? I mean, does he have a big scar or anything?"

"Child, please. That man don't have a scar."

"He doesn't?"

"No," Bo calmly replied after a sip of tea. "He has a reminder."

48

Revelations

Having eaten their fill at a seafood restaurant, Hope and Frieda window-shopped as they walked around Seaport Village. It was a beautiful day in San Diego—a soft wind blowing, bright sun shining, and boats bobbing gently in the marina waves.

"It's beautiful here," Frieda said as they strolled. "I should come down more often."

"Yes, and you should keep driving a few more miles and visit your cousin more often, too."

"Whatever, chick. Same distance going north on the freeway as it is going south."

Hope laughed. "True that. What brought you down here anyway?"

"Trying to track down a dude I messed with a while back. Ran into a friend of his while shopping in Long Beach and he told me to come down, that he didn't have a number or address on old boy, but if we rode around we might find him."

"By the sound of your voice, I take it you didn't?"

Frieda shook her head. "I think his friend was just trying to make a move, if you know what I mean. I don't hollah at hoopty drivers. Boyfriend should have known."

"So was this another—"

"Possible baby daddy? Yep. And the last one I'm going to try for too. After Gorgio and Shabach came back negative I just knew

Jonathan was the child's father. He's the one I thought had the birthmark. But come to find out, it's more of a mole. Even if that hadn't ruled him out, that DNA test sure did."

"I'm sorry, cousin. I know you want to know the identity of Gabe's father."

Frieda shrugged. "I didn't know mine and it messed me up. At least Gabe's got Gabriel."

"He still going for full custody?"

"Our lawyers are trying to work out something a little more agreeable, maybe not fifty-fifty, but definitely with me having more of a presence in my son's life. I might not be the best mother, but I am his mother. Nobody is going to take that role from me, believe that."

"So you and Gabriel are still not talking? No chance that you'll work it out?"

"No. I hear a little this and that from a sistah who works at the hospital, one I befriended a year ago after she'd had her baby. All her family is down south and her husband was overseas so I kept her company a little bit."

"What did you hear?"

"That Amber is working extra shifts and shit, trying to be at the hospital every time he drives up. They're probably screwing."

"You don't know that."

"I don't not know it, either." They reached their cars, which were parked side by side. "I don't care. She can have his nerdy be-hind."

Hope knew that Frieda didn't mean that, but she felt no need to point out the obvious. "What are you doing for Labor Day?"

"I don't know. What are y'all doing?"

"Cooking on the patio. Simeon is coming down."

"Cy's fine-ass cousin?"

"Yes, Mrs. Livingston. He's coming down with a guest, a woman he wants us to meet."

"I should have got me some of that at your wedding, when I had the chance."

Getting "some of that" is what had gotten Frieda in trouble in the first place. But, again, Hope chose to not sing to the choir. Instead, she reached over for a hug. "Love you, cuz. You're more than welcome to join us for the holiday. A few of our neighbors are coming over, and some of Cy's friends. You'll be fine."

"Okay, Hope. I'll let you know."

"Call and let me know you made it home safe, okay?" Hope turned to get in her car, and stopped. "You know what?"

"What?"

"I don't think I've heard you use the b-word lately. In fact, today you barely cursed. Are we trying to turn over a new leaf?"

Frieda smiled. "Something like that." She got into her car, having decided early on not to share the fact that she was consulting with a life coach. "When change is genuine," her life coach had told her, "you don't have to tell people. They'll see it and know."

As Frieda hit the I-5 ramp on her way back to Los Angeles she thought of someone else she'd like to see, wondered whether he'd notice anything different. And if so, if it would matter.

Gabriel nodded as Amber rambled on and on about pathophysiology and clinical assessment, classes she was taking at UCLA on the road to a masters in nursing. Gabriel was happy that she was continuing her education and that she was excited about medicine—he really was. But truth was, he'd done thirty-six hours at the hospital, slept for eight, and then agreed to have dinner with Amber to get away from medicine, not talk about it from appetizer to dessert.

"Gabriel? Are you listening? Do you think my volunteering with Doctors Without Borders is a good idea?"

Gabriel rubbed a hand across his face; stifled a yawn. "I'm sure it would be a valuable learning experience."

"Oh my. I'm sorry. Here I am prattling on and on about work and you're probably sick to death of dealing with this stuff. It's just that I'm so psyched about . . ." And off she went again.

Gabriel looked at her with interested eyes. And didn't hear a thing. He was too busy getting a revelation. *That's what I loved about her. And that's what I miss.* Sitting there, he tried to remember not only the last conversation he had with Frieda about his profession, but any conversation he'd had. None in-depth, that was for sure. Whenever he'd begun a conversation about the hospital, Frieda would inevitably turn it into a conversation worthy of a reality show. She'd always focus on the people involved in whatever he was talking about, wanting to know the dirt of their personal lives and imagining some if none existed. When with her, he learned more than he ever wanted to know about hip-hop performers and movie stars, about vacation destinations and designer labels. Yes, she was materialistic, even shallow, to use his mother's term. But in his somewhat stodgy community she was also a breath of fresh air, a delightful change in the norm with a different perspective and a plethora of opinions. *And a plethora of men, don't forget.* Yes, there was that. She'd never hidden her promiscuous past from him. And while he wasn't excusing her behavior, he felt somewhat responsible for her feeling the need to look elsewhere for what he couldn't give her after performing a ten-hour surgery.

"Doctor Livingston?"

"Uh, I'm sorry, Amber. What were you saying?"

"Never mind. It's obvious that you have a lot on your mind." She reached over and grabbed his hand. "Is it the divorce? Has it been finalized? Do you want to talk about it?"

"Thanks, Amber, but no. It's not something that I want to discuss."

He didn't want to discuss it with Amber, but the bigger question, he later realized, was whether or not he wanted the divorce to happen at all.

49

A New Day

Stacy and Frieda sat on Hope's massive patio, catching a beautiful breeze as they took in the picturesque view of the Pacific Ocean that served as Hope's backyard. It was the day before the big Labor Day bash. The three friends were grateful to spend time alone before the crowd arrived. "It's beautiful out here," Frieda mumbled, adjusting her sunglasses as she lay back on the chaise.

"Sure is. If I lived somewhere like this, I'd never leave home."

"Girl, for real."

Both looked toward the sliding glass door as it opened. "All right, ladies," Hope said, carrying a large tray toward the canopied table. "Lunch is served."

Stacy rolled off her lounge chair and stretched. "Hope, you should have told me you needed help." She walked over to where Hope was removing the dishes from the tray to the table. Nibbling on one of the tempura-fried vegetables, she commented, "These are good."

"Thanks, sis," Hope replied. "I'm glad they turned out this time because my first attempt was a failure to the nth degree and my second try wasn't much better. I guess the third time is the charm." She picked up a crispy cauliflower and plopped it into her mouth. "Come on, your highness," she said to Frieda, who was still lying on the chaise.

"Aw, hell," Frieda moaned. She walked over to the spread, taking in the sliced baked chicken and kaiser rolls for sandwiches, the vegetables, and German potato salad. "Dang, Hope," she said, after eating a slice of chicken. "Did you cook this?"

"Why, what's the matter with it?"

"It's good!"

Hope gave her a look of indignation. "You say that like you're surprised."

"I am!"

The women laughed, sat down, and fixed their plates. While Hope opted for sparkling water, Stacy and Frieda enjoyed chilled chardonnay. Soon eating replaced conversation, punctuated by the lapping water and an occasional screech of a bird overhead. After finishing off her first helping of vegetables, Stacy reached for her glass, sat back and sipped thoughtfully as she again took in the beautiful day.

"A penny for your thoughts, Stace," Hope said, reaching for her glass as she too sat back.

"I was just thinking about what a difference a year made. This time last year I was in Phoenix, happily married. Tony was playing for the Cardinals and life seemed good. Then bad stuff started falling like dominoes. Tony got hurt, then cut from the team; he lost hella money on that stupid Ponzi-scheme, and started taking steroids. Did y'all know that taking that drug can make it difficult for a man to get hard?" Hope and Frieda shook their heads. "It can. A few times, we had problems in the bedroom. I thought it might be another woman. Never dreamed it was because of what is sometimes called 'juice.' I did research and found out that aggressiveness can be a side effect of over using. Guess that's how Tony turned into a monster and beat me up. Now, here I sit. Back in LA, alone, unsecure and my future unsure." She shrugged. "It's a trip."

"Are you still shopping your resume?"

"No. When Darius found out I was looking for work, he increased my child support, said he wanted my primary focus to be our child. I still want some type of career though; something that I can do from home."

"Darius stepped up for real," Frieda said, finishing a bite of chicken and picking up a tempura-battered asparagus tip. "Good for him. Let's see, last year this time," she continued as she thoughtfully chewed, "I was kicking it with Clark Pratt, living in Brentwood, and feeling that my husband and son were weights I could do without." She finished her glass of wine and reached for the bottle. "If only I knew those weights were treasures that I'd give anything to feel right now."

"When is the last time you talked to Gabriel?" Stacy asked.

"Over the phone, about a month ago. Other than that our conversations take place through e-mails or via his assistant and only involve arrangements for picking up Gabe."

Hope finished her water and poured wine into her glass. "Is Cordella still living with them?"

"Yes. And I can't even say I'm mad about that. I was blaming her for being in my business when, since I was screwing her son, she could say that she was minding her own. I was mad at her for not being down with my scandalous mess. But looking back at it, she was really trying to get me to pay attention to what I had right in front of me. She loves my son and whether I like it or not, he loves her. I don't doubt that at all."

Hope stared out over the ocean. "Do you think there's a chance of y'all getting back together?" And then, "What about the letter? Did you write it?"

"More importantly, did you send it?" Stacy added.

"Yes and yes," Frieda said, a soft sigh escaping before she could hold it back. "After a couple days I sent a text asking if he got it. He said yes." She shrugged. "That's it. So . . . it looks like I'll have a new title in about three months—divorcée."

It went without saying that in time, Stacy might be wearing that title too.

"Last year this time I didn't know Trisha Underwood," Hope said into the silence.

"Good thing she's left the country," Frieda said with a huff. For once, Hope was in total agreement with her cousin's brash remark. "I still wonder whether that chick even had cancer."

"She had it," Hope said quickly. "We've had extensive conversations with Dr. Adzikiwe about her condition, Cy more than me. She was a very sick woman and she's not out of the woods yet."

"Well, at least she's out of your husband's life," Stacy said.

"But she's still in that wallet, isn't that right, Hope?" Frieda asked.

"Yes, Cy is handling her medical expenses. There's no way she could afford this treatment otherwise. It's very expensive."

"You're a better woman than me," Frieda admitted. "If it were my man and my money, chick would be at the county clinic... maybe."

"I'm glad we decided to help her. She's not a bad person."

Clearly, Frieda wasn't convinced. "Whatever. What about Crazy Millicent? Will we be seeing the ebony and ivory tomorrow?"

Hope nodded, understanding Frieda's interracial couple reference. "She's finally over her morning sickness. Their daughter, Sarah, is staying with friends in Los Angeles but Millicent, Jack, and both sons will be here."

"I never thought I'd see the day when Millicent would be eating a meal at your table," Stacy said with a chuckle.

"Me either," Hope replied. "Life is full of surprises."

"Well," Frieda said, once again reaching for the wine bottle and emptying it by topping off all of their glasses, "it looks like it's a new day for all us sister-girls."

Hope lifted her glass and her friends followed suit. "To a new day."

"A better day," Stacy added.

"And better decisions," Frieda said.

The women clinked their glasses and hoped for the best.

50

The Woman I AM

The setting was the Gibson Amphitheatre located in Universal City and the place was standing room only. It was the final evening of the Sanctity of Sisterhood's autumn conference titled The Woman I Am and, as requested, the attendees had dressed in white. The tableau created was majestic, almost heavenly in its appearance, over six-thousand women singing and dancing before the Lord.

The guest moderator for the conference, a former first lady in Los Angeles and current talk show host, walked across the stage and grabbed the microphone. Her double-breasted white suit with big bold buttons and an oversized collar made quite the statement as she stood before the women and lifted her hands to the sky. "Praise Him, sisters," Carla Chapman extolled as she walked back and forth. "He made you the woman that you are, and you are made in the image of the great I AM." Her declaration caused another uproar in the crowd, one that D & C, Darius Crenshaw and Company, quickly punctuated with riffs on the keyboards, strings, and drums. Realizing that this was a time of worship, not words, Carla gave an almost imperceptible nod to Darius, who broke out in a song taken from Psalm 8.

"Oh Lord . . . how excellent is Your name above all the earth; who has set Thy glory above the heavens. When I

consider Thy heavens, the work of Thy fingers, the moon
and the stars, which Thou hast ordained. What is man,
that Thou art mindful of him, and the son of man, that
Thou visits him? For Thou hast made him a little lower
than the angels, and hast crowned him with glory and
honor . . . O Lord our Lord, how excellent is Thy name in
all the earth!"

Reactions varied throughout the arena. Some cried, some laughed, some simply raised their hands in adoration. Others sat in their seats and rocked. This was a personal moment between attendee and God, a time to reflect on what He had done, and why they should be thankful. Darius's baritone flitted among the praise, the instruments in one accord with the anointing. When the song ended, Carla waited until most had taken their seat and then again attempted to move forward in the service.

"Yes, His name is excellent," she began, her voice naturally authoritative. "And since we are created in His image, so are we! As we discovered in this conference's sessions, it doesn't matter who you are or where you've been, what you've done or who has judged you. Your membership in the kingdom has deemed you excellent and whole before the almighty God. Oh, yes, sisters. Some of you don't believe it. But I stand here as a witness that He can take your feet out of the miry clay and set it upon a solid rock. What do I mean, you're asking? What is miry clay? That's just a fancy King James saying for dirt, y'all. Doing the dirty. Watching the dirty." Various reactions from laughter to applause to shaking heads accompanied her statement. Still, others had looks that showed the listener seemed less than appreciative of what was being said. "I appreciate the applause, but not all of y'all are happy. Oh, I see the frowns and raised brows. And I know why. It's because y'all think I'm talking about you." She paused, looking over the crowded space. "Well, news flash, baby. I'm talking about me! I was the sinner, a wretch undone. Hey! A promiscuous teenager who became an unwed mother, an adulterer when I thought I was way past that kind of sin. Yes, I may be pointing one finger out, but there are three that are pointing back at me, and—hallelujah!—I'm so thankful to know that I am not what I've done. I am all that I AM!"

This statement brought out a praise party that lasted several minutes.

When the audience calmed down once more, she continued. "We have a special treat for you as we bring this conference to a close, and we want you to tell all of your sisters who couldn't make it about the next major conference that will take place next August. Mark your calendars because you won't want to miss it. We're going to leave land behind, and our husbands"—Carla paused amid the snickers—"and set sail on one of the seven seas. That's right, saints. Our next conference will happen aboard a cruise ship and will feature some of the most powerful women of God in the country along with some of our finest praise and worshippers, including who we've been blessed to have in our midst this weekend—Darius Crenshaw and Company!" Darius smiled and bowed to the crowd to acknowledge their applause. When it subsided, Carla continued. "Once again I'd like to thank this year's cohost, Mrs. Vivian Montgomery, who pulled herself away from that fine husband long enough to talk to us about who we are in God." Vivian smiled and waved. "I'd also like to thank Tai Brook who, while she couldn't be with us in person, contributed in spirit and in monies by funding yesterday's luncheon. Y'all, show Mrs. Tai Brook some love so that she'll see it on the DVD! Oh, and we can't forget her daughter, Princess Petersen. How about that workshop: Jesus Is My Boo; Let Him Be Your Boo Too. And Mamma Max!" Again, a nice round of applause was offered up by the attendees.

After thanking the other ladies who'd assisted with the conference, Carla motioned to the side of the stage. Out walked Hope and seven other women, also all dressed in white. "To close out this miniconference, I'm pleased to once again introduce Hope Taylor, back by popular demand, y'all, doing an encore of the praise dance to "In the Land of I Am." Let's put our hands together for Hope Taylor and the Women Who Worship!"

Hope walked up to where Carla stood waiting as the other seven dancers spread across the stage. The sound of a Ricky Byars original masterpiece filled the room. The crowd was on their feet as the words delivered above African-inspired music filled the women's hearts and heads, reminding them of all that God is and because of being made in His image, of all that they were as well.

The conference ended and the conference speakers and co-hosts prepared to go their separate ways. Vivian and Hope walked the short distance to their cars. "That was wonderful, Vivian. Thanks for asking me to participate. I'd never thought about it, but I loved speaking to and encouraging the women. It felt good."

"They loved you, too," Vivian replied. "Your topic, 'I Am Hope,' was perfect! Your story gives them faith to believe that their dreams can come true, too. It was also good that you included the challenges that have come with marriage, especially to someone as desirable as your husband. It's good for women to see that we may live in big houses but we don't live on big pedestals. We have problems, challenges and issues the same as them. Your story showed them that. The DVD from your session is selling very well."

"I'm thankful for that."

"We're thankful for you. And I'm delighted that everything has worked out with your and Cy's situation. It takes a big woman to do what you've done; to not only embrace a former lover of your husband, but to help her get better."

"It's not me, Lady Viv," Hope said sincerely. "It's the God in me. He is the reason why I am who I am."

51

A Pledge of Allegiance

"**Y**our Aunt Gladean is a mess!" Darius and Bo had just returned to their Manhattan luxury hotel suite after a day of love,
laughter, liquor, and good home cooking. Instead of the traditional
fare, this island-born clan of Trinidadians had brought out chicken
pelau, curried shrimp, zucchini corn bake, macaroni pie, callaloo,
fish stew, plantains, peas and rice, and coconut bread pudding. At
Darius's request, Bo's Aunt Gladean had also made what she called
a yam pie. "I think I'm forever spoiled by her sweet-potato pie. I
hadn't had any that tasted that good since my grandmother died."

"Yeah, old girl can throw down, that's no joke!" Bo placed his
pouch on the dining room table and proceeded to the bar, where
he pulled out a bottle of Courvoisier. "You want some?"

"Just one finger; lots of ice."

Bo nodded and yawned. "Lord have mercy, I love my family,
but they wear me out!"

"I love them too. Growing up, I never experienced the type of
environment that you took for granted. Grandma was superstrict
and our house was literally a house of prayer—no music other than
gospel allowed and even that was played low. No loud talking; I
never remember her laughing out loud, you know, one of those
good belly laughs like your Aunt Phyllis let loose all day." Darius
smiled; the memory alone felt that good. "I swear her laugh could
be a prescription for depression."

"And if that didn't work, her punch sure could!" Phyllis's punch was famous throughout their Queens neighborhood. A mixture of Hawaiian Punch, orange juice, lemons, and a blend of liquors known by her alone.

They walked from the dining room into the bedroom. Darius began undressing before they reached the room. "Man, I'm tired. That was the most fun I've had in a long time," he said around a yawn. And DJ's been in heaven these past two days. He was knocked out, wasn't he?"

"Gonna be hard getting that boy to leave their house tomorrow. My sister's place has been like heaven for that only child."

At this comment, Darius plopped down on the bed and perched himself up on his right elbow. "What are we going to do about that, baby? It's time for us to have another child, before DJ gets too big. Man, if Stacy had said yes, that would have been perfect!"

"Yeah." Bo joined Darius on the bed, bringing their drinks with him. "It would have been nice if DJ's brother or sister could have had the same mother. But this visit back home has me thinking." Bo paused and sipped his drink. "We've got a little Darius. I think we need a little Bo."

Darius sat up, laughing as he did so. "Oh, Lawd, no. One of you on the planet is enough, man." When Bo didn't join in on the joke, Darius sobered. "I'm sorry, baby. I thought you were playing. Do you really want a child of your own?"

"I know. I never thought I'd want that either. But DJ changed my life. I like that little boy like my own, and watching him laugh and play with all of his cousins got me thinking of how nice it would be to have my own seed, in the home, living with us. Maybe two."

"Whoa, now wait a minute, baby. Don't forget our crazy schedule."

"Hell, if Celine and Beyoncé and J. LO and all them heifahs can drop babies and keep it moving, we can too."

"Ha!" They were silent, sipping their liquor. "Do you have a mother in mind?"

Having finished undressing, Bo climbed onto the bed and positioned himself so that he faced Darius. He lazily ran a finger up
and down Darius's chocolate toned arm. "I've thought about it and
I think that one of those surrogate agencies is the best way to go.
You know, look through a catalog of women and their pedigrees
like we're shopping for designer clothes, and pick the one that will
give us our dream baby."

"I was kidding earlier," Darius whispered, leaning over and
placing a kiss on Bo's waiting mouth. "I'd love to have a baby Bo."

The lover's innocent touches and light kisses soon turned
more amorous. Bodies touched and hands roamed, until Bo
squeezed Darius's butt cheek and came in contact with the proof
of prior anger. He began a journey along Darius's body, kissing
every square inch of exposed flesh—arm, chest, stomach, hip,
thigh. When he reached Darius's firm, round backside, he outlined
the scar with his tongue, massaging the sensitive area just above his
husband's buttocks as he did so.

"Ooh, baby, you know I'm ticklish there," Darius said, after Bo
had licked a particularly sensitive spot of Darius's lower anatomy.
He returned to the scar, first licking and looking at it, really looking at it, for the first time.

"You know what, Dee? I think you need to get this scar tatted,
memorialized. I don't mean to be funny, but, baby, this kinda looks
like a bow. I think you should add an arrow and let me forever be
immortalized on your ass."

"Ha! You are such a nut!"

"No, I'm serious. Hold on, let me get my phone." Soon, Darius was looking at the scar that remained from Bo's channeling
Norman Bates in *Psycho,* when scissors instead of a knife punc-
tured his soft flesh.

"You know what—it really does look like a bow. That's crazy.
I've wanted to get a tattoo. I think this might be the time . . . and
the place."

"Well, you know I'm down with that," Bo said, making a show
of rubbing the name "Darius" that was written in calligraphy across
his lower back.

Darius outlined the name emblazoned across Bo's caramel toned body, skin that was baby smooth and blemish free, first with his finger. Then with his tongue. The lovers traveled familiar territory across each other's bodies, their mutual desire clearly evident by raised flagpoles pledging allegiance to each other.

"You know I love you, nut. I thank God for giving me you." Darius positioned himself over his heartbeat, taunting, teasing, kissing his neck.

"Yes, and I love what the Lord made that's tickling my backside," Bo replied sarcastically. "Now let's get this private party poppin'!"

52

Marriage Vows

Cy and Hope cuddled in the backseat of the town car that squired them around the snow-covered streets of Washington, DC. When the Taylors had suggested they wanted to spend some time alone with their grandchildren, they'd quickly taken them up on the offer. Cy had arranged a town car so that after taking in some of the historical landmarks, they'd meet Simeon and his date for some drinks at a jazz club and maybe even find a dance club where, as Cy put it, they could "bust some moves."

The car crossed 14th Street heading for Pennsylvania Avenue and within minutes they were passing 1600, the most famous address in the country. "It looks so imposing, almost majestic," Hope said, as they took in the gargantuan Christmas tree in front of the stately, Hoban architecture that had been built more than two hundred years ago. The subdued lighting gave the building an intimate feel, yet power fairly oozed between the wrought-iron fence.

"Think our president and first lady are home?" Cy joked. "Think they'd mind if we came for a visit?"

"Naw," Hope replied, nestling closer into Cy's warmth. "They're probably spending the holidays on some exotic island, or back in Hawaii." They continued riding, passing the Washington monument, the Congressional office building and other famous landmarks. "Let's let them enjoy the holiday. I'm sure our dear president will call you when he comes to California." Hope's comment was only partly in jest. Cy had met President Obama last year, at a pricey fund-raiser. Not one for celebrity photo ops, the picture of the two smiling men was proudly displayed on Cy's office wall.

"Ah, here's somebody calling with even more clout than the prez." He tapped his phone's screen. "What's up, cousin?"

"Wondering where y'all are at?" Cy could tell that Simeon was already at the club; his voice was raised above the din.

"We're on our way." Cy reached over and kissed Hope as he listened to Simeon. She kissed back, passionately. After listening to Simeon, he answered. "That sounds like a plan because, uh, there's something I need to do first too." He finished up the call and then spoke to the driver. "Let's head uptown."

The driver nodded.

Hope looked at Cy. "I thought the club was on U Street, where we were last night." Cy smiled, looking like a brother with a secret that he wasn't ready to share. "Cy Anthony Taylor," Hope said, in as stern a voice as she could muster with Cy's thumb playing a light symphony on the sensitive side of her arm. "What are you up to?"

"I'm not up yet," he whispered, nibbling her ear in the process. "But that will all change in about ten minutes."

Nine minutes and forty-five seconds later, they pulled up to the Mandarin Oriental in Washington, DC. This luxury chain had quickly become one of Cy's favorites, and he was more than happy to introduce it to his baby.

"Cy!" Hope looked out the window upon the opulent hotel entrance and the doorman already opening her door. "You told me they were sold out," she whispered, smiling at the doorman and waiting for Cy to come to her side.

"It is," Cy said, nodding at the doorman and placing a light hand at Hope's back. "But I've got connections. The president, remember?"

"Whatever, man," Hope said, a squiggle forming at the core of her heat as Cy's hand made an almost imperceptible circular motion at the small of her back. She was duly impressed when they bypassed the check-in counter and headed straight to the elevators. "I see someone's been busy," she said, as a bellman appeared from nowhere and accompanied them to their suite. "As you know, Thanksgiving night signals our start of the Christmas season. The present I wanted to give you tonight was best done out of the sight of my parents and our kids."

Just as they were getting settled into the Oriental Suite, Hope's phone rang. She reached for it and immediately, her playful mood vanished.

Cy noticed immediately. "Who is it?"

Hope showed him the screen: Trisha Underwood.

"Just ignore it, baby," Cy said. They'd already had the conversation with Trisha about not being able to continue the friendship, seeing that she was improving, and wishing her well. Especially now, since it appeared that she wouldn't be leaving this earth, not in the near future anyway, Cy had done so without feeling guilty. He sincerely felt that given the circumstances, he'd done everything that he could. "Whatever she wants can be said in a message. We can check it later on."

Hope had different plans, as evidenced by her answering the call. "Hello, Trisha." She pressed the speaker button.

"Hello, Hope! It's still Thanksgiving there so . . . I hope you, Cy, and the children have had a happy one."

"We did," Hope replied. "And you?"

"It was great. My parents came over to Australia to spend time with me. That meant the world."

"I'm sure it did."

"Hope, hold on a minute." There was a pause where the garbled sound of a man was heard in the background.

Is that Trisha's father? Cy thought, telling himself to relax as a feeling of guilt surfaced, something that he'd sworn he'd gotten over. Why would he be suspicious of Trisha calling and wishing them a happy Thanksgiving? Especially since she'd called Hope?

Obviously, she wasn't trying to be underhanded. "Hey, Trisha," he said, to let her know they were on speakerphone.

"Cy! Please give a hug to your parents for me. I've thought of them often over the years; they were always so kind."

"I will."

Cy and Hope became silent then, waiting to hear the reason for Trisha's call. She quickly obliged them. "You're probably wondering why I'm calling."

"Yes," was Hope and Cy's simultaneous reply.

Trisha's laughter was genuine and heartfelt. "Well, since you guys indirectly played a huge part in what just happened, I wanted you to be the first to know." During the next few seconds of silence, Cy's brain raced with possibilities and Hope held her breath. "I'm getting married!"

What!? Cy and Hope looked at each other, stunned. Hope recovered first. "Congratulations, Trisha."

Cy leaned toward Hope's phone. "Wow, Tricky, that was fast. Who is it? I mean, where did you meet him? How?"

"Maybe I can best clarify." A deeply accented voice wafted over the phone.

Again Hope and Cy shared a simultaneous moment. *The doctor?*

"Kendrick?" Cy's joy was genuine. "I mean, Dr. Adzikiwe."

"No," the man said. "My name is Allen Adzikiwe. I'm Kendrick's brother."

"Allen," Cy repeated, still shocked at this quick and unexpected turn of events. "Nice to meet you."

Kendrick, who was with the recently engaged couple, joined the conversation. "They met when I invited Trisha to a family dinner. One look at each other and it was love at first sight!" After talking a bit longer, Kendrick and Allen extended the Taylors an invitation to the Adzikiwe-Underwood wedding, planned for Valentine's Day in Sydney, Australia, where Trisha now lived. Surprisingly, the Taylors found themselves saying yes. They'd been around for the beginning of this unbelievable turn of events—the search for a cure that turned into a love affair. It seemed only right that they'd be there for the ending.

Once Hope ended the call, Cy immediately took her hand and pulled her toward the closed bedroom door. "I think we should take full advantage of all of this love that's in the air." He opened the door and smiled at Hope's gasp. The already beautifully appointed room was awash in lit candles, and there were several presents on the bed.

"Cy! What's all this?"

"Only one way to find out."

She opened the first box and pulled out a lovely negligee. It was a powdery pink number with satin straps, a satin hem, and a gauzy, see-through material in between. She smiled, remembering the first time he'd bought her negligees, the ones she'd worn on her honeymoon. "Great taste as always, baby," she said, kissing him softly on the mouth. "Can't wait to put this on."

"Can't wait to see you in it."

She reached for the second box, a smaller one containing a perfume bottle—shaped somewhat like a curvy woman, but with a flat bottom allowing the container to comfortably sit on a vanity. She tilted the label to read it in the subdued lighting. Tears came to her eyes as she read the single title: Hope. "You didn't," she whispered, already unscrewing the cap to smell the essence inside the crystal decanter. It smelled divine: ylang ylang, vanilla, what smelled like a spice that Hope couldn't quite define, and a hint of cinnamon. She immediately tilted the bottle, but Cy grabbed it before the liquid spilled. "Here," he murmured, his eyes darkening as he stared at Hope's chocolate skin. "Allow me." He tilted the bottle and dabbed amounts of the custom-made cologne on Hope's wrists and temples. "I've got a few more places in mind," Cy whispered. "Later."

Hope sat on the bed and pulled the third box to her. She opened it, and smiled as she saw a smaller box. "What did you get me?" she asked. Cy shrugged. She opened another box, and another, three more times until she got to a box that was smaller than the others... and colored blue. *Tiffany!* "Cy, it's not even Christmas yet!"

"Doesn't matter. Since I get to enjoy my present every day." He shrugged, "Maybe I got carried away, but you know I'm one of those rare brothers who loves to shop."

"That you do," she murmured as she slowly lifted the lid. "Oh, my goodness, Cy," she exclaimed, pulling the modern-day mother's ring from the black velvet case. "It's stunning." In lieu of the gems the setting astrologically called for, Cy used colored diamonds to tell the story of the family that he loved. "Everything is so gorgeous, so perfect," Hope whispered, suddenly hot and ready for the only man she'd ever loved like this. "Thank you, baby. Thank you so much."

"You're welcome, baby. Now, can I see you in your presents?"

"Absolutely!"

Within minutes, Hope was dressed in her signature cologne, the mother's ring, the silky negligee... and nothing else. The only thing Cy wore was his wedding band. They climbed onto the massive king-sized sleigh bed and after kissing her thoroughly, in a manner that almost took her breath away, he eased himself down to the bottom of the bed and sucked a freshly showered toe into his mouth. Hope moaned, having not known until she was married how sexy sucking this particular appendage could be. A soft moan was all it took for Cy to continue his journey upward, spending long, languid moments around and in her heat, his tongue parting and pushing, his teeth nibbling her nub, his mouth covering her paradise, giving her pleasure until she began to shake from the intensity of the oncoming orgasm, and her love of the man who'd once again showed her what an exceptional husband looked like.

Before she could catch her breath, Cy had raised himself over her, nudged apart her legs with his own, and entered her. Hope gasped at the incredibly delicious girth of him, a sound that was caught in Cy's mouth as he kissed her. Soon, his tongue mimicked his pelvic thrusts, before twirling with Hope's as they settled into a rhythm perfected over the past six years. With each thrust, memories of the confusion, insecurity, and friction that Trisha's reappearance had caused was replaced by the love, commitment, and honor expressed in their marriage vows. Cy's rhythm increased and before long, Hope felt the familiar buildup in her core, felt herself begin to shake with anticipation at her inevitable release. Cy soon joined her, a long hiss escaping from his lips as he released inside her. For the next several seconds, heavy breathing and rapid heartbeats were the only sounds.

Cy kissed Hope's nose before rolling off her. "That was delicious."

"Simply scrumptious," Hope agreed, nestling into his side. "Oh, no! What about Simeon? Aren't they waiting for us at the club?"

"Don't worry." Cy wrapped his arms around Hope. "I told him that we'd take a rain check and do breakfast instead."

"When did you tell him that?"

"Texted him when you were in the restroom."

"Hmm, I see that you're full of surprises."

"I knew that one round wouldn't be enough for us." Hope laughed. He smiled and pulled her even closer. "I love you, Mrs. Taylor."

"I love you, Mr. Taylor."

They spent the rest of the night showing each other just how much.

53

As Long As It Takes

"**Y**ou're cheating!" Stacy stood up, reached over and bopped the middle brother, Damien, on the head. "You know good and damn well that wasn't your book!"

"Watch your damn language!" Stacy's mom shouted from the other room.

Everyone laughed.

"She's just mad," Damien told his brother, Brent, as he raked up the cards and shuffled for another hand of a family favorite, bid whist. "The only way she and Scully are going to see Boston is if they pack their bags and go with us!"

Damien and Brent high-fived.

Stacy rolled her eyes.

"Forget both you nuckas," Scully mumbled."

"Mama, Scully's in here cursing," Damien yelled.

"Stop lying, punk! I said forget!"

Their mother walked into the dining room with her hand on a slim hip. "I tell you, some things haven't changed in twenty years. Am I going to have to break up this card game?" She placed a hand on Stacy's shoulder. "Do you need some more girl power in this room?"

Stacy placed her hand on top of her mom's. "I can handle these clowns."

"Come on and sit down," Scully said, rising from his chair. "I need to go check on the nieces and nephews."

One of their cousins sat down and soon the trash-talking, and bantering across the table began again. Amid raucous laughter, Scully reentered the room. "Stacy, you have a visitor."

Stacy's brow furrowed. "Who?" Her answer walked into the room, carrying two dozen roses. She stood and faced him, indignation written across her face. "Tony, I told you that I didn't want drama today. What are you doing here?"

"It's on me, sis," Brent said, rising. "He called me, asked if he could come over, and I said that it was okay."

"Oh, so when did you start speaking for me and when did I stop being able to speak for myself?"

"Listen, I'm not trying to get in your business—"

"I can't tell—"

"But I know that both of you are missing each other; both of you are hurting. I figured that since this is the day we're being thankful and all, that we could call a truce for a minute."

"I can't believe you did this, Brent. You of all people. It was just a few short weeks ago that you were on the verge of getting arrested for assault!"

Brent fixed Tony with a determined look. "I'm still not far from it. If he ever puts his hands on you again, Tony knows how it's going down." He turned to Stacy. "But what you don't know is that he also called two weeks ago and asked to meet with the family. Without you." Stacy looked from Brent to Tony, with a confused expression. "He shared what had brought him to that awful place with you, and what he was doing to make sure it never happened again. He also wanted our forgiveness. I'm one of the ones who gave it to him."

"I'll only stay a few moments," Tony said, the conversation now finally with him instead of about him. "But I wanted to see you, Stacy. And give you these." He held out the roses.

Several seconds went by without her moving. Brent finally stepped forward. "Girl, are you going to just let the man's arm fall off?"

Stacy took the flowers. "They're lovely, Tony. Let me put them in some water."

When Brent left the room, an awkward silence followed. Unlike Brent, Damien still had nothing to say to the man who'd dared put his hands on his sister. His and Scully's was the forgiveness for which Tony was still waiting. "Time will tell," was Damien's answer when Tony insisted how sorry he was. Even now his fingers were itching to open up a can of whoop ass and use it on the man who hurt his sister. As for hotheaded Skully, he was only two seconds and about five feet away from let-me-handle-this-punk-ass-fool, so he again left the room.

He'd left, but Stacy didn't trust Skully. He was likely to get to thinking about what happened and bum-rush a brother. "Let's go outside," she suggested, turning and leaving without waiting for a response. While walking to the sliding doors just off the dining room, she tried to sort out the myriad of feelings that seeing Tony had brought on.

"I didn't mean to upset you," Tony said, as soon as they were alone in the Gray's backyard. "But you haven't answered your phone all day. Or returned my calls."

"Maybe that should have told you something," Stacy quietly replied.

"I guess. But the last time we talked, you said that you weren't going to close the door on us, that you were going to give me time to prove to you that what happened was a once-in-a-lifetime mistake."

"I said that, Tony. And I meant it. But that doesn't mean I want to talk to you on the regular, because I don't. Yes, I've forgiven you, but I haven't forgotten. I'm not going to fake the warm and fuzzy feelings when they are not there. I always said that if a man ever hit me, it would be one hit too many. And I'd be gone without looking back. Whatever you said to my brothers may have softened Brent's position, but two of my brothers are still very angry. And, quite frankly, so am I."

Tony took a deep breath. "There are no words for how sorry I am. If I could take back that night—"

"But you can't...."

"But if I could, I would never, ever have put my hands on you. If I knew then what I know now, I never would have begun taking the steroids; and I would have listened when my supplier told me to back off."

"Woulda, shoulda, coulda..."

"Doesn't change a thing. I know."

The two were quiet as they watched two yellow-rump warblers flit between the bird-of-paradise bush. One seemed to be chasing the other before both stopped and had a chirping conversation. Stacy imagined the one doing the most chirping was female because as soon as the other bird jumped on the same branch, the chirping bird took off again. Observing the birds' shifting for closeness and distance, Stacy wondered whether or not she and Tony would ever again be on the same page.

"I know you're trying," Stacy said at last, her back to him as she continued to look for where the birds had gone. "The flowers are nice. Thank you."

"You're welcome."

"So..." She finally turned around and looked at him. "Did you have a nice time with your family?"

"It was good, the usual. Mom asked about you. She's still mad at me too."

This elicited a slight smile from Stacy. She loved the feisty Mrs. Johnson, admired her courage in battling back from cancer. The day after the incident, she'd called Stacy and let her know in no uncertain terms that her son was one-thousand percent wrong, that she didn't condone what he'd done, and that she would totally understand it if Stacy filed for divorce. After they'd talked for almost an hour, she'd also admitted that Tony had never been a violent man and that what had happened was totally out of character. Stacy had continued the relationship with his mother, even when she and Tony were not speaking.

"The family is thinking about going somewhere together for Christmas and New Years....Maybe renting a large cabin in Big Bear or a house in Palm Springs."

"That sounds nice." For them, not Stacy. She hadn't been to Big Bear since her debacle there with Bo and Darius. And she couldn't remember the last time she'd been to Palm Springs.

"Do you know what you and little man are doing yet for Christmas?"

Stacy shook her head. "Haven't even thought about it."

"I probably don't have to tell you what I'd like—for us to spend it together."

"Tony—"

"I'm not looking for an answer today," he said, putting his hands up in surrender. "I know I'm going to have to work hard to earn your trust, for you to let me back into your life."

"You're right. And I honestly don't know how long it's going to be before that happens. Besides, I've been in this game long enough to know what the deal is. It's probably not like you're hurting for company of the female persuasion."

"Listen, Stacy." He placed a hand on her arm. She didn't flinch or pull away. "I'm not even looking at any other women right now. And I'm not being unfaithful. You're my wife and you're the one I want. Good things come to those who wait. You're worth waiting for."

Stacy looked in his eyes and saw honesty, sincerity, and vulnerability. In short, she saw the man that she married. Her heart flip-flopped, revealing the love for him that was still there, and the room to believe that their marriage could be saved. "You say that now. But how long do you think you can wait for me to get over what happened?"

Tony dared to take one step, and then another, and then there it was: Stacy wrapped in his arms. "I love you. I miss you. And I can't see myself living without you. So I will wait as long as it takes."

54

Love Unconditionally

In the similar vein she'd adopted these past few months, of doing different things to yield different results, Frieda was spending Thanksgiving alone. She'd seriously considered joining Hope, Cy, and family in Oklahoma and dining at the table of her dear Aunt Pat, who would be there with Uncle Earl and Hope's stepmom, the woman who'd used an uncanny amount of chutzpah and diplomacy to bring the three together on one accord. But at the end of the day, Frieda didn't want to face the inevitable questions of where her family was, specifically her son, Gabe, and her husband, Gabriel. Which led to the second invite she'd contemplated, and declined—the one from her mother in Kansas City, who'd said that her cousins would be joining them for the affair. While she'd recently learned how to forgive, she had no desire to break bread with the man who'd raped her, the one who even after Frieda had come clean with the sordid details had continued to have an open relationship with her mother, and who Frieda was ninety-nine point nine percent sure would be breaking bread in Kansas City this holiday season. Finally there was the last and most compelling invite—one from Stacy and the rambunctious and always entertaining Gray family. This was an invite that she almost accepted. After all, she could count on the renowned Gray brothers to let her get her flirt on, and the love-their-liquor relative that every family has even if they don't acknowledge, Uncle Boomer, was well into his cups at not even nine in the morning. Stacy had even offered to have Lamar pick her up. Her youngest, still-single brother lived not far from Frieda's condo, and had a sparkling personality sure to put a smile on Frieda's face. Plus, he was fine. It was a sorely tempting offer, but in the end, Frieda declined. It wasn't too long ago that she couldn't stand having only herself for company. Now that she was learning to love herself, she could actually be alone with her thoughts, sans weed or alcohol, and contemplate them. Doing so had led to the revelations she'd shared with Hope and Frieda—that she missed being a mother. Even more surprising, she missed Gabriel too. Not his money or the lifestyle; she missed him.

Looking at her watch and realizing the day was quickly getting away from her, Frieda went into the kitchen and took a minicooler from the walk-in pantry. Within minutes she'd filled it with some of the items she'd bought the day before specifically for this solo beach trip: turkey salad, potato salad, Hawaiian rolls, and sparkling apple juice. After placing ice packs around her personal picnic spread, she pulled a container of Thin Mints Girl Scout cookies from the freezer and placed the roll on top of the ice packs before closing the cooler.

On her way out of the kitchen, her home phone rang. Frieda checked the caller ID before answering. "Hey, Mama." The smile on her face was genuine. It was enough that she was learning to forgive herself. That she was also learning how to forgive her mother and reestablish a real relationship with her was a bonus.

"Frieda, I can't believe you're going to spend the day by yourself."

Frieda laughed. "I know, huh? Not the typical Thanksgiving, for sure."

"I called Pat earlier, talked to Hope. She assured me that you are all right." A pause and then, "Are you?"

"I'm good, Mama, seriously. I just didn't want to spend the day around a bunch of people. I wanted to—" Frieda hesitated. The one topic she hadn't discussed in detail with Sharon was her family. Sharon's general distrust in men (even as she entertained a plethora of them) had inadvertently fueled Frieda's attitude. She really didn't feel like hearing anything negative about Gabriel right now.

"You wanted to what?"

I wanted to spend the day with the two most important men in my world. "I wanted to spend the day . . . by the ocean. There's a place in Rancho Palos Verdes that is away from the crowds but has beautiful views of the Pacific. That's where I'm headed."

"What about your son? Are you going to see him today?"

"Later," Frieda lied. "They're spending the day at his grandmother's house. That's not a dinner I want to join."

"You need to be with your child, Frieda."

I wish you'd remembered that when I was young. Rather than become angry or worse, get into an argument, she decided to end the conversation. "I need to run, Mama. I want to get on the highway. With this being a holiday, there will probably be heavy traffic."

"Girl, I don't see how y'all stand it out there, all those people, the cars, threats of earthquakes."

"You get used to it," Frieda said as she walked to the hall closet and grabbed a collapsible lawn chair. "You'll have to come out for a visit. Maybe Christmas."

"Girl, I don't have that type of money."

"Then you could consider my buying your ticket as a Christmas present. Look, Mama, I gotta go."

"Okay, Frieda. I worry about you." There was a long pause, during which time Frieda wondered if her mother was going to say those three words that coming out of her mouth were all too rare. "Take care of yourself," she finally muttered.

"Love you, Mama," Frieda said.

"Bye, girl."

An hour later, Frieda was at one of her favorite spots, an elevated area with an unobstructed view of the Pacific. Having skipped breakfast, she made quick work of the lunch she'd packed and in between reading pages of another book, she took in the beauty around her. The scene was postcard perfect, the food tasty...but the joy that Frieda felt the area would bring her remained at bay. That is, until her phone rang with a familiar number on the caller ID. It was the one call she'd been too afraid to hope for, yet the one that she wanted most of all.

"Hey, Gabriel."

"It's me, Mommy!"

Frieda laughed. "Oh, hey, baby!"

"Happy Thanksgiving, Mommy!"

"Happy Thanksgiving, Gabe. Did you eat lots of turkey?"

"No, we had pizza!"

"Pizza?"

"Yeah, and it was good too. Grandma said she made them just for me because she said I don't like real food."

"Well," Frieda said, surprised that she was tearing up. In the moment, however, she realized that there was another grandmother that Gabe barely knew. "I hope you thanked your grandmother for being so nice to you."

"Yeah," Gabe replied, his voice in a pout. "But I forgot at first and Daddy scolded me."

"Where is Daddy?"

"He's right here. He wants to talk to you. Bye, Mommy. Love you!"

"Love you too, Gabe."

"Why don't you come over, Mommy? We have lots of food and we can share some with you."

"That's so nice, baby. Let me speak to your father." Her heartbeat tripled as she waited to hear Gabriel's voice.

"Hello, Frieda."

"Hey there. Sounds like you guys had a good time—but pizza for Thanksgiving?"

"That was a part of the kiddie menu—turkey pizza made with a stuffing crust. It was pretty good actually."

"Hmm, that sounds like something I might like. Dressing has

always been one of my favorite parts of this holiday." Frieda became quiet, thinking of how different this day might have been for
her . . . if she'd only recognized the treasures she had.

"What did you do?" Gabriel asked.

She told him. "I'm still here, actually," she finished, placing her
empty containers back in the cooler. "But I'm getting ready to
leave." Gabriel was silent for a long moment. "Hello?"

He cleared his throat. "I'm sorry you spent the day alone,
Frieda."

"It's cool. I had invites, just felt like chillin' out. No, really, I
wanted to see my son, but your mother hates me and you probably
do too, so—"

"I don't hate you. I hate some of your actions and what you
did to our family, but I don't hate you."

"I'm sorry, Gabriel. But I couldn't really love you because I
didn't love myself. I'm working on me though. I'm tired of the
person I used to be, so I'm inventing a new me."

"Good luck with that."

Frieda heard the smile in his voice. "Right? I know it sounds
like a tall order, but everything is possible."

"It is." There was a companionable silence for a moment before Gabriel spoke. "Have you eaten dessert?"

"No, but I've got some Girl Scout cookies with my name on
them!"

"Why don't you come have dessert with us? Mom baked a
pineapple upside-down cheesecake and insisted I bring home half
with me. It's way more than Gabe and I need to eat."

"I'm not sure that's such a good idea. Cordella hates me and I
can't say that I blame her." And seeing Cordella would remind her
of Clark, the now ex-lover who'd quickly moved on as soon as
both of Frieda's pocketbooks closed.

"All of the house staff have the day off. It's just Gabe and me."

"In that case," Frieda said, rising from the chair and gathering
her things, "I'll see you guys in about an hour. Is that cool?"

"We'll see you then."

Frieda arrived at her old home and had a pleasant time with the two men she wanted back in her life. She watched Gabe splash in the pool and then helped him to bathe before assisting Gabriel with an early tuck in. "We're up bright and early for a trip to Universal Studios," Gabriel explained. "It's sure to last all day."

When she arrived back at her condo at around 8:30 p.m., there was a smile on her face. It had been a different kind of Thanksgiving, but it had been a good one. And while Gabriel hadn't invited her to join them, or said anything about their getting back together, he hadn't mentioned the divorce either. He still loved her. She could see it in his eyes. For the first time since that night she came home to changed locks, there was hope that she hadn't totally ruined the best thing that had ever happened to her.

"Don't go there, Frieda," she whispered, heading to her bedroom to take a shower. *You've forgiven yourself, remember?* Upon entering the bathroom, she changed her mind about the shower and decided on a long bubble bath instead. She started the water, then went into the bedroom for some vanilla-scented candles. On the way back she passed the mirror and the plaque that hung beside it:

> *You should know yourself*
> *And uphold yourself*
> *And let unconditional love*
> *Be the only kind that you show yourself.*

She stepped up to the plaque, ran her hands over the raised lettering. Continuing on to the bathroom, she felt a peace that was hers for the first time in life. When told about it, Hope had insisted that there were only ten commandments. Maybe so. Frieda didn't know anything about scripture. But this one, called the eleventh commandment, was helping her change her life.